RICK PARTLOW
DROP TROOPER BOOK THIRTEEN
WEAPONS FREE

www.aethonbooks.com

WEAPONS FREE
©2023 RICK PARTLOW

This book is protected under the copyright laws of the United States of America. No part of this publication may be reproduced, stored in a retrieval system, or transmitted, in any form or by any means, without the prior permission in writing of the publisher, nor be otherwise circulated in any form of binding or cover other than that in which it is published and without a similar condition including this condition being imposed on the subsequent purchaser. Any reproduction or unauthorized use of the material or artwork contained herein is prohibited without the express written permission of the authors.

Aethon Books supports the right to free expression and the value of copyright. The purpose of copyright is to encourage writers and artists to produce the creative works that enrich our culture.

The scanning, uploading, and distribution of this book without permission is a theft of the author's intellectual property. If you would like to use material from the book (other than for review purposes), please contact editor@aethonbooks.com. Thank you for your support of the author's rights.

Aethon Books
www.aethonbooks.com

Print and eBook formatting by Steve Beaulieu.

Published by Aethon Books LLC.

Aethon Books is not responsible for websites (or their content) that are not owned by the publisher.

This book is a work of fiction. Names, characters, places, and incidents are the product of the author's imagination or are used fictitiously. Any resemblance to actual events, locales, or persons, living or dead is coincidental.

All rights reserved.

ALSO IN THE SERIES

CONTACT FRONT
KINETIC STRIKE
DANGER CLOSE
DIRECT FIRE
HOME FRONT
FIRE BASE
SHOCK ACTION
RELEASE POINT
KILL BOX
DROP ZONE
TANGO DOWN
BLUE FORCE
WEAPONS FREE
COLLATERAL EFFECTS

[1]

"Do you know," my father asked, "why we named you Cameron?"

I was used to looking up to Papa, but he was eye to eye with me at the moment, down on one knee so he could reach the loose board at the base of the chicken coop. He paused to hammer in a nail before looking back to me, wiping sweat from his brow. Papa had always seemed old to me back then, but looking at him through different eyes, I could see how young he was.

I didn't have an answer for him. I *should* have. I knew it, but for some reason I couldn't bring myself to speak, afraid of breaking the spell, of losing this moment with Papa. He answered for me.

"It was your great-great-uncle," Papa confided, leaning closer as if it was a secret. His brown eyes flickered side to side like he was making sure Mama wasn't around. "Your grandmother's sister's husband. He was a Yankee, you know. It's a bit of a controversy in the family. He lived in south Texas back when it was a state, back before the war, and when things began to fall apart, when the trucks stopped running and the riots burned the cities, he came down here and married Laura, your grandmother's sister, and lived among us." His smile took on a sad tinge. "He passed away saving your grandmother and her family from bandits. His name was Cameron Anderson, and we decided to name you in his honor. He was a hero, a leader, and I know you will be as well."

Papa set his hammer beside the door to the chicken coop and squatted, his dark eyes level with mine.

"I know you're going to do the right thing, not just for you, but for all those people counting on you." He clapped me on the shoulder. "You'll get them home."

Tears blurred my vision, smoothing out the smile lines in his face, then wiping it away completely in a haze of blinding, white light...

"Wakey, wakey, eggs and bakey!"

I blinked, rubbed at the gunk in my eyes, and fought back a shiver. The face of my long-dead father morphed into the plain, doughy face of Dr. Hallonen. She was grinning broadly, and I abruptly realized I was naked.

"I hate this shit," I murmured, sitting up and taking the uniform Hallonen offered me, using it to cover up strategically. "I thought waking up from the auto-doc was bad, but I never dreamed in the auto-doc."

"Yeah," she agreed, turning away as a concession to my modesty as I pulled on my clothes in the narrow confines of the stasis chamber. "I'm just glad this is the last go-around for a while."

I rubbed at my eyes again, the words not quite penetrating. Around me, the figures of the other crew climbing slowly and painfully out of their stasis chambers were still a blur against the harsh lights.

"What do you mean?" I asked her, thoughts still coming slow and muddled. We'd been running two thirds of the crew in stasis at a time, one third on duty, every three months for... how long had it been? Close to five years now.

Holy shit. Five years. Just thinking the words twisted cold talons in my gut. Had I done *anything* for five years? The Marines. The war. I'd barely gone past five years with my birth family.

"She means we're here, Alvarez."

I didn't *need* to see the face that went with that voice, it was burned into my memory, lined and sagging like a hound dog, though the beard was new.

"Isn't that facial hair against Fleet regs, Captain Nance?" I asked the man, swinging my legs over the side of the chamber, grabbing at the cold metal and hauling myself up to my feet. The deck was as cold as the stasis pod and I found the boots Hallonen had left beside it for me, socks stuffed into the end.

Nance chuckled, running a hand through the close-cropped beard, shot with tendrils of gray.

"Maybe," he admitted, "but I've been on watch for three months, and I'll be damned if I haven't consumed every piece of entertainment in the ship's database. Anyway, if we were going by military regulations, a Marine captain wouldn't be in charge of the entire expedition."

"Point," I granted him, tightening the boot's fasteners, then straightening. A little too fast... the blood rushed to my head, and I had to steady myself against the side of the pod. "But what do you mean we're here? Aren't we still in T-space?"

Or at least that was what I'd assumed from the Earth-normal gravity I was feeling. We could only generate artificial gravity in T-space, using the warp field generator, though why it wouldn't work in normal space was a question a hyperdimensional physicist might be able to answer, but I couldn't.

"No. I spun up the habitation drum."

That was something I still wasn't used to, even after all this time on the *Orion*. Fleet ships didn't have spinning drums for artificial gravity as a rule, since the complexity of the structure made the vessel more vulnerable, created gaps in her armor. But the *Orion* had been sent out for long-term patrol, and she'd been specially constructed by Fleet Intelligence designed to sit out in normal space, waiting. And leaving the crew in free fall for that whole time would have been bad for health, morale, and readiness, hence the rotational drum at the center of the ship. It could be locked in place for Transition, the furniture and control stations shifted for the shifting gravitational direction.

"You locked us in for rotational gravity?" I asked, though it was a stupid and obvious question and I blamed the fog in my brain from the stasis. But that could take hours, and he wouldn't have done it unless... finally, the reality of the situation penetrated. "We've found a habitable?"

"Not just a habitable," he corrected, a grin splitting his new whiskers. "It's a whole damned *civilization*. Which is why we're tucked into the outer asteroid belt, all nice and silent, watching." He jerked a thumb over his shoulder. "Go grab a shower and we'll meet in the Ops Center so I can go over the whole thing with you."

I nodded, ignoring the casual insubordination as he turned on his heel and headed out of the compartment. Yeah, I was in charge and everyone had agreed to it, but that didn't change the fact that this was Nance's ship and he was king here. Instead, my attention went back to Hallonen and the next stasis pod over. Shutting one of the things down and waking up the occupant was, I'd discovered, a long and involved process, and I didn't envy the medical crew having to do it every three months. Hallonen had insisted she be the first one wakened and that she supervise every single shift change, which meant she'd been awake longer than any of us.

The clothes for the occupant of the next pod were stowed in

a drawer built into the base of the thing and I grabbed them, waiting patiently behind Hallonen as she finished the revival process. The doc shot me an annoyed look over her shoulder but didn't bother saying anything. We'd gone through this before too many times, and she had to know I wasn't going anywhere.

The lid opened with a pneumatic hiss and Vicky Sandoval sat up, disgustingly awake and aware without the minute or so of disorientation I always experienced. I knew reactions to the hibernation process varied by individual, but that didn't mean I had to like it.

"Morning, Cam," she said, smiling as she took the clothes, not seeming the least bit squeamish about her nudity, something else I envied. I'd been raised in a more conservative environment. Not that *I* didn't appreciate her lack of clothes, but I'd rather have kept it private. "So, where are we this time?"

"Hopefully, the end of the line," I said, and her head came up sharply, eyes narrowing. "We've found an inhabited system. Meeting in the Ops Center as soon as everyone's awake."

"Oh, good," she sighed, pulling on her shirt. "My favorite place."

I think my own loathing for the Operations Center on the *Orion* was compounded by how much I'd hated the constant meetings there that Colonel Hachette used to preside over. Now, in the latest evidence that God was the supreme ironist, I was in charge and had to call those damned meetings myself.

It was strange being at the center of the round table, the controls for the displays at my fingertips, even stranger because of who *wasn't* at the meeting. No Hachette, of course. He'd sacrificed himself to eliminate the threat from the Skrela. No Top either. Sgt.-Major Ellen Campbell had died in action even earlier, and no disrespect to Hachette, but I missed her presence more than his. She was a prop kicked out from beneath us, the only reason Vicky and I had agreed to come back into the Marines for this mission.

No Captain Solano, who'd been lost on the Resscharr world of Decision, which had put me back into a leadership role, replacing him as CO of the Drop Trooper company on the ship. Technically I was still their company commander with Vicky as my XO, though in practice she commanded the company, because I'd stepped into Hachette's position through the very unmilitary expediency of everyone voting me in.

And now, no Kyler Dunstan. He'd been with us nearly from the beginning of this whole fiasco, though he'd originally been working for the Corporate Security Force as a private military contractor, flying one of their repurposed, military-surplus missile cutters. We'd brought him into the mission and, consequently, back into an active Fleet commission, and then dragged him halfway across the galaxy. He'd asked to stay behind back on the Island World with the human settlers there along with his crew chief, Beckett, who was pregnant with his child and didn't want to chance the stasis pods. I'd left them one of our landers, arming the thing with some fabricated missiles and coilguns and hoping its presence would be enough to discourage the Tahni on Yfingam from trying to take the world at some point in the future. I wasn't sanguine about that in the long run, but there was nothing else we could do, and we didn't want to stay there and try to build a new civilization.

I hadn't realized how much I was going to miss the big goofball. Without Dunstan, there was no one left I felt I could trust completely except for Vicky. She was here, of course, and so was Nance. Of the rest... well, Commander Brandano was the senior Intercept pilot, with Lt. Villanueva his newly appointed junior, promoted to fly Dunstan's old bird from her previous spot as an assault shuttle pilot. Brandano was a stiff, by-the-book type, which was reflected in his stern, hawk-like face, although like all of us, he'd had to bend to the circumstances of being stranded thousands of light-years from home. Villanueva looked uncomfortable being here and was trying—badly—to hide it through a too-deliberate casual air.

"So," she said, smiling too broadly, "did we find the Northwest Passage already? Somehow I thought it would take more effort."

"I'm afraid not," Captain Nagarro said without the slightest trace of a sense of humor. "It's much more complicated than that." She shot a look at me, then at Captain Nance. "If I may, sirs?"

Which she didn't have to call me, since we shared a rank, but did anyway because I was in charge and Nagarro was all about decorum, as if she'd taken the banner from Hachette when he passed.

"Go ahead," I told her, beating Nance to the punch. Not that it was a competition or anything...

Nagarro tapped at her 'link and the holographic projector set in the center of the table flickered to life with an image of a star system, assembled, I presumed, through a combination of optical telescopes, spectroscopy, as well as thermal and gravimetic sensors and drones.

"It's a fairly standard system for a habitable," the Intelligence officer said, gesturing to the projection. "G-class star, a couple of large gas giants that attract detritus, three terrestrial planets, only the second one habitable, also the only one with a large moon."

"A large moon?" I asked, eyes darting toward the representation of the planet. "Dwight, didn't you tell us once that was a sign of a world terraformed by the Predecessors?"

The AI had immersed itself into our ship's database and

could have just answered over the compartment's speakers, but since the first time he'd infiltrated the *Orion*, he'd represented himself in the holographic display as a generic-looking Fleet crewmember, uniform and all.

He leaned against something that didn't exist, the edge of the projection, a strange affectation for something that didn't have an actual body.

"Possibly," he replied, shrugging. "The Predecessors supplied moons to all the habitables they terraformed because they assumed one was necessary for complex life, but they also had a total of one sample to draw from. This system is thousands of light-years away from your world... it could simply be a coincidence."

"A large moon *is* necessary for complex life to evolve," Lilandreth interrupted, and either her command of our body language and intonation had improved to the point where I could sense her irritation with the AI, or maybe I just assumed it because it seemed the natural state of affairs between the two of them. "Experiments were done. The likelihood of life-ending asteroid strikes is much higher without a moon to intercept them."

It still freaked me out sometimes how *old* Lilandreth was, over six thousand years, and yet she still had only been around for a bare fraction of the Resscharr civilization, right at the end before the Skrela had overwhelmed them and forced them out of the Cluster. The fact *that* freaked me out and having a two-meter-tall humanoid dinosaur sitting at the same table *didn't* was just a hint of the shit we'd been through.

"Nevertheless," Nagarro interrupted, glaring at the two of them with annoyance, "whether the world is terraformed or natural, it's inhabited and from all indications, their level of technology is similar to the Commonwealth's prior to the First War with the Tahni." She touched her 'link again and red dots sprang up scattered throughout the system, moving slowly in comparison to the sheer space between the planets yet still perceptibly. "The thermal signatures are definitely fusion drives. Nothing as advanced as the main drive on a Fleet ship, more in line with the pulse drives we used a hundred years ago, but enough for them to spread through the system. We've detected signs of outposts or maybe even colonies on both of the other terrestrial planets and several of the moons of the two gas giants, as well as indications of mining and manufacturing in their primary asteroid belt."

I sighed, unable to hide my disappointment, and Vicky matched it with a scowl.

"Shit," she muttered. "It's not the Predecessors then. They wouldn't be using fusion pulse drives. Hell, they might not even be *connected* to the Predecessors."

"That was my first thought as well," Nagarro admitted. "And then I saw *this*."

Her fingers danced over her 'link display and the projection zoomed into a spot in the asteroid belt. Fusion drives were swarming toward it like it owed them money, a large swathe of white and red points gathered around it as if there were stations orbiting something. Something that glowed Cherenkov-blue on the sensors, something I recognized very well after all this time in the military.

"Holy shit," Villanueva blurted, eyes wide as she stared at it. "Is that...?"

Nagarro nodded.

"A wormhole jumpgate." She smiled thinly. "And I suppose that answers the question of whether they're connected to the Predecessors."

[2]

"I still don't know if this is a good idea," Nance complained, eyes fixed to the screens as if the sensor data was going to tell him something he didn't already know. "We could be starting a war."

I very deliberately did *not* sigh in exasperation, but it was tough. We'd been through this a dozen times already, all the way back to the interminable Ops Center meeting.

"That doesn't prove the Predecessors were here," Brandano had argued, his strident voice penetrating the general hubbub upon the revelation that this system had a jumpgate. "If they could engineer something like the wormholes, why couldn't someone else? Maybe these people did it themselves."

"The jumpgates *don't* occur naturally," Lilandreth had informed him curtly, sounding as if she resented the implication that any species except her own could have been responsible. "And engineering them requires either a pair of neutron stars shaped into a cylinder and spun at relativistic speeds or the absolute control of microscopic black holes. The former we would have noticed immediately upon entering the system, and the latter would obviate the need for fusion drives... or for the gate itself. So, your choices are either accepting that my people did this or postulating some *second* civilization sophisticated enough to create the gateway and leave it for another intelligent species."

"Occam's Razor, Commander," Nance had piped up, the first time he'd spoken in the meeting, which I assumed was because he already knew everything Nagarro was telling us. "The simplest explanation is the best one."

"Are we getting any EM transmissions?" I'd demanded, trying to cut through all the chatter. "Something that'll give us an idea who we're dealing with?"

It was an open question. The Predecessors had brought along humans and Tahni wherever they went, and they'd also engineered a particularly nasty hybrid of the two that we'd encountered along the way, the ones who had killed Top.

"Negative," Nance had answered. "There's some EM wave activity, but it's not modulated for communication. Likely sensors of some kind. As far as we can tell, they're using hard-wired fiber for data and laser line-of-sight for long-range comms in space. There's microwave activity on the planet, but nothing aimed outward. Probably for private communications via something like our 'links."

"Or maybe like the old cellular phones they used back a couple hundred years ago," Nagarro had added. "Either way, we can't intercept their comms. We have no idea who we're dealing with until we meet up with them face to face."

"Yeah, that didn't turn out so well with the Khitan," I'd pointed out, the memory of Top stinging. "I think we need a better plan than just knocking on the door. We don't even know if we'll be able to speak their language."

"What's that reading way out at the outer edge of the asteroid belt?" Vicky had asked, standing and pointing at a faint thermal signature at the edge of the belt closest to the gas giant.

"I *think*," Nagarro had replied, "that it's a small mining operation. There's a ship out there working some kind of solar smelter." She'd shrugged. "Probably has a live crew, given that I've seen the ship move twice since we started monitoring."

I loved Vicky dearly, but the smile she'd given to that answer scared the shit out of me.

"Then I think I have a better plan."

And here we were.

"I don't think they've seen us," Wojtera said. A lot of the crew had let themselves go a little during our time in and out of stasis, their hair longer, wilder, some with facial hair, but not Wojtera. The tactical officer was straight-backed, clear-eyed, his uniform neatly pressed, his hair just at regulation. "Their ship hasn't moved since we Transitioned in. If I had to guess, no one's keeping watch for traffic since they don't expect any company."

"Well, that'll make things simpler," I said, unstrapping from my seat. It had once been Hachette's seat, and it was a constant struggle to make myself go to it instead of the spare acceleration couches at the edge of the bridge where Vicky and I had plunked ourselves for over a year, looking over the colonel's shoulder. "I'm heading down to Intercept Two."

"You know you're in command now, Alvarez," Nance reminded me, giving me a baleful glare. "Just send Campea and the Force Recon to handle this."

Pausing at the hatch to the bridge, I chuckled back at the captain.

"You were the one just worrying about starting a war," I countered. "And you want me to let a bunch of Force Recon door-kickers handle this? They'll wind up shooting holes in everything that doesn't have an IFF transponder." I shrugged. "Besides, if you guys wanted a mission commander who'd sit around and lead from the rear, you should probably have picked a Fleet officer... not a Marine."

Nance did *not* shoot me a bird in front of the entire bridge crew, but I could tell he wanted to.

"Is it just me," Vicky asked, staring at the Intercept's main screen, "or is that thing the biggest piece of shit you've ever seen masquerading as a spaceship?"

Commander Brandano didn't reply, either because his attention was absorbed with maneuvering Intercept Two into a docking orbit or maybe because, unlike Dunstan, he wasn't the type to bullshit during an operation. His copilot wasn't so reticent though.

"Got nothing to compare it to," Lt. Tinsley mused, "so I don't know if they're all this bad, but yeah, that's one ugly fucking collection of spare parts."

They weren't wrong. The ship reminded me of the cobbled-together vessels I'd seen out in the Pirate Worlds, though this one hadn't been designed either to land in any sort of atmosphere or to maneuver in combat, which meant there wasn't the slightest bit of streamlining to it. Fuel tanks bubbled out around the drive bell like cancerous tumors, solar panels tucked into every spare centimeter of its surface like the rain barrels my parents had left under the drains of every roof on our property. A battered communications dish threw the nose of the ship into shadow, but there were no other protuberances to indicate armament of any kind.

The ship wasn't where we intended to dock, however. It was in a tight orbit around a small asteroid, the rock not much larger than the *Orion*, and if the ship looked cobbled together, then the facilities dug into the surface of the rock could have been a shanty town built by refugees.

"They aren't mining that thing," I said, nodding at the tiny asteroid. "Not unless they're digging into it by hand from the inside."

"It's a shelter," Brandano declared, apparently satisfied that this conversation was serious enough that he felt comfortable taking part in it. "That ship isn't armored enough to protect them from cosmic rays or solar storms, and at this level of technology, they probably don't have deflectors. They live on this rock while they maintain *that*."

A waggling finger indicated what *that* was, as if I needed anyone to point out the blinding glare coming from a few hundred kilometers away. The curved, mylar panels were kilometers across, not solar collectors but solar *reflectors*, focusing the rays of the far-off star on a more respectable rock, melting it into a vapor that was sucked up by machinery not very different than I'd seen at any asteroid mine from the solar system all the way out to the Pirate Worlds. The setup was bulky, awkward, and ungainly, but simple and cheap. It separated out the ores and stored them in storage cylinders for collection and transport, probably designed to be towed back to the habitable planet, or its moon, by the ship.

"They're not at the mining site," I decided, eyeing the readout from the scanners. "Not with the reflectors lined up. They'd get cooked. They're either on the ship or in the shelter. What are we getting on thermal?"

"The ship's reactors powered down," Mendez, the Intercept's crew chief, announced from his position off to our right, his eyes flickering back and forth from one display to another, "but they've got all those solar panels..."

"I'd go for the rock," Brandano said without a hint of uncertainty. "The ship's gonna get hot, no matter how many collectors she's got on her. The rock is insulated, safe, comfortable. This is a shit job with shit equipment. The people running this thing are probably content to do just as little as they can get away with and not get fired."

There was, I thought, an argument to be made that he was looking at it from the point of view of someone born and raised in our own society and theirs might be different, but I had no idea, and starting with one was just as good as the other.

"Take us down as close as you can," I told him, yanking the quick-release for my harness. "We'll be venting atmosphere in the utility bay and going out the ramp, so seal up the cockpit tight."

"Not my first rodeo," Brandano grunted. I didn't snap back at him as much as I wanted to. It *was*, in fact, the first mission of this type he'd been on since we'd joined the operation, which was close enough. But we didn't have time to argue it out now, though I put a pin in it for later.

The Force Recon squad Lt. Campea had brought along was already sealed into their helmets by the time Vicky and I floated down from the cockpit, through the narrow passage where the ship had her berthing compartments and galley, and into the utility bay. Gentle bumps nudged us first against one bulkhead, then another as Brandano maneuvered Intercept Two into place above the asteroid, and I steadied myself with a hand briefly before fixing my boot's magnetic soles to the deck and pulling on my own helmet.

"Everybody ready?" I asked Campea over my helmet radio, sliding the latches into place to secure the thing at my suit's neck yoke.

"What's the ROE, sir?" Campea asked, his faceplate an opaque mystery under the lights of the utility bay.

"Don't fire unless fired upon," I told him, checking the service pistol in my chest holster. "And even if you *are* fired upon, make damn sure it's something that's going to actually be a threat. I don't want to start a war over some peashooter that couldn't penetrate my uniform shirt."

"Yes, sir." He didn't sound too sure of himself, and I could understand why. It was easy for me to say not to fire unless they knew there was a threat, but not so easy to be the one getting shot at.

"Don't worry," I assured him. "I'll be going first."

"Dammit, Cam," Vicky smacked me on the arm, which I barely felt through the armored pressure suit. "You're doing this just to piss me off, aren't you?"

"This is diplomacy, sort of," I said, not bothering to shrug because it wouldn't show through the suit. "Isn't that supposed to be my job?"

"Yeah, you keep telling yourself that."

"Captain Alvarez, we're as close as we're going to get," Brandano told me, the words punctuated by one last blast of the belly jets that sent me into an involuntary crouch before free fall took back over. "Cockpit is sealed."

"Vent atmosphere," I told him.

Air rushed out of the vent fans with a nerve-rattling hum that thankfully faded as the medium conducting it was ejected into space. The light over the ramp controls shifted from green to yellow to red, letting us know we were in vacuum, and I motioned to Campea.

"Stick close behind me. Dwight, are you there?"

"Always, Captain Alvarez," the AI reported, and maybe I was only imagining the patronizing tone in his voice.

"If their airlock is sealed, can you penetrate their security?"

"Undoubtedly, as long as you can make contact with a conductive surface... and as long as the lock is electronic. This facility is primitive enough that they may utilize something as simple as a metal bolt."

"A metal bolt," Campea cut in, yanking a plasma cutter up by its top grip, "we can handle."

The hatch cranked open in eerie silence, the glint of reflected sunlight off of metal and faceted rock sending rays of yellow into the utility bay, darkening the polarization of my faceplate. We hadn't landed, of course. There wasn't enough gravity for an actual landing, not on a rock this small, and trying to touch down would have just sent the cutter bouncing off the surface. Instead, we hovered about ten meters up and getting down was going to be… well, calling it *tricky* was an exercise in understatement. Even though there wasn't significant gravity, Isaac Newton's First Law still applied and momentum was still a thing.

Nothing to be done about it though. Disengaging my magnetic soles, I pivoted around, my inner ear lodging a formal protest that I'd probably have to file a report on later since I had to file reports on everything else. I planted my feet at the overhead and pushed off. I'd never gone swimming until I joined the Marines and wasn't a huge fan, but this felt a lot like the few times I'd dived off a high board into the training pool, except it never ended.

Ten meters wasn't much. I was barely in space for five seconds, with a big-ass rock beneath me and the bulk of the Intercept cutter above, yet even the hint of empty space around me speared through my gut with the agoraphobia I thought I'd banished years ago. Too much muchness, and I forced myself to concentrate on rotating my body around, on getting my feet beneath me. I barely got into position before I hit.

Damn that momentum. The impact drove me into a deep crouch, my ass almost touching the rock, and I was deathly afraid I was about to spring back up, bouncing off the surface and back into space to die of asphyxiation… eventually, days later. Or worse, to force Brandano to rescue me and then have to listen to him hold that over my head for the next few months.

Thankfully, there was just enough of a gravitational pull from the rock to keep me from doing more than rising a meter above the ground before I settled back down, clutching at outcroppings of rock. Cursing myself for the flashback of agoraphobia, I shuffled to the side, making room for the next Marine out. That turned out to be Vicky, though I hadn't planned it that way, and her landing was more graceful than mine, though to be fair, that might have had to do with watching me try it first.

At least I did better than most of the Force Recon troopers, who were encumbered by their weapons and equipment. Some of them landed flat on their back, and only Campea showed any sort of agility, hitting in a three-point landing like a gymnast.

"All down," he reported to me. "No casualties."

I checked myself, just to make sure, then turned my attention to the airlock. It wasn't much, just a metallic dome barely the size of a groundcar sticking up from the rock, the door an oval set in the side of it. I needn't have worried about picking any locks, as it turned out. Rather than any sort of electronic security pad or biometric reader, there was just a wheel. I'd seen this sort of lock before, mostly in the Pirate Worlds or the Periphery, where people who couldn't afford better just had to make do, and the only question was, clockwise or counterclockwise?

"Should we flip a coin?" Vicky wondered, apparently reading my mind again.

"I'll try left first," I decided. Yeah, it would be a coincidence if these guys' wheel locks were designed the same way ours were, but it was a fifty-fifty chance.

Left worked and it wasn't even that hard to turn, though I did have to brace my feet on chocks set beside the door. It was hinged on the opposite side from what I expected, but nothing about the interior surprised me. A tiny room, barely large enough for three or four humans in suits, with vent fans built into the walls to pump oxygen in or out and a crude lamp display. It was blue at the moment, so at least they used different colors than we did, or I might have started getting paranoid that the whole system had been settled by the Commonwealth.

"Vicky, Campea, and one other Marine," I said, motioning for them to join me inside. Keep the others outside unless we call for them."

"And what if there are more troops than we can handle inside?" Campea asked, pulling the door shut. He tightened the wheel while I searched for the control to fill the lock with air.

"The ship's unarmed," I reminded him absently, most of my attention on a lever set in the wall beside the blue light. "There's no security, and the mine is small-scale automation. What about this place screams 'troops' to you?"

Campea grunted, sounding unconvinced, but I'd finally figured out which way to pull the lever, and it went into place with a vibration that traveled up my arm. I wasn't sure if I'd guessed right because I couldn't hear anything, but then I saw the fan blades moving inside the vent. The thing filled slowly, and it was minutes before there was enough air in the lock to conduct the sound. If I'd thought the fans in the utility bay of Intercept Two were loud and annoying, this thing was a banging cacophony of disrepair, loud enough that I was sure anyone inside had to be able to hear it, and I started feeling as paranoid as Campea.

Finally, the blue light turned to orange and the external atmospheric reading in my suit told me the air was breathable. I didn't take my helmet off, but I did turn the wheel on the internal door. Campea and the NCO who'd come through with him shouldered their Gauss rifles and Vicky pulled her handgun, holding it at low ready.

"I'm opening it," I told them. "Remember, don't fire unless fired upon."

There was another chock beside the interior door, and I braced my boot against it and put my shoulder into the hatch, pushing hard not because it resisted but just to get it open quickly. The less time whoever was on the other side had to react, the less chance they'd take a shot at us.

As it turned out, there was little chance of that. There were a grand total of two people on this station and both of them were standing on the other side of the airlock, shock written on their faces. Neither was in any sort of armor, neither was carrying a weapon—in fact, what they were wearing looked more like brightly colored pajamas.

And neither was human. Nor Tahni, nor Khitan, nor Resscharr. Certainly not Skrela.

They were humanoid. Two eyes, two ears, a nose, a mouth... *almost* human. But not quite. The color of their skin was a tan so deep it was almost golden, not the natural hue of any race of humanity that had ever existed, and the eyes were slitted vertically, the hair fine and feathery.

One of them, the taller of the two, gabbled at me in something that sounded like a cat coughing up a furball and raised his hands, palms out in obvious surrender. Well, at least the hands looked fairly normal, four fingers and a thumb even.

"Dwight, any help?"

"Sorry, Captain Alvarez," he said, and for once he actually sounded apologetic. "Whatever they're speaking, it's unrelated to Tahni, Resscharr, or any human dialect. They look close to human, but from what I can tell, they're not related to you in the slightest."

"Oh, joy." I sighed. "Campea, get a couple more of your guys in here and start looking for space suits for these two. We're taking them with us."

[3]

I don't know how I expected the aliens to react to being abducted off their asteroid station and stuck in a ship full of strangers, but this wasn't it.

The talkative one, the one who'd gabbled at us back inside the rock, still hadn't shut up, two days later. Like our old neighbor back in Tijuana, Mrs. Castellano, he talked with his hands a lot, and watching him sitting in the small compartment with the Fleet Intelligence language specialist, the alien looked like he was conducting an orchestra only he could see.

Lt. Vargas, the Intelligence officer, had a bemused smile on his face, his hands folded, only contributing the occasional nod as he sat across from the golden boy, just letting the cameras in the room record the gestures and words, feeding them into the database. The other guy was slumped in a chair behind his friend, content to watch silently, and behind Vargas an armed Force Recon Marine was his counterpart, still as a statue.

"We got names for them yet?" I asked. I wasn't worried about being overheard since the image on the bulkhead display was merely a projection from the next compartment over, insulated and soundproof. I'd been asking Major Nagarro, but I wasn't surprised when Dwight answered.

"We were able," the AI told me, "to glean enough data from the computer systems your Marines took out of the ship to come up with a basic understanding of their language. Thankfully, it's mostly vocal and subvocal rather than relying on chemical pheromones or elaborate body language. There's *some* body language involved, of course, as you can see by watching the subject under study, but it can be bypassed through syntax."

I looked upward, though I wasn't sure if I was doing it unconsciously because that was where Dwight's avatar was located in the Ops Center or if I was appealing to God for patience.

"I asked if had names for them."

"The one speaking," Dwight replied, lacking even a hint of awareness of his own capacity to irritate, "has a designation that roughly translates to *Judge My Virtue by My Deeds*, while the other is *Driftwood Floating Lazily at the Shore*."

"Poetic," I said, snorting a laugh. "But that's gonna make for some long conversations."

"We've been calling them Jay and Bob for short," Nagarro confided with a shrug. "It doesn't matter since the translation software can substitute their actual names for whatever designation we give them."

"And what's Jay saying?"

By way of answer, Nagarro touched a control on the display and sound from the other compartment blared over the speakers. Jay's actual voice came first, a series of clicks and clucks and glottal stops interspersed with warbling sounds from deep in his throat just for a moment before the translation overpowered it. Whoever had chosen the voice for the translation of his voice had decided on a generic Trans-Angeles surface-dweller accent, which was both familiar and grating for me. The Underground didn't care for Surface Dwellers, mostly since the only time we saw them was when they came down to buy drugs and act tough, like they belonged down there with us.

"So yeah, dude," the translation drawled, and oddly enough, the cadence and the tone seemed to match Jay's mannerisms almost exactly. "We were, like, just doing this work until something better came along, y'know? I never really wanted to work the rocks, right? And I know Bob doesn't even like low gravity."

Bob grunted agreement and no translation was needed.

"Anyway," Jay went on, "we don't got any special connection to the place, but we like, gotta get that ship back to the mining company or we'll be on the hook for it, y'know? I don't want to be working the rest of my life for free just to pay off that piece of junk."

"Isn't Vargas going to say anything?" I asked Nagarro. She seemed amused by the suggestion.

"So far he hasn't had to."

I frowned, checked my 'link. Time of day had no meaning on a starship, particularly one that had been out as long as we had and ran constant shifts on watch, but we had to keep a consistent ship's time anyway and it was, technically, sixteen hundred hours. Vicky had told me she'd meet me here in the Intelligence section ten minutes ago. I tapped a control on my 'link.

"Vicky, you still coming?"

"Sorry," she said immediately. "I got stuck down in the cargo bay. First platoon Bravo had a problem with the coilgun rounds we've been turning out from the fabricators and I had to show Sgt. Darlon how to file a report for the engineering and armory crew." Her sigh was a burst of static in my earbud. "And if you thought admin reports were boring, try teaching them to someone who didn't even know what a computer was two years ago."

"Ouch," I said sympathetically. "You still tied up with that?"

"I should be done in a few minutes. You want me to head on up?"

"No, it's almost dinnertime. I'm gonna go ahead and talk to Jay."

"Jay?" I could hear her frown and I chuckled.

"I'll explain later. See you in the mess." I ended the call and then offered Nagarro a nod. "Let's do it."

Vargas and the Marine both came to attention when I entered the compartment, but I waved it away.

"As you were." I motioned to Vargas. "Go take a break, Lieutenant. I want to talk to them for a while."

The officer didn't need to be asked twice, apparently having had his fill of Jay's monologuing for the day, and I fell into his chair, waiting until the hatch shut behind him before I turned my attention to the aliens.

Something I hadn't noticed back in the rock had been the smell. Not like an overpowering stench, but simply a faint, unpleasant musk reminiscent of the Tahni, not by the particulars of the scent but more in their difference from what I was used to. I resisted an urge to pinch my nose shut, resolving to get accustomed to it.

"Hi, I'm Cam Alvarez. I'm the acting commander of this... mission." It had taken effort not to call it a fiasco. "And I wanted to apologize to you for taking you away from your asteroid base and your ship without your permission. We just arrived in this system from very far away and we had to figure out a way to learn your language before we approached your government." The translator reworked the words into the hoots and clicks of their language, trying to distract me from what I was saying, and I had to concentrate to shut it out.

"I get that, dude," Jay said, nodding, which surprisingly meant the same thing to them that it did to us. The translation came close on the heels of the hoots and clicks, close enough that I could put the gap out of my mind and let the English synch with his mouth movements. "No problem at all. We're completely chill with answering your questions and shit. Like I said to your bud, Vargas, we're just worried about our jobs."

Bob said nothing.

"Do you work for a private company or for your government?" I was worried the question wouldn't translate right, because it wasn't a given that their society *had* private companies and I was prepared to expound, but Jay grasped it just fine.

"Consolidated Mining is a private company, but we're contracted to the Confederation government. It's like, easy money, you know? But they have a hard time getting anyone desperate enough to spend a year out here alone with no one else to talk to. Shit, even trying to do laser comms back home, there's a half an hour delay. You can send vids and letters and stuff, but no way you're having a conversation, y'know?"

Jay seemed determined to just keep talking until I interrupted him, so I did and hoped he wouldn't be offended.

"The Confederation is your planetary government?"

"Well, dude, it's like, *one* of the governments on our planet. What? Do they have just one government where you come from?"

"Kind of." I didn't feel like explaining our long, convoluted, and ugly history to him. "Our Commonwealth supervises our system and a bunch of others we've colonized. How many governments do you have?"

"Well, we got just the one," he replied, grinning, "because we're both from the Fed, but there's the Grey too."

"The Grey?" I repeated, frowning in confusion. I turned my eyes upward. "Dwight, is there some kind of translator error here?"

"I'm afraid not. I don't know the significance behind the

appellation, but the records from their ship do have multiple references to some entity which corresponds with the color humans refer to as gray."

I shook it off and tried again. If Jay had been disturbed by the exchange, he didn't show it. Bob remained silent.

"This... Grey? Are they your enemies?"

Jay made a face that I guessed meant diffidence, though there was no help from the translator and it might have been indigestion.

"Sometimes... we've never actually fought a war against each other, if that's what you mean. But it's been close, and there's been a bunch of proxy wars with the independent nations, like both sides provide the guns and those poor sons of bitches do the actual killing and dying." Jay's shoulders shook. "It's pretty nasty. But so far, everyone's too scared that if we started shooting at each other, then the fusion missiles would fly and we'd drop asteroids on each other until there was nothing left of the planet."

That sounded familiar, like something I'd read in the history books during my online studies for OCS, except for the dropping asteroids part. It sounded a lot like the Cold War between the United States and the Soviet Union back when both those nations had existed.

"Like, I wouldn't want to live in the Grey," Jay went on. "They got some serious authority issues there, like the whole deal is run by this council of maybe twenty people who just happen to be the richest guys in the country." He glanced around the room. "Say, you got anything to eat or drink? Feels like I've been talking for hours here." Jay twisted around to look back at his companion. "What about you, Bob? You want anything?"

Bob shook his head wordlessly.

"Can we get some water and maybe some snacks for these guys?" I asked loudly, hoping someone outside was listening.

They were, and it was barely ten seconds before Vargas returned with a couple bulbs of water and a bag of something crunchy.

"Is our food edible for them?" I asked, suddenly concerned as the Intelligence officer handed the snack to Jay. "It's not going to poison them or something, is it?"

"We checked that when they first got here," Vargas assured me. "Their biochemistry isn't that different than ours."

"It wouldn't be," Dwight put in. "They're warm-blooded oxygen-breathers. There's only so many ways they could evolve, and your Marines brought samples of their food along for me to analyze."

Jay wasn't paying attention to my concerns, just munching down on peanuts and popcorn while Bob drank from a bulb of water. I nodded thanks to Vargas and he left the compartment.

"And what about the Confederation?" I asked. "What sort of setup do they have?'

"Just like any civilized people, dude," Jay told me around a mouthful of food. "We vote on shit. Any time a decision comes up, we all get polled on our tabs and we vote." He reached into his shirt pocket and pulled out something that looked like a larger, more primitive version of a 'link and shook it demonstratively.

"Direct democracy, huh?" I said, raising an eyebrow. "I don't think we've ever tried that. How well does it work?"

Not that we *couldn't* have done it, but it would have required too many powerful people to give that power up, something that wasn't likely.

"Pretty good, I guess," he said, shrugging. "I mean, everything runs pretty smoothly most of the time. Everyone has to stay informed, which means keeping plugged into the net most of the time." He sniffed. "I kinda think the Grey try to influence our votes sometimes though."

"You're paranoid," Bob said with an amused snort.

"Who controls the jumpgate?" I asked. "The Confederation or the Grey?"

"We share it," Jay said, shooting a glare at Bob. "The Grey discovered it first but they couldn't figure out how to open it again without us, so we share it. We have like two colonies and we share those too. I mean, they're whole planets, man."

"Do you guys know who made the gates?"

Jay's brows went up.

"Well, dude, I didn't think *anybody* made them. The scientists all say it was just natural."

I made no comment on that. If any of their scientists suspected the gate *wasn't* natural, they'd probably keep it to themselves if they didn't want to get laughed out of academia. And speaking of laughs, now I had to get to the questions that might get *me* laughed out of the room.

"Are there are any legends of some ancient, lost alien civilizations?" I asked them. "Maybe ruins or carvings or anything?"

And Jay, of course, *did* laugh, but not as hard as I would have thought.

"Naw, man. The only aliens around are the Nova."

"The Nova?" I repeated. "What are the Nova?"

Jay shared an uncomfortable look with Bob.

"Nobody likes to talk about them much. I mean, the Grey don't *let* their people talk about them, but no one in the Fed wants to because it's embarrassing. We got to the second star system through the gates, the Confederation I mean, one of our exploration ships, and then once we'd hit the third, the Nova showed up. They told us that everything on that side of the gate was theirs and we weren't welcome." He shrugged. "The government didn't listen, of course. They came back with armed ships and tried to set up a colony anyway. The Nova showed back up with like a hundred ships and blew the hell out of us and that was the end of that. We got two star systems and we can't go any further."

"Did anyone ever try negotiating with these Nova again?"

"No, man, they don't want to talk to us. They never said another word after we left that system. They don't even try to colonize it, y'know? It's got *two* planets you can live on, that's what the news I saw on the net says, but the Nova don't even go near it. They just don't want *us* there."

"And do you know what these Nova look like?" I asked, still holding onto the faint hope they might be remnants of the Resscharr who went out this way—the Reconstructors, Dwight had called them.

"Well, yeah, man. When they warned our ships away from that system, they sent out a video call and the picture was all over the nets."

Jay tapped at the screen of his tab, then held it up for me. The image definitely *wasn't* a Resscharr. It wasn't anything I'd ever seen before, anything *any* of us had seen before. If I squinted hard, I could kind of make-believe Jay and Bob were human. These Nova, though, no amount of blurry vision or low light could have made them look like anything so much as bald-headed octopus people.

That's not entirely accurate, but I was no kind of scientist and there wasn't any other comparison I could make. There were three of them in the image, standing at the center of what had to be the bridge of one of their ships, a head-to-toe shot except they didn't have toes. They had what looked more than anything like tentacles, except they were stiffer than an actual octopus or squid, like these guys had a skeleton underneath them. Their arms were the same sort of setup except they split into squiggling worms at the end of the tentacles, what I guessed were their equivalent of fingers.

They weren't wearing clothes, per se, but they did have some kind of harness with pouches for storage, and despite their nudity, I still couldn't tell if they were male, female, or hermaphrodite.

"Dwight," I said, staring at the image wide-eyed, "have you ever heard of anything like this before?"

"No." The computer didn't elaborate, which was pretty much a first for him. Did AI feel emotional shock?

"Hey, um, Cam?" Jay said, digging through the bag for the last of the food. "What are you guys gonna do with me and Bob?"

"We're not going to hurt you," I assured him. "We can just put you right back out on that mining station if you want."

Jay exchanged another look with his friend, then leaned over and whispered something low enough that the translators couldn't pick it up. When he turned back to me, he was smiling.

"You're gonna head to Homeworld now, aren't you?"

"Homeworld?"

"That's the approximation of the name they use for their planet," Dwight said, seemingly over his brush with amazement. "And they call themselves, not surprisingly, *the* People. It's not very imaginative, but then you humans named your world *dirt*."

"Yes," I answered Jay's question, pointedly ignoring Dwight's barb. "We're going to talk to your people on Homeworld now that we can understand their language."

"Do you think maybe you could take us with you?" Jay's tone as interpreted by the translator was hopeful, like a child asking his parents for a pet. "Like, you know the language, or at least that tab thing you're carrying does, but we could still help you with the ins and outs, right? I mean, there's a lot of little things about living in the Fed that people don't know, a lot of who-you-know type stuff, right? You need someone's help, and we could do that." He wiggled his finger between himself and Bob. "We know people." Jay shrugged. "Well, we know people who know people. People who could get you in to see the right people."

"Wouldn't we just talk to your government officials?" I asked, amused by the offer. This guy was a fast talker, and they were alike whatever the species. "Your president or chairman or whatever you call it?"

"Aw dude, the Chairman is a figurehead, everyone knows that." He waved the idea away dismissively. "The real power's in the influencers." At my confused frown, it was actually Bob who explained it.

"The social influencers. They package the news on the net, do interviews, let people know what's going on so they can vote the right way." If the interpreter program was accurately portraying his tone, Bob didn't sound crazy about the setup, but he didn't elaborate.

"So, whaddya think, man?" Jay asked, spreading his hands. "You wanna give us a job? To be honest, we could use the work. Do you guys offer a medical plan?"

[4]

"Are they going to shoot at us?" Vicky asked, staring at the greens and blues of the planet.

From someone else, there might have been concern in the question, but she sounded more curious than worried, and not just because our ship had defense shields designed by an alien civilization millions of years old. Vicky and I had stared death in the face so many times, we'd both memorized every wrinkle and wart.

"Both the Feds and the Grey have orbital weapons," Wojtera reported, taking the question to heart rather than just as shooting the shit. *That* was daunting, the idea that the two of us had real authority. I was too used to being a strap-hanger on the bridge. "Lasers, I think. Maybe particle accelerators, but definitely powered by fusion reactors from the thermal signatures. They're aiming them our way."

Nance shot me a look.

"They won't shoot at us," I decided, though all I had to go on was talking to Jay and Bob. "Not until they know who we are. For all they know, we're the Nova coming back to kick their ass.

Lt. Chase, they're not going to be set up for EM transmissions. Can we do laser LOS to one of their antennae?"

"Yeah, there are major laser rectennae in orbit," Chase said, squinting at the sensor readouts. "I don't know which of them belong to which of those two nations you told us about in the briefing, but I could send transmit simultaneously to both if you want."

"I want. Run what I say through the translation program, but make sure they see my face. Like I said, they might assume we're Nova, and I want to make sure they know we're not."

I stood, wishing the bridge was in the habitation drum. That wasn't practical since we had to crew the bridge during maneuvers, which meant it had to be in line with the drive. The sticky plates in my ship boots would hold me in place, but no one looked as dignified in free fall. Chase nodded, then pointed to me. My instinct was to try to look at the camera, but there wasn't one. Fleet ships were fancier than the officers' quarters on a troop ship and the video intake was holographic, the cameras scattered around the perimeter of the bridge. Wherever I stood, they'd find me.

"You're up," Chase said, pointing at me.

Taking a deep breath, I stared straight ahead and tried to look stern and official. It was a con, of course. I was rarely stern and far from official. But I was an old hand at running cons.

"Greetings. We are representatives of the Commonwealth, a collection of star systems from far across the galaxy. We mean you no harm and only seek to return to our home. For that reason, we're searching for signs of an ancient civilization that may have passed through this area thousands of years ago. We need any information you have, any archaeological remains, any astronomical indications of high-energy events nearby. And we're willing to pay for any information you give us. You saw us appear as if out of nowhere just outside the orbit of your moon.

We did that using a means of interstellar travel called the Transition Drive. It uses the same principles as the wormhole jump-gates you've already discovered, but it lets you bypass those gates and go directly to a connected system. From what I understand of your current situation, this would be very important to you. We'll be waiting for a reply. The first ones to contact us will get the deal."

I slashed a hand sideways in Chase's general direction and he touched a control at his station.

"And that's it," he said. "It's sent."

"Are we sure this is smart?" Vicky asked, holding onto the back of her acceleration couch, using it to keep her in place. "I mean, remember how bad we thought it was when Colonel Hachette gave that tech manual to the Vailoa? How is this any different?"

"Wait, what tech manual?" Nance asked, eyes narrowing.

"This is different," I told her, putting off answering that question in front of the entire bridge crew. "They already have the method of opening the gates and the gates to study. They're going to figure out Transition Space soon enough, and even if I give them the specs, they won't be able to manufacture the exotic matter for the drive for decades."

And yeah, that sounded lame to me too, like something Hachette would have said, but it was all we had to offer these people. I put those concerns aside and stared at Chase, waiting for the reply. I was sure it would come almost immediately, and I was hoping it would come from the Confederation, since the Grey seemed way too much like an oppressive oligarchy and I knew I'd feel dirty dealing with them. Not that I wouldn't have done it anyway because it was my job to get these people home, not solve every world's political problems, but it was also nice being able to look at myself in the mirror.

Either way, *someone* was going to call back. Except no one did.

I shifted, frowning at the main screen and the planet displayed on it.

"What's going on?" I wondered. "Could they be trying to signal us back but we're not receiving?"

"Not a chance," Wojtera told me. "If someone's shining a laser on this ship, it's no brighter than a flashlight."

"Captain Alvarez," Nagarro's voice buzzed in my ear. "Jay wants to talk to you."

Wonderful. Maybe he wanted to ask to work for us again. I hadn't actually given him an answer, and damned if those two weren't bound and determined not to go back to that Godforsaken rock. But I didn't have anything else to do for the moment...

"Yeah, put him on."

"Hey, dude," Jay said almost before I got the last word out, "you're going about this all wrong!"

I sighed. This was all I needed right now, being lectured by a half-assed miner about political strategy.

"What do you mean, Jay?"

"You're playing right into the hands of the Grey! They're gonna start doing the shit they do on the net, on the public media, and trying to get the Fed turned against the idea of making a deal with you."

"If that's the case," I said, trying to keep myself from getting angry at the man, "then why haven't the Grey already got into contact with us?"

"Well, that's obvious, it's because they ain't got anything and they think the Fed does. They're going to get the people to vote down any deal with you and that'll give them time for their spies to steal anything we *do* have, then they'll trade for your drive and freeze out the Fed."

"Jay..."

"Dude, if you don't believe me, tie into the Fed-net right now and check what's trending."

Vicky frowned at me, only privy to half the conversation and obviously unhappy about it.

"Chase," I said aloud, realizing that no one else on the bridge could hear what Jay was saying either, "can you tie into the public data network in the Confederation?"

The younger man shrugged, fingers dancing in the haptic holograms of his station.

"I think so. It's a little tricky since they don't broadcast it on any EM bands, but I think I can read the microwave tower-to-tower transmissions from the surface. Give me a second."

"Hold on, Jay," I added, lest he start chewing my ear off again.

"I got it," Chase said. "Running it through the translator. You want it up on the screen?"

I didn't answer immediately. Hachette might have checked it privately first, worried about the effect on morale if it turned out he'd fucked up. Which was exactly why it passed through the crew like wildfire and killed morale every time he fucked up.

"Yeah, put it up."

I wasn't sure what to expect, but what filled the lower right quarter of the main screen was a two-dimensional display filled with smaller images, and if the computer was even attempting to provide a translation of the blocky, alien writing that coursed across the screen or the half-dozen people talking over each other, I couldn't understand a word of it. There were images that were clearer than others, radar screens with a single, large blip on them, telescopes showing us, the *Orion*, floating in high orbit. The ship had a unique look to it, and from that far away it reminded me of an angel hovering over the world.

Finally, dribs and drabs of conversation filtered through as the flood of information slowed. A female, young, about the age for a high-school student if it had been a Commonwealth world.

"How can we trust them? They're just like the Nova. This is some kind of trick to make us vulnerable to attack."

Another, this time an older male, and if I looked at him out of the corner of my vision I could imagine him as a farmer on one of the colony worlds telling trespassers to get off his lawn.

"It's ridiculous! We've already risked the future of our entire world defying the Nova and now we're going to make a deal with these weird-looking creatures? It's asking for trouble!"

"And this is just the latest in a series of incidents that have occurred due to our interference in matters that are none of our business." Older female with the air of a professional. "We're playing with fire here. We need to keep our attention on our own problems."

"Wow, they're really laying it on thick," Vicky commented, laughing softly. "Does that shit *work* on them?"

As if some ill-tempered god had been listening, a multicolored chart popped up on the screen. I couldn't make heads or tails of the thing, but the voiceover explained it for us.

"The most recent polls in advance of the public vote shows opinion running against the proposal of helping the humans of the Commonwealth with fifty-four percent of respondents against. The actual vote will take place in two days..."

"Shit," I murmured. "Cut it off, Chase." I touched my earbud, taking it off mute. "Jay, what do you suggest?"

"Dude, we have to go down there. The two of us and you. Just you though, no guns, no Marines, no armor. You have to get on the public nets and get your side of this story out. And you don't have a lot of time to do it."

"Right. I was afraid you were going to say that." I turned to Vicky and Nance. "I need a lander prepped. I'm going down to their capital to try to salvage this shitshow."

"That is a terrible idea, Alvarez," Nance blurted, "This is a possibly hostile world, and the only advantage we have over them is this ship and your hard-shell Marines, our technical edge. You're about to give all that up and put yourselves in their hands alone without so much as a fucking handgun?"

"No," Vicky agreed, the corner of her mouth turning up in a grin. "He's not going alone. I'm going with him."

Shit.

"Vicky," I said, keeping my voice even and steady, "it'd be a pretty bad thing for the mission if both of us got in over our heads. Besides, if things go bad, I was counting on you to come bail my ass out."

"And I still will. Besides, I've been training on how to fly a lander, so we won't have to even risk bringing a pilot with us."

Shit, shit, shit.

Shit.

"Nagarro," I said into my earbud, "get Jay and Bob to the hangar bay. We leave in half an hour."

[5]

"I think that was my best landing yet," Vicky said, powering her acceleration couch back from the lander controls.

"You're getting better," I agreed, eyeing Jay and Bob out of the corner of my eye. Bob was still sunk into his seat, golden face a few shades paler than normal, while Jay was puking loudly into the spacesick bag from the pocket of his chair. "Are you guys gonna be okay?"

"Oh, yeah, man," Jay assured me, folding up the bag and looking around for a place to stow it. "I mean, I may never fly again, but I'll live."

"Fuck," Bob put in earnestly.

I scanned the viewscreen, checking out the 360-degree cameras, and frowned. The spaceport at Two Rivers was a busy place even at the crack of dawn, the landing field crowded with shuttles, more coming in every minute, and there were service vehicles and crews winding their way around the entire ten-kilometer perimeter of the installation. But none heading our way.

I'd expected military troops, the landing area cordoned off and isolated, but there was no one waiting for us, not even a crowd of curious onlookers.

"Are we going to have to call a taxi?" I asked, looking back at Jay.

"No, someone'll be coming. I called my friend Benny and he called his old girlfriend Nadia and she called Frost."

"And Frost is...?" Vicky asked.

"Frost," he told her, setting the bag full of vomit in a corner and shrugging, "is *the* influencer, the chair of Fed Net Incorporated. She's the biggest of the big, the brightest of the bright, and she's the only one who can help you pull this off."

"Then where the hell is she?" Vicky wanted to know.

"She'll be here, man. You gotta have faith."

I was fresh out of faith at the moment and was about to tell him so when I saw the vehicle approaching. I'd seen all sorts of cars and trucks and busses on dozens of different planets, used by four different species, and ten or twelve separate cultures and, after a while, they all took on a certain sameness despite their cosmetic differences. They were all built to haul people or cargo as comfortably and efficiently as possible over some kind of road, be it gravel, dirt, or pavement, which meant tracks or wheels of some kind.

In the colony worlds, some people used hoppers for short-range air transport, but I'd never seen anyone except the Resscharr who used airborne vehicles for everything. And they had anti-gravity, which made it easy. Everyone else seemed to realize that the logistics and traffic-control issues of individual air transport for general use made it impractical.

But not these guys. The car that came to pick us up flew. I couldn't tell if it was a ducted-fan helicopter like our hoppers or maybe a VTOL jet of some kind, but it cruised in at a sedate speed and touched down right beside the lander. It was the bright, sparkling silver of a starship from the ViR movies but with the luxurious lines of a limousine, screaming a message of conspicuous consumption that crossed species barriers. A door near the front opened and one of the People hopped out, a male in some sort of uniform that looked surprisingly like puttees from early 20th century England along with knee-high black boots.

The driver, I assumed, or should I have said *pilot*? Either way, he rushed to the rear of the car and touched a control, opening a clamshell door for a female. Sexual dimorphism worked for the People in the usual way among warm-blooded humanoids, and this one was making the most of it in a low-cut black gown, her feathery, dark hair styled into a tall, swept-back cut.

"Oh, wow," Jay breathed, staring at the viewscreen. "She showed up in person! It's Frost."

"Let's not keep the lady waiting," I said, slapping the control to lower the lander's ramp.

Frost was waiting for us at the bottom, a polished, silver slipper tapping impatiently. A breeze across the tarmac teased at her long dress, cool, bracing. It might have been early spring here, maybe late fall. There were trees on the edge of the spaceport, a green belt between it and the squared-off skyline of Two Rivers, but I didn't know if whatever foliage had evolved on this planet changed colors with the seasons.

"You must be the one they call Cam," she said, hazel eyes looking me up and down. "My God, you're a weird-looking bastard." She shrugged. "Kind of cute though, in a lost-puppy sort of way."

"Nice to meet you, Ms. Frost," I said, keeping myself from stumbling over the words only through a supreme effort of will. I motioned to Vicky. "This is my wife and second-in-command, Victoria Sandoval."

"Good, good," Frost said, nodding curtly. "Good move, bringing your wife along. A power couple will sell this better." She made a gesture between the two of us. "Are you in love?

Children perhaps? Children would be best... doesn't matter how pale and ugly you are, kids are always cute."

"No children," I told her, staring bemused. She was every stereotype I'd ever seen in the ViR-dramas of a Corporate Council PR executive gone wild. "This is a military operation and we generally don't bring kids along. But yes, we are in love."

The woman sighed deeply.

"Oh, well, I suppose it'll do." She clapped her hands, then waved toward the aircar. "Inside. We have much to do and not much time to accomplish it. We'll speak in the air."

Vicky was, at least, *trying* to become a good pilot, which was more than I could say for Frost's driver. The air traffic was getting thicker as the primary star rose higher in the sky, but this guy didn't seem to care, barreling straight ahead as if the car had its own private defense shield. The other cars flying by in a mosquito-swarm stream must have thought so too, because they got out of the way in desperate haste.

Vicky took it all in with aplomb, grinning at the cars racing by outside the canopy only meters away like this was the best virtual reality rollercoaster she'd ever experienced, but I was just putting up with it. After so many years in drop-ships, so many space battles, I was inured to it, though I didn't enjoy it. Jay, on the other hand, looked as if he was reminiscing fondly on his out-of-stomach experience on the lander, and Bob's lips were skinned away from his teeth like he wanted to jump right out of the cockpit.

"What do you know about the history of your world?" I asked Frost, mostly to distract myself. "How did there get to be the two power blocs you guys have today?"

"Oh, I'm not a historian." Frost waved the question away.

The woman rummaged in a container recessed in the seat in front of her and came up with a bottle, popping the top cap back and taking a swig. She didn't offer us any. "I can suggest some books for you to read, if you like. All I know is what they teach children in school. Supposedly, we all evolved down in Land of the Sun…"

"That's the southernmost continent on this world," Dwight supplied. "Also the largest, though the climate there has become much more arid in the last few thousand years."

"I don't know about *that*," Frost went on, "but however it happened, we all wound up here in the north, on the Great Forest Glen."

"Their name for the continent you're on right now," Dwight told us, always helpful no matter how little I wanted to be interrupted.

"That was, I don't recall, a few hundred years ago maybe? But there was a split between two religious factions and the Grey emigrated east and founded their own nation. The Confederation is beyond all that superstitious nonsense now, but the Grey still clings to it and we've had nothing but trouble with them since." Another deep drink of whatever was in the bottle, and I began to suspect it wasn't water. "Oh, of course there are various other theories about why we wound up so different, geographical features, resources, diseases, demographics… but it all comes down to the fact that they still bow down to some magical god in the sky and it's made them backward. The Confederation has far outstripped the Grey in every field of science and technology. We built aircraft, spacecraft, developed fusion power well before they did, and they stole every innovation from us. They're leaches on our society, devouring resources, polluting our world, and shoving themselves into our advances. Thankfully, we developed computer technology first as well, or we'd never have our current system of government."

"How did they wind up finding the jumpgate first then?" I asked. "If they're so backward?"

"*Because* they're so backward," she snapped, features screwing up as if she found the question offensive. "While we were smelting asteroid ore in the belt with sophisticated solar reflectors, *they* were using fusion bombs to propel them into lunar orbit. It was reckless and stupid, and only blind luck allowed them to accidentally open the gate the first time." She sniffed, tossing her head haughtily. "Even then, *our* scientists had to explain how it had happened and repeat the process until we found a way to keep the gate open permanently."

Which was amazingly close to how *we'd* discovered our own gate, but I suppose if you go around setting off fusion bombs around a Predecessor wormhole, eventually you'll open the damned thing.

"Then, of course, they intimidated us into signing the treaty to share the gates and the resources on the other side of them, despite the fact that it was mostly Confederation infrastructure that exploits them."

"For someone who isn't a history student," Vicky interjected, "you certainly know a lot about history."

"Very recent history, darling. And recent history is what made me devote my life to building this company." She smacked the arm of her chair as if demonstrating which company she meant. "The Grey have been meddling in our politics, hamstringing our attempts to expand our resources, doing everything they can to drag us back into the dark ages when they ruled this world. I've made it my life's work to fight their intrusion into our lives, and I'll be damned if I'm going to allow them to steal this away from us."

"You mean the Transition Drive?" I asked. Maybe that was obvious, but I had my suspicions that just us being there and being featured by her network was nearly as important to her.

"Of course!" she said, gesturing expansively, spilling a few droplets of the pink liquid in her bottle on the seat in front of her. "We're trapped, you see. Yes, it's three star systems, three habitable planets, which should be enough room and resources for centuries, or even a thousand years, but that's not the point. We're trapped with *them*, with the Grey, and they don't care how much space they have, they don't care that they don't *need* to take our land or our mines or our asteroid claims. It all has to be theirs because their god tells them so."

And *that* sounded very familiar, too, and from a much more recent example.

"That's not even mentioning the Nova, of course, who aren't as important to you at the moment." Frost punctuated the change of subject with a long, slender finger jabbed at my chest, as if this was all my fault. "But they're the ones keeping us hemmed in, and we're helpless against them. If we want to do anything but fight and scrape for a chance at second place, we have to get around them, get some sort of edge. And that's where you come in, Cameron, Vicky." Frost smiled fiercely. "And that's where *I* come in."

"So, what do you want us to do?" Vicky asked her, and I got the sense that the question was more to get a word in edgewise than from any curiosity. Frost was a talker, even more than Jay, and if there was any benefit to the gut-wrenching flight, it was that it kept his jaws clenched for a while.

"Interviews, of course. In-depth and personal. You tell your story, not just about your ship and your mission but about *yourselves*. That's important. This has to be personal to win people over."

I raised an eyebrow, suddenly frightened in a way I hadn't been by the reckless pilot.

"You want us to go in front of your whole planet and talk about our personal lives? What does that have to do with your people deciding whether or not to trade information for the Transition Drive?"

"You're still thinking like we're dealing with a government, Cam," Vicky admonished, offering a smile to take the edge off the words. "Government officials, Corporate Council execs, they think about things like foreign policy, economic growth, military deployments. The normal people read the scansheets and gossip about celebrities. They want to know about other *people*, not about events, not about threats and resources. You were a street kid, so maybe you didn't live that life, but my mom and sisters sure did."

"I can see why you married her," Frost told me, laughing. Or at least that was what the translator *told* me she was doing. To me, it sounded more like a cow mooing. "She's obviously the smart one."

[6]

"Dude, this place is *really* nice," Jay enthused, gawking around the high-rise apartment like a tourist. "I always dreamed of having a place like this."

"Well, don't get used to it," Frost snapped, standing in the doorway, arms crossed. "This place is one of my leases, and you'll be staying here only as long as it takes to get this vote done." The woman checked her tab, which she'd done at least a dozen times on the elevator ride up to the top floor of this building. "Which will be the day after tomorrow, which means your interview has to be tomorrow."

"Isn't that cutting it close?" I asked her.

"The closer the better. The public has a short memory." She checked her tab again. "And now I have to go prime the pump for you." Frost waved in a circle around her. "There's food in the kitchen you can warm up in the oven, but if you want anything else, just push the button by the door here and call for service."

She didn't wait for us to confirm we'd heard her, just stalked out, the soles of her platform shoes clicking off the hardwood floor.

"She's intense," Bob said, watching Frost as she closed the door behind her.

"You said it," Jay agreed. "I feel like she's gonna chew us up and spit us out." He turned to me and shrugged. "But she's the best."

I wasn't paying attention, pacing over to the wall-sized window looking out over Two Rivers. I'd been too caught up with the flight and the conversation to sightsee along the way, but now, looking out from forty stories up, I was impressed. It wasn't a megacity like Trans-Angeles, but neither was it one of the cookie-cutter cities the Commonwealth had laid down in the colonies, where none of the buildings were over six stories and everything looked like it had been designed by a military engineer.

Two Rivers had character. There was art and style to the design of the skyscrapers, not like the towering spires and obelisks of Tahn-Skyyiah or the brain-twisting architecture of the Resscharr on Decision. This was more human, but like if we'd taken a different turn, maybe like there'd never been a Sino-Russian War and the nukes had never flown. Like the old cities hadn't burned, hadn't been replaced by the new Commonwealth and their megalopolises but instead had evolved into something else over decades. Something more artistic and elegant. It made me appreciate these people—*the* People—more. I didn't know if it was all of them or just the Confederation.

"You know, I was born not twenty kilometers from here," Jay said, pointing east toward the rising sun. "My mom and dad still live out there. Bob, he's from all the way across the continent in Mountainside, but we met when we did our two years in the national militia."

I chuckled.

"You were in the military?"

"Everyone is, man." Jay shrugged. "I mean, most of us don't

stay in, but we can all get called up if there's an emergency. That's the way we gotta do it because the Grey has a huge army."

"Jay, come check out the size of the screen on this entertainment center!"

That was as excited as I'd heard Bob, including when he'd been abducted by aliens, and Jay's face lit up with the news.

"Be right there, dude!"

He ran to the bedroom like a child on Christmas morning and Vicky sighed, watching the two of them, hands on her hips.

"After the last two years," she told me, "none of this feels real."

"I know you weren't speaking to me, Captain Sandoval," Dwight pitched in, "but I quite agree. Until we arrived here, I would have been willing to swear—as your people say—on a stack of Bibles that the only places in this galaxy that life had evolved were Earth and the Skrela homeworld. The Resscharr wiped out the Skrela tens of thousands of years ago, and all the other life was engineered from Earth DNA."

"Yeah," I agreed, not bothering to express for the millionth time how much we didn't like him listening into our conversations. "That's a hell of a lot of parallel evolution, isn't it? I don't know that we're going to have the chance to run any genetic scans on them, but I'll admit, I sure as hell want to."

"Maybe these'll help." Vicky had walked into the next room, and I followed her into what had to be a library.

I hadn't seen a physical book until I was out in the colonies in the Marines, and even then they were a curiosity fabricated from local wood and pulp and cotton by eccentric purists. I liked the feel of a book, and when we'd lived on Hausos I'd always meant to have some printed out for myself, but I'd never gotten around to it. These weren't exactly like the volumes I'd seen in Dak Shephard's study on Brigantia, but they were close, bound with cloth-wrapped wood, the characters the same hieroglyphic-looking writing I'd seen in the scrolling on the Fed-net.

Vicky had pulled one off the shelf and was thumbing through it.

"It's so weird," she said, shaking her head. "The translator is working with the readout in my contact lens so I can read the original script in my left eye and English in the right." She raised the book demonstratively. "This one's a history book, I think. Something about the original settlers on this continent."

I closed my left eye experimentally and scanned the books on the shelves, searching titles. Some of them didn't make much sense even translated to English, any more than some random English titles would have meant anything to a Tahni looking at them. I saw something that mentioned biology and pulled it out, opening to a page near the middle. Then I opened both eyes and shook my head because it still didn't make any sense.

"It's a genetics text," Dwight told me. "Open it to the beginning and scan through it quickly. I'll be able to read it through your enhanced vision lens."

"Are you telling me you can access what we see in our contact lenses?" I demanded, the book suddenly forgotten.

"I *can*," Dwight admitted, "but I would never do that without your permission, of course."

And I could believe that as much as I wanted. Sighing, I started at the beginning of the book.

"No, it reads from right to left," Dwight informed me.

It only took a few minutes to flip through the text, though if I'd spent hours poring through it, I would have learned just as much. I'd *tried* to delve deep into science and math courses in my continuing education as an officer, but that seed had fallen upon stony ground as Mama would have said, and I'd done better with history and psychology.

"This is fascinating," Dwight enthused. "We may not need

to run any genetic samples after all. They've done it *for* us. Not just for themselves, but for the rest of the life on this planet."

"So, are they based on Earth life too?" Vicky asked. "Is this whole place another experiment by the Resscharr?"

"Their physiology is *not* based on DNA, but it *is* based on RNA."

"Well, how the hell is *that* possible?" I shook my head, wanted to throw up my hands but I was still holding the book. "Isn't RNA just as much an Earth thing as DNA?"

"Not necessarily," Vicky told me, setting down the history book and raising a finger, her eyes clouded in thought. "I read something about how RNA might have been carried around the galaxy on comets or asteroids, going from one planet to another. Panspermia is what it's called. It was just a theory, but I think they've actually found RNA strands on comets since then."

"It's more than a theory," Dwight informed us. "The Resscharr confirmed it millennia ago, but they'd never found another sentient species that had arisen from panspermia. Until now, of course. But there's something incongruent about their theories of evolutionary biology... they seem to have an accelerated idea of punctuated equilibrium. Their dating methods only take life on this planet back a few million years, which is patently impossible. The greatest likelihood is that the entire ecology here was transplanted."

"Which would fit the large moon," I reasoned. I shoved the biology text back into its niche in the shelf. "More terraforming. This has all the earmarks of the Predecessors. But you said millions of years ago. That would have put it back near the beginning, wouldn't it?"

"It would. And I would expect that knowledge to be in my database, but it isn't, which I would take to mean that it was a well-kept secret."

"The question is, do we care?" Vicky asked. "All we want is

to find the Northwest Passage, right? Does it matter whether these guys are natural growth or transplant?"

"No," I agreed, although a bit reluctantly. It was all beyond my understanding, which might have been why I found the whole thing so fascinating. "But it might be a clue to how close we are to the Reconstructors. If they *did* put the People here on this world, there had to be a reason for it. It's right there in their name, the Reconstructors. They were trying to rebuild what they had back in the Cluster with the Tahni. If the People were their new Tahni, then maybe they've come back to check on them."

"Not a bad line of reasoning, Cam," Dwight allowed, sounding as if he was surprised I could come up with it. "Which also means the Resscharr might be part of their legends and lore, whether they recognize them for what they are or not. Perhaps gods or angels."

"And maybe it means we aren't wasting our time here," I added. "That'd be nice."

"You guys want some food?" Jay asked. At some point during our conversation, he and Bob had made their way from the bedroom to the kitchen and they were rummaging through the cabinets, pulling out prepackaged meals. "I know you're on a different schedule and all, but it's lunchtime and we're starving."

"Aren't you on a different schedule too?" I asked him. "You were living in the asteroid belt until a couple days ago."

"Yeah, but we kept our local schedule to Two Rivers' time. Just out of the faint hope we might wind up back here someday." He grinned broadly and spread his hands. "And here we are! Best jobs we ever had!"

"I still don't know how we're going to pay you," Vicky told him. "We don't have any of your money."

"We'll figure out something," Jay said, waving it away. "I

mean, almost anything you guys have up there is better than what we have. Like those hologram projectors you use—we don't have anything as good as that. You give us just one of those and we'll be set for life!"

"Until the Grey steals the design and starts selling them at half the cost," Bob added, not looking up from the instant-heat meal he was unwrapping.

"And you called me paranoid," Jay shot back.

"I could eat something," I told them, rubbing at my eyes, "but then I think I'm going to grab some sleep. It might be your lunchtime, but it's pretty far past *our* bedtime."

"You're getting soft in your old age, Alvarez," Vicky teased, pushing at my shoulder.

"Naw, I just learned the same lesson *you* should have, Captain Sandoval." I grabbed her around the waist and pulled her along with me to the other bedroom. "Never turn down a meal or a nap when you can get it."

―――

I'm not sure whether I was sleeping when Dwight spoke. I don't remember waking up, just being suddenly aware of my surroundings, as if I woke up a moment before the words with a prescience that they were coming.

"Captain Alvarez, there's a problem."

"What?"

Vicky sat up at the same time as I did, and I knew Dwight had invaded her earbud and her sleep simultaneously. We were both fully dressed since it was sometime in the afternoon, locally, and we hadn't wanted to be unprepared if Frost returned to yank us into some publicity shoot. The room was warm for me, so I hadn't even retreated beneath the covers.

It was dark, but not the dark of night, just the shadows of a place well insulated from the light of day. Enough light slipped beneath the door to reveal the details of the walls, the outlines of the furniture.

"Someone's coming up the elevator to this level."

"Couldn't it be some of Frost's people?" I asked, not looking up from pulling on my boots.

"It could be, but it isn't. I have access to Ms. Frost's schedule and the list of approved visitors, and these six people are definitely not on it. Check your 'link."

I patted at my belt for a second before remembering I'd left the thing on the small night table beside the bed. The display was small, so I hit the control to transfer it to my enhanced-vision contact lens and closed my left eye. The half dozen men crowded into the elevator *could* have been maintenance workers or just some guys coming back from a party, but they weren't. Their clothes didn't give them away, the dark-colored tunics and trousers not that different from what I'd seen of Two Rivers fashions on their Fed-net. Their features might have been slightly different than Jay and Bob, but I wasn't familiar enough with the cultures on this world to make out ethnic differences.

No, what made them stand out was universal, whether it was Tahni, human, or whatever. They were ready. Every single one of them was alert, standing straight, shoulders relaxed, elbows just slightly bent, like they expected some enemy to attack at any moment. They were trained soldiers, nearly a full squad of them, all in an elevator heading for this floor. It was too big a coincidence to be anything but enemy action.

"I've analyzed their facial structure against the records on their public nets," Dwight informed me, "and I can say with perhaps eighty-five percent certainty that all of them originated from lands under the control of the Grey."

"Shit," I murmured.

"Well, that's the downside of a culture that puts everything on social media for everyone to see," Vicky commented, looking around the bedroom. "You think there's any weapons in this place?"

I didn't answer immediately, throwing open the door and stalking down the short hallway. The apartment was arranged with the living area as the hub of a short-spoked half wheel and I circled clockwise around it, checking the library along the way.

"Jay?" I called. "Bob?"

Nothing. Damn, could the two of them have been in on it? I hoped not. I kind of liked those guys.

"I estimate you have thirty seconds until the elevator reaches this floor, Captain Alvarez, Captain Sandoval," Dwight announced. "You should take appropriate precautions."

"Thanks, Dwight," I ground out. "How about you try calling the police or the army or whatever?"

"I've notified building security," Dwight told me. "But this city doesn't have a central law enforcement agency, and each district hires their own private security. They're hesitant to become involved in international political machinations which might result in their own deaths."

"Oh, good," Vicky cracked from the kitchen, rummaging through drawers. "They're so damn useful. Why don't you ask them if they'll loan us a couple guns?"

The last door was the bedroom where Jay and Bob had discovered the entertainment center, and as it turned out they weren't traitorous, just indolent. Both of them were sprawled out on reclining chairs, decked out in earphones and some kind of virtual reality goggles, weaving patterns with wireless controllers. Up on the screen, giant robots were fighting with flaming swords, but I didn't bother to ask who was winning, just yanked the goggles off their faces. Wide eyes looked up at me in shock.

"We got an elevator full of Grey soldiers heading this way.

Either of you two worth a shit in a fight?"

"I haven't picked up a gun since I got out of the militia," Jay squeaked, the color going out of his face. Bob tossed away his controller and jumped out of his chair, looking through the open door like the bad guys were already there.

"That's just as well," I said, shrugging, "because we don't have any guns unless Frost keeps some hidden in this place."

"Well, if she does, she didn't tell me, man!" Jay said in a plaintive tone edged with panic. "I'm not like a soldier or anything! I did maintenance on fucking cargo planes!"

"Here," Vicky said, handing me a long, silver kitchen knife. I looked at it doubtfully, then at her. "Hey, it's the best we can do," she said, waving around a broad, chopping blade. "Unless you want to start breaking up furniture."

I took a deep breath, let it out. This was bad. I was a Drop Trooper, not Force Recon and definitely not some kind of commando, not like the guys coming up the elevator.

"Will they have guns, Dwight?" I asked. "Are there sensors or something in the building?"

"There are metal detectors and millimeter-wave radar in the lobby of this building," the AI informed me. "However, if these are military or intelligence operatives, they may be carrying weapons designed to avoid detection."

"You're very reassuring," Vicky told him. "Any chance you can shut down the elevator?"

"It's controlled by a closed system for safety reasons," Dwight told me. "Manual operation only."

"Jay, Bob," I said, "get in the closet and hide. Don't come out until we tell you to."

I was about to tell them not to argue, but I needn't have bothered since they nearly tripped over each other sliding open the closet door and ducking inside. I shook my head. Two against six then.

"Dwight, can you at least turn off the lights and keep them that way, bypass the manual switches?"

By way of reply, the apartment plunged into shadow, the late afternoon sun filtered by the surrounding buildings providing the only light... until the shades slid shut, plunging the place into total darkness. Not for us, of course. The enhanced-vision contact lens flickered to life with infrared and thermal filters. It was only half my vision, but the human brain, amazing thing that it is, somehow managed to make it look three-dimensional.

"Thanks."

"They're out of the elevator, heading down the corridor," Dwight informed us. "They'll be at the door in ten seconds."

"You take the left," I told Vicky, motioning to the alcoves to either side of the front door. "I'll be on the right. Let the first two get inside."

"We're probably going to die," Vicky informed me, stepping into the shelter of the niche in the wall.

"You always say that," I murmured, turning the knife in my hands. I'd fought with one before, way back in the day, but only long enough to get away from the other guys. Everything I'd learned about actual combat tactics with a knife had come from Marine boot camp and a few sessions with Top during the course of the last few months.

"I do. And eventually, I'm going to be right."

"I'll bet you twenty bucks we live."

"What kind of a bet is that?" she asked, leaning out to frown at me. "If you lose, neither of us will be around for you to pay off!"

"They're at the door," Dwight said.

"All right." I leaned back into the wall. "Dwight, there's one more thing you can do for me..."

[7]

The door had some kind of electronic lock, but it didn't stop them.

A muffled, metallic *thunk* told the story, and I didn't need to know *how* they did it. They were spies, assassins probably, and they wouldn't have come here without the right tools to do the job. Which likely meant they had guns too, the detectors notwithstanding. If the gang hitters in the Underground could do it, I was sure the Grey could pull it off too.

I wanted to talk to Vicky, wanted to tell her that they'd probably enter in teams of two, but that was just my innate desire to be doing something, to be in control. She knew the situation as well as I did, was probably as good with a knife. I kept quiet, waited. A black-clad arm pushed the door open and the fat-muzzled barrel of a handgun pushed through.

I still waited. The man was short, slender, like most of the truly dangerous people I'd met in my life. The big ones didn't *have* to be dangerous because their size intimidated everyone. He moved like a cat, stalking through the door, not opening it all the way. Careful. Methodical. The light from the hallway spread out through the opening, leaving both sides dark, and he wasn't going to barge in. That was a shame. This would have been easier if he'd been careless, headstrong.

I held my breath, willing him to step inside. Mama had told me once that my abuela on her side, who'd died before I was born, had believed in psychic powers, had told her that her own grandmother had been able to influence others with just her mind. I didn't buy it, but I wished it were true, wished I was actually dragging him inside.

Maybe it was, because he took two more quick steps, scanning left and right, the barrel of his gun tracking with his eyes. His face was narrow, angular, his head shaven, a scar white on the side of his neck. He looked right at me and saw nothing in the deep shadows of the alcove because I willed him to see nothing. He looked away, moving inside, motioning behind him, and the next one followed. This one was a woman, though her clothes were identical to his and so was her gun. For a race of humanoids who only shared RNA with us, their sexual dimorphism worked about the same way.

She stepped through and I moved. The guy was on my side and so was the back of the door, and I slammed into it before I slammed into him, shoulder into his ribs, and as I knocked him off-balance I slashed the knife downward into his right arm. It was a kitchen knife and not an incredibly expensive one and the blade snapped, leaving the point stuck in his arm.

He was tough and didn't drop his gun, but his grip had loosened enough for me to rip it out of his hand. He swung at me with his left hand but I dropped, knowing there was no way I could take this guy hand-to-hand and not even trying. I hit awkwardly on my right shoulder blade, not worrying about my balance, not worrying about leaving myself open to his attack, just worrying about getting a grip on that gun.

It was mostly plastic, light and poorly balanced, but I wasn't trying to make a long-distance shot, and all that mattered was that its trigger was in the right place. I jerked it over and over. The report was a hoarse cough, suppressed, the sound of the bullets smacking home drowning it out. The assassin jerked and stumbled, falling off to the side, blood spattering on my legs. I didn't try to jump up—that would take seconds I didn't have. Instead, I shifted the muzzle of the pistol to the other side, to where Vicky was struggling with the woman.

The woman was fast, faster than the guy in front had been, or maybe she'd just had a microsecond's warning because of my attack on her comrade, but she'd managed to grab Vicky's knife hand, while Vicky had control of her wrist. She had the gun pointed up at the ceiling and the two were doing a high-stepping dance, each trying to stomp on the other's leg.

I shot the woman twice in the side, and that was all the time I'd been able to buy slamming the door shut. It burst open and the other four exploded through.

"Now!" I yelled, but Dwight was already on it.

The apartment was high-end, befitting the preeminent Ms. Frost, and thus came with a state-of-the-art fire suppression system. A spray of white gas shot out of the ceiling and right into the faces of the Grey commandos who were coming through the door. The squawk of confusion that came from the man in the front was satisfying, but what was even more satisfying was the full three seconds the choking cloud of gas gave me, and the smoke screen that my thermal lens could see through but their flesh-and-blood eyeballs couldn't.

Still lying flat on my back on the hardwood floor, I didn't try to aim, just fired into the white and red silhouettes the thermal imaging provided. What I hit was a mystery, but the results weren't. The four of them tried to turn and run, but two fell, one motionless except for a final jerk of nerves, the other trying to crawl on hands and knees until I fired off the rest of the rounds in the pistol's magazine and he slumped to the floor.

The fire suppression gas swirled into the climate control vent fans and the room began to clear, and I rolled to the left, getting myself out of the line of fire in case the other two were still out in the hallway, waiting to pick us off.

They weren't. The corridor was empty, the last two Grey hitters gone.

"Are you okay?" I asked, coughing and choking the words as I finally rolled onto my feet, dropping the empty gun. It clattered with a hollow, plastic sound, a discarded toy, but before the echo had faded I'd already grabbed a fresh weapon from the hallway just outside the door.

Vicky didn't answer immediately, hacking out the last traces of gas, gulping down air until she could speak again.

"I'll live," she estimated. "And I guess I owe you twenty dollars."

"Dwight, do me a favor," I said, leaning against the doorway, trying to catch my breath. "Call those damned rent-a-cops again and let them know we did the hard part, see if you can get them to come clean up the mess."

———

"What the hell do I pay you for, you cowardly piece of shit?" Frost bellowed at the hapless security officer, bracing the uniformed man like the meanest DI at boot camp. "I should suspend your fucking contract right now! You *know* who these people are!" She pointed at me and I waved, not getting up from the kitchen chair. Not that I didn't want to, but the post-adrenaline-spike shakes had hit and I wasn't confident in my ability to stay on my feet.

"You know how important they are," Frost went on, "what they could mean to this country, to this company, to *me* personally! And you were just going to sit back and watch them get killed by spies from the Grey without doing so much as lifting a finger? Tell me why the hell I shouldn't just terminate your entire organization and sue you for your last red cent?"

"Ma'am," the security police officer said, his words clipped and precise, as if he was a private being dressed down by a general, "I have no excuse other than that I was not on duty and my second in command was poorly trained and lacked discipline. He will, of course, be fired immediately, and you'll have a full, written apology and a refund of this month's payment."

The rest of the security commander's squad was still swarming around the apartment and through the hallway, collecting evidence, digging bullets out of the walls and floor, and taking statements. I'd already given mine under the direction of Frost's legal counsel, who was now sitting next to Vicky, guiding her answers to questions being recorded on a small video camera. The man had introduced himself as The Road Runs Straight, which I'd immediately told Dwight to change to Gary because he *looked* like a Gary. Gary was pleasantly professional and ruthless in his defense of Ms. Frost's interests, which I found refreshingly honest.

Three of the bodies had been carried away by a crew in white biohazard suits, but they were still working on the last one, the woman. She'd created quite a mess, not just from where I shot her. As it turned out, Vicky had buried the knife in the woman's throat the second the assassin had let go of her arm, and there was a lot of blood on that side of the room.

"And that was when my client acted in self-defense against the Grey assassins," Gary told the security officer, emphasizing his words with a knife-hand gesture. "I want the record to show that these people were armed and came in with murderous intent."

"That's perfect, sir," the investigator said, shutting off the camera and giving the lawyer a nod. "If we need anything else, we'll get back in touch with you, but I think the evidence speaks for itself."

I snorted a cynical laugh. These guys were a lot different than the police I was used to back in Trans-Angeles.

"Are you injured, Captain Alvarez?" Frost asked, putting a hand on my shoulder. I blinked, realizing I must have zoned out because I hadn't noticed her finish her dressing down of the commander. "Do you need me to call in medics to attend to you or Captain Sandoval?"

She was acting solicitous, but I got the sense it *was* just an act. Not that she didn't care whether we lived or died, but she cared for her own reasons and was heavily invested in getting us to believe it was altruistic. Either way, we needed her and there was no point in pissing her off by making it obvious I didn't buy her schtick.

"No, we're both fine," I assured her. "I could use some water though." Cotton mouth, another symptom of the post-adrenaline crash, one I was very familiar with.

"Oh, I got ya, dude!" Jay said, running to the kitchen.

He'd been spastic since we'd retrieved him and Bob and from the closet, practically bouncing off the walls with excess energy, and I'd seen that before too. Surviving a brush with death was a high that some people got addicted to. Bob, on the other hand, was sitting on the couch, staring straight ahead through the wall, hugging his arms to himself. He was close to shock, and he hadn't even been out here for the really bad parts.

"Tell me something, Ms. Frost," I said. "Are we going to be in any trouble for this?"

"This?" she scoffed. "Oh goodness, no! This was very definitively justifiable homicide. You'll be totally cleared once the city magistrate sees the evidence and the recorded interviews."

"And they'll just take your people's word for it?" I

wondered. "Even though this is just a private security company?"

"Of course. The company is completely bonded with the city and national government. Is this not how it works where you are from?"

"Not at all," I assured her. "There, both of us would have been sitting in police headquarters for hours until they went through every piece of evidence ten times and checked us out all the way back to birth. And *then*, we'd have to practically get down on our knees and beg to get cut loose." I shrugged. "And that's not even taking into account the whole part where we're aliens and this is an international incident."

"Oh, the State Security Service will investigate the Grey assassins," Frost said. "But there's no reason for you to be held. You certainly don't know anything pertinent about them." The woman smiled in a very catlike way. "But I have to say, this will play *very* well in our interview. Not just a love story but a spy story as well! I have security camera footage of the whole thing and the ratings are going to be through the roof!" Frost leaned in closer to me, a conspiratorial tilt to her eyebrow. "Tell me something... you're both soldiers, correct?"

"Marines," Vicky corrected automatically from the next chair over. "But basically, yes."

"So, you've done this before? I mean, shot people, had people shoot at you?"

"Oh, yeah," I said, laughing humorlessly. "Not the first time. Or the tenth time."

"Or the hundredth time," Vicky added. "We fought in an interstellar war with another species for nearly eight years."

"Ooh, maybe we should leave that part out," Frost decided, pursing her lips. "We want you to be capable and slightly dangerous for an air of mystery, but not warlike and deadly.

Remember that for tomorrow—noble, mysterious, slightly dangerous, but not warlike. You come in peace and all that."

"We *do* come in peace," I said, taking a bottle of water from Jay. I sucked down a long swig and then sighed, the sandpaper dryness in my mouth finally gone. "How sure are you that these guys were from the Grey government? Have they ever done anything like this before? I mean, snuck into your country and killed people?"

"Oh, dude," Jay said, shaking his head. "It's all over the nets all the time! They send kill teams across the border to take out anyone who defects out of Grey territories. I mean, there are whole movies about that shit."

Vicky rolled her eyes.

"I'm sure your spy movies are great sources of intelligence."

"Yeah, *our* movies are full of bullshit about ancient aliens," I murmured. "None of *that* could ever be true."

"Spy movies aside," Frost interjected, "yes, the Grey *have* been known to take direct action, as your friend said, mostly against defectors who've shared intelligence with the Fed government." She ran a hand over her eyes. "What a fucking mess this place is. It's going to take days to get it cleaned up. I'll find you another place to spend the night, of course." Frost glared at the security officer. "Someplace with security that *isn't* useless."

[8]

I squinted at the studio lights, fighting back a headache. Frost had provided a replacement for our room, this one halfway across town, but sleep had proven elusive for both of us. You'd think, after all this time, I would have been able to shrug this kind of thing off, but some things didn't change. No matter how soft the bed or how comforting the white noise, my brain wouldn't turn off, so Vicky and I had just held each other into the night, waiting for the sun to rescue us.

It probably hadn't helped that Jay and Bob were up all night long gaming, but I hadn't had the heart to ask them to stop. They were dealing with shock and post-traumatic stress too, just in their own way. I knew a Marine who used to dance around the barracks all night naked after we got back from a mission, and thank God neither of these guys had tried anything like *that*. I didn't need to know if the similarities between them and us went that far.

They were sitting off to the side, out of the camera shot, munching on the breakfast sandwiches that had been left for us in the lobby of the studio. It was a small office in a high-rise building. These people seemed to love high-rise buildings, and as much as I appreciated their architecture, I was starting to get tired of long elevator rides. Or maybe it was just the headache.

"Chill out," Vicky whispered aside to me, leaning to the side of her chair and brushing her shoulder against mine. "You look like you're about to get called into the division commander's office for an ass-chewing."

"If only," I hissed back.

This whole place gave me the creeps, between the bright red curtains behind us to the clownish makeup Frost wore. I was surprised she hadn't made *us* wear makeup, but she'd assured me that our strange coloration and weird faces were part of the draw, that if we looked *too* much like the People, they'd doubt that it was real, think it was all some kind of scam.

Then there were the lights, the cameras with their oversized, fisheye lenses pushed way too close to us, and the microphones hanging down from the ceiling.

"This shit looks way too old-fashioned for a society with fusion power and interstellar space travel," I said softly, hoping the translator wouldn't pick it up.

"Different societies develop along different lines," Dwight explained patiently, like he was speaking to a slow child. "Don't make the assumption that every civilization will progress at the same rate that yours did in every field."

"The Tahni didn't," Vicky reminded me. "Their computer technology was way behind ours."

"All right," Frost said, descending into the chair opposite ours with the grace of a gymnast, a sandhill crane descending into her nest. "We're all set up and we have monitors in place to gauge public reaction in realtime." She gestured at flat-screen displays on the walls, each showing some kind of multicolored chart that even the translators couldn't decode adequately for me to understand it. "If I abruptly change directions in this interview, don't be alarmed, it's in reaction to the results. Go with it and follow my lead. We ready to go?"

Vicky nodded and I sighed, rubbing at my temples.

"Ready as I'll ever be," I said.

"Going live in five," Frost said, "four, three, two, one." She nodded sharply. "Good evening, concerned citizens of the Confederation. This is Frost bringing you another exclusive, the hottest news, the latest developments in what may be the biggest story in the history of this planet. Today, on a fine, sunny, Two Rivers morning, I bring to you Cameron Alvarez and Vicky Sandoval, representatives of the human Commonwealth from the far-off world of Earth. They've come to our system to make us an offer, an offer that could change the very course of our history and turn the Confederation into the preeminent space power in this part of the galaxy."

Which was laying it on thick, but she was a media specialist and I assumed she knew what she was doing.

"Before us is the chance to vote on whether to accept their offer, a chance to receive the power of the gods. Before we do that, I felt you deserved the chance to meet our new friends, to let them explain their circumstances. But others are not interested in allowing our guests to speak to you, the voters, in giving you that choice. Agents of the Grey infiltrated one of our buildings last night and tried to assassinate them, but they overestimated their own ability... and underestimated their prospective prey. The whole thing was captured via security cameras and I'll play it for you now."

The video played out on one of the screens on the wall behind us, and I turned to watch almost against my will, my eyes drawn to the carnage. It was beyond odd seeing myself in the third person, as if I was watching it happen to someone else, as if the scene playing out before me was a movie starring someone who just looked like me. It had felt awkward when it had happened to me, felt desperate and stumbling and imprecise, so unlike operating in the suit. In the Vigilante, everything was separated from reality by a layer of machine, insulating me. This had been raw, personal, uncomfortable. Too much like my life before the Marines.

On the screen, though, it looked as if I knew what I was doing, moving precisely, professionally. What I also hadn't seen the first time around was how close we'd come. Pistol suppressors lined up straight at my chest, and maybe the bullet-resistant material would have stopped the rounds and maybe they wouldn't have. I wouldn't have wanted to find out the hard way but I'd come damn close to it. I was getting the shakes again just looking at it.

"The two surviving Grey assassins were apprehended by the Confederation Intelligence forces trying to get out of the city, but they refused to surrender and were killed by our heroic agents. It's obvious what the Grey was trying to do. They intended to blame the deaths of our visitors on our government, to make us seem duplicitous or incompetent. Instead, they've merely revealed themselves as the scheming, murderous devils they are and given us the opportunity to make an alliance with our new acquaintances... and to get to know them better."

For an alien, Frost had a very human smile, one I could almost believe was genuine.

"Tell us about yourselves, Cameron, Vicky."

I cleared my throat and tugged at the collar of my uniform, which suddenly felt tight. For a moment, I wished spies were shooting at me.

"I'm from a small town," I said, trying to remember what we'd gone over earlier this morning. Keep it simple, keep it honest. "Near the ocean. My parents were farmers who raised..." Would *chickens* translate? "... small animals for their eggs and meat. And a few for their milk. I lived with them until

I was about seven. That was when they died." My throat closed up at the words, the surge of pain surprising me. It had been decades now and it should have shrunken into nothing by now, a little ball of anguish and desperation I could easily handle. It *should* have, but it hadn't. "The town was in a... bad place. A forgotten place, run by criminals, and they killed my family."

Vicky's put a hand on my arm, squeezed, just letting me know she was there. I gave her a grateful nod.

"I was on my own, close to death, when I was found and brought to the nearest large city. I had a... *safer* life there, if not an idyllic one. I joined the military at a young age and that's where I met Vicky. We've been together since then. We were recruited for this mission by one of our old friends from the Marines, trying to hunt down a terrorist. In the process, we followed them through a gateway, not too different than the jumpgates you have here, except it was one-way. It led us out here and we're desperately trying to find our way home. That's why we've come to you. We believe the same ones who built the gateway are somewhere out here and they can get us home. All we're looking for are any records you might have of suspicious thermal or spectroscopic activity and perhaps any legends from far in your past of visitors from the stars. No matter how outlandish any of it might seem, it gives us a place to start."

"That seems so little to ask," Frost said, a twitch in her cheek as she glanced at the charts in the readout the only hint that things were going wrong. "What about you, Vicky? Tell us your story."

Shit. Things were going bad in the polls. That was the only reason she would have cut me off. I didn't look back at the display, not because I wasn't curious but because I wouldn't have gotten anything useful from them.

"I was born in the same city as Cam," she said, taking it up smoothly, much more of a natural at this than I was. Once upon a time, I'd been good at this, been good at the small-time con, talking my way through things, but it had been too long. "But it's a huge place, three times as large as Two Rivers, and we never met of course. I joined the military because we were at war and I was a patriot... I believed in my nation and wanted to defend it against unprovoked attack."

Again that twitch, and again I knew why. Frost had told us *not* to discuss the war, but Vicky was sharp, better with people than I was, although that wasn't a high bar. To Frost's credit, she ran with it.

"I know it must be hard for you, Vicky," Frost said, putting a hand on her leg, "but could you tell us about the war?"

"It was the formative event of my life," Vicky said easily, casually, like she was speaking to a friend. "I was a young girl fresh out of school, no jobs, no experience. I'd never been into space, never left the small section of the city where I was born until the Marines. In the war, I saw two dozen planets, saw more of the galaxy than most people ever dream of... but at the price of seeing so many other things. Horrible things. War is a tragedy, even when it's fought for the best of reasons, even when there's no other choice. And there wasn't. Our enemies were religious fanatics who believed the galaxy had been created for them, that we were trespassing on *their* worlds even if they'd never set foot on them."

The corner of Frost's mouth turned up. Score.

"Yet you and Cam fought bravely against them and prevailed. And you met your husband."

"Cam and I were in the same company." Vicky smiled at me. "He was the new guy, quiet and reserved but confident... almost cocky. Like he just knew he was the best. And he was right. I resented him for that a little, at first, but after I got to know him I understood he was a good man, despite everything that had happened to him. He didn't have a family, but he made *us* his family, all of us."

My ears were warm. I didn't like talking about my life, and I sure as hell wasn't crazy about hearing someone else talking about it, particularly not in front of hundreds of millions of people, even if they were aliens. I knew it was ridiculous. I'd likely never see any of these people again and most of this was in my official file, which meant that most of the crew of the *Orion* already knew.

"Tell us how that made you *feel*, Cam," Frost said, leaning toward me like an owl about to pounce on a vole.

I grabbed the bottle of water from the table between us and took a swig to buy myself a few seconds. How did it make me *feel*? What kind of bullshit question was that? She sounded like the military psychologist I'd seen briefly.

"Vicky's right," I said, finally. It was an easy go-to since Vicky was usually right. "After I got to Trans-Angeles, I was put in a group home for orphans but I didn't fit in. I was an outsider, didn't even speak the language at first, so I didn't get along with the other kids. I ran away. A lot. Went from one home to another, then finally ran away for good, was living on the street, a small-time criminal stealing from other criminals. If I'd stayed out there, I'd have wound up dead. Instead, I wound up arrested and given the choice between confinement or joining the Marines." I shrugged, took another drink. "At the time, joining the Marines and maybe dying didn't sound so bad compared to staying on my own. At least in the Marines I had a big metal suit and could shoot back. I wasn't especially patriotic like Vicky, had never thought about joining the military. I didn't know much about the war except that we were losing and it looked bad. When I got to the actual fighting, it was different than I thought, much worse. Not because of the danger it put me in but because I started caring about the other people around me."

The words were tumbling out now at an alarming pace, like an avalanche going down a mountain, and I wasn't sure I could stop it. "Not just Vicky. I had friends, people I could trust, as close as brothers and sisters. And I lost a lot of them. Most of them. And every one of them was like a strip of flesh pulled off of my soul, like the worst thing that ever happened to you times ten. When the war ended, I didn't feel so much victory or accomplishment as just pure relief that I wouldn't lose any more people. That Vicky and I could be together and not have to worry about each other getting killed."

"And yet you're back in the service, Cam," Frost said, her intonation encouraging, her eyes lit up like she was on drugs. The numbers were trending up, or she wouldn't be trying to get me to go on. "You *and* Vicky. How did that happen?"

I ran a hand through my hair, feeling tired, not just from the lack of sleep but from the recognition of how long this had been going on. It felt like forever.

"We were trying to make a living as farmers." Vicky laughed at the idea and, upon reflection, so did I. If there was a little bitterness behind the laughter, it was well hidden. "It was a long shot, but we had to try. It was obvious after a year or so that we weren't cut out for it, so when we got recruited back into the service for this mission, we pretty much jumped at it. I think we're... well, I think *I'm* a Marine by birth. I think Vicky could move on to something else, but I guess I wasn't ready for it. But I think maybe, after we get back—*if* we can get back—that I might be ready to try again."

Vicky was looking at me, and I wasn't sure if there was hope behind that expression or doubt. Probably both.

Frost's expression was easier to read. Her jaw muscles were clenching from trying not to grin from ear to ear.

"Thank you *so* much for coming onto the show with us, Cameron, Vicky. We very much appreciate your candor." She turned toward the camera. "And thank you all for watching. Be sure to do your public duty and vote tomorrow on the policy initiative!" She inclined her head toward the side and her producer nodded.

"And we're done," he said, straightening.

Frost sprang from her chair like a twisted spring, fist pumping in the air.

"Yes! Oh, yes! Look at those damned numbers! This is the best work I've ever done and you two were magnificent!"

I blew out a breath, shoulders sagging. I felt more ragged out than I had after the gunfight with the Grey assassins.

"I never want to do that again."

"I don't think the situation is going to come up again," Vicky said with a chuckle.

"Don't worry," Frost said, practically dancing. "The vote is a shoo-in. And we need to go have a drink to celebrate! In fact, I need *several* drinks!"

"Can we go too?" Jay asked, grabbing Bob by the arm and pulling him up from his chair like he wanted to make sure they didn't miss out because the other man was too slow. "I've always wanted to go to a Frost party!"

"You brought them to me, you dear, sweet, dimwitted man," Frost said, running a finger down the younger man's cheek. Jay looked as if he was about to float right off the floor. "I'll even find you a nice girl." She eyed Bob. "Or two."

"I just want some sleep," I moaned.

"Come *on*," Vicky urged, pulling me up from the chair. "Duty calls."

"Yeah," I sighed, following Frost and the others to the door. "Duty."

[9]

"Wake up!" Vicky urged, shaking my shoulder.

It was a tribute to the years we'd been together that I didn't spring out of bed reaching for my gun. Well, a tribute to that *and* the killer hangover I was nursing. I hadn't intended to drink much, not just because I was technically on duty but also because I'd once gone a little too far into self-medicating PTSD with alcohol and I didn't want to fall into old habits.

That hadn't proved possible, however, because whatever their other virtues and vices, the people of Two Rivers had perhaps the strongest alcoholic beverages I'd ever attempted. I think there was some sort of extra pop to them, some kind of narcotic, because I did *not* taste that much alcohol. The flashing, multicolored lights and the writhing dancers on the rotating floor of the club hadn't helped any, and by the end of the night—or maybe it was the morning—I was the one spinning rather than the dance floor.

I didn't actually remember going to bed, and I obviously hadn't taken off my uniform because I was still wearing it. And it smelled.

Somehow, Vicky was as bright and bushy-tailed as a golden

retriever, eyes wide open and alert. She pointed at the screen built into the far wall of the bedroom. This place was even higher-class than the high-rise, or at least it seemed that way to me, though I was probably missing some archaeological and artistic subtleties unique to the People that made the high-rise worth more.

The screen was huge though, and leaving aside the indecipherable charts and graphs that were on all of their net broadcasts, I could tell what the news was by the attitude of the talking head reporting it.

"The vote went our way," Vicky said, shaking my arm like she was trying to drain the inebriation out of me. "They're going to make the deal! We did it!"

"Yeah, I got the idea," I said, relieved it wasn't bad news. "Frost said that the decisions were implemented immediately, so I guess we're going to get the data within the next couple days, however long it takes them to put it together." I plopped back down onto the bed. It wasn't too different than beds on Earth, though it was a lot nicer than the bunks on the ship, even in the officer's quarters. A little soft for my taste, but at the moment I didn't care. "I'm going to use that couple days to sleep, if you don't mind."

"Maybe you should take a shower first," she suggested, holding her nose as she climbed back into bed beside me. She had taken off her uniform and was dressed in shorts and a t-shirt. "I took one last night, but I couldn't even get you undressed."

"Do I *have* to?" I pulled a pillow over my head, shutting out the light from the screen. "I really need to get some more rest. I feel like I haven't had a full night's sleep in days."

"All right," she said, putting a hand up between us. "Go back to sleep then. I mean, *I* was in the mood to celebrate on a more personal level, but not until you get a shower."

I pulled the pillow down and raised an eyebrow at her.

"Oh, really?" I offered her a crooked smile. "I may be hung over and exhausted, but I'm still a Marine."

"Oh, Lord," Vicky said, rolling her eyes. "I fell in love with you because you *weren't* one of those jarheads with more balls than brains. If that's suddenly changed just because we're back in, you need to let me know now so I can start the divorce proceedings."

"Oh, come on! You're one of those jarheads too. And don't tell me you don't have your fair share of balls, because I know better."

"All right, you've convinced me," she relented, offering a hand. "We'll *both* take a shower."

I scrambled out of bed, about to follow her to the bathroom when something beeped for our attention from the nightstand. I glanced around for the source, frowning in confusion until I recalled the tabs Frost had gifted to us last night. They were primitive compared to our 'links, but they were tied into the local nets and she'd wanted to be able to get ahold of us quickly in the event of any emergencies, like Grey hit squads coming after us.

Rolling back over the bed to the other side, I grabbed the thing and struggled for a second to remember what to push to answer the call. I tried the triangular icon near the top since it was pulsing a dull orange for attention, and once I slid it downward the beeping stopped. I awkwardly held the thing to my ear, which seemed like a crude and primitive way to talk to someone, but I didn't have an ear bud connected to the thing and even if I had, getting the adhesive off the semi-permanent one already in my ear would have been a pain in the ass.

"Yeah?" I replied, unsure what the protocol was for answering calls on this planet.

"Captain Alvarez, this is Frost. I assume you've seen the

news?" Another anachronism. Their comms connection made her voice sound distant and tinny, and I wondered how they put up with it.

"We have. I guess it worked, congratulations and thank you. What do you think the timeline might be for us to get access to your astronomical data?" And if I was being pushy, maybe it was because I was getting a little tired of being a show pony and ready to get this over with.

"Immediately, but I'm afraid there's a more pressing issue currently. This hasn't been released to the public yet until there's confirmation, but satellite imagery has picked up substantial military maneuvers by the Grey. I'm afraid they're not taking this whole business lying down. The assassination attempt didn't work, so they've been forced to ramp things up."

My stomach cramped up and I squeezed my eyes shut against sudden nausea. This was exactly the sort of shit we'd run into on Vailoa, and I'd been all over Hachette's ass for how he'd handled that.

"Hold on a second, Ms. Frost." I waved off Vicky's curious stare and touched my ear bud. "Captain Nance, you reading me?" He *should* have been since we were using the Confederation's satellites to bounce my signal off to reach the ship, but there was no reply. "Nance? Anyone hear me? Dwight?"

"That's the other thing, Captain Alvarez," Frost interrupted, impatience thick in the words as if she didn't like being interrupted. "Several of our satellites have gone offline in the last hour. Again, we have no confirmation, but our analysts assume they've been targeted by Grey weaponry. We're calling in shuttles from our lunar base to investigate, but it'll take hours, and I have disturbing instinct that whatever's happening will have happened by then."

"Shit," I murmured. "Get us a flyer and get us back to our lander. Right now."

"Are you going to tell me what the hell's going on?" Vicky demanded, grabbing her uniform off the back of a chair.

"Let's just say," I told her, grabbing my boots, "that I'm glad your piloting skills have improved."

I didn't realize how accustomed I'd gotten to having Dwight around until he wasn't. The entire flight out to the port, Jay and Bob were staring at me like I was nuts because I was calling the *Orion* over and over and must have looked to them like I was mumbling to myself. I think the only reason Jay wasn't asking me about it was that the two of them were too busy holding onto their arms of their chairs and gritting their teeth. The pilot had taken Frost's orders to get us to the spaceport as fast as possible to heart in all the worst ways, and oncoming air traffic had no say in it. I was beginning to understand why aircars had never caught on back in the Commonwealth.

"Are we sure the Grey are going to invade?" Vicky asked, her eyes fixed on the spaceport. We were only a couple klicks out, but from this far up we'd been able to see it for a few minutes now and it still seemed like we'd never reach it. "Maybe it's just posturing. They're obviously not happy about us making a deal with the Confederation. They could just be trying to get the Feds to blink."

"And if they're not," I pointed out, "then there's about to be a global thermonuclear war and we're going to be caught in the middle of it."

"Not just nukes," Jay said, finally squeezing words out past his clenched teeth. "The Grey have those rocks they're mining out in lunar orbit. They can destroy Two Rivers with just one of those things."

"We're landing," the pilot announced. "Hold on, gonna be bumpy."

The woman wasn't lying about that. It wasn't so much a landing as a controlled crash, and I barely had time to tuck my chin into my chest to avoid biting my own tongue. The yelp from the bench seats behind me told me that either Jay or Bob hadn't been so lucky. I didn't bother to compliment the pilot for her alacrity or daring, just pushed the lever to lower the door and scrambled out onto the tarmac.

The wind was chillier this time than when we'd landed here, and I decided it must be late fall instead of spring because the weather was heading the wrong way. I was hoping we wouldn't be around for winter because I hadn't brought a jacket... and this place might be a nuclear hellscape in a few days.

A slap on the security ID plate opened the side hatch, but the steps took years to lower, or at least that was how it seemed to me, and I couldn't keep my eyes off the skies. Gray clouds hung low, blocking off the sun and everything else above them, and I imagined ballistic missiles descending through them, about to turn everything to ash. They were primitive weapons compared to what I was used to during the war, but they could kill billions of people just as dead.

Vicky must have felt it too, because she didn't even wait for the hatch to open all the way, vaulting through the gap when it was just a meter wide and leaving those of us less graceful to wait until the steps descended. Jay and Bob tried to crowd past me, and I had to elbow past them.

"Why the hell did you two come along anyway?" I asked, falling into the copilot's seat beside Vicky. Her fingers swept across the controls in a sequence I'd seen her practicing in the simulator during our watches on the long Transition. "We're not making any media deals up here, we're trying to stop a war."

"Yeah, dude, we know," Jay said, buckling himself into his acceleration couch. *"That's* why we want to go with you. I mean, I love the Fed and Two Rivers is a cool place, but that don't mean I want to burn up with it."

The turbines screamed to life, drowning out whatever Jay might have said next, and the belly jets lifted us on columns of fire. Skyscrapers descended, bowing to the rising lander, but I only saw them from the corner of my eye, concentrating on the lander's comm console.

"Can I get them with this thing?" I wondered. "I mean, without the satellites?"

"If they're on this side of the planet," Vicky said, shrugging with her eyebrows alone because her shoulders were completely involved controlling the spacecraft. "We can do microwave or laser-LOS from the lander. Give it a shot."

I'd figured out how to use the controls in the shuttles during this mission but I wasn't an expert, and it took me a few seconds to set the thing for broad microwave transmission. By the time I looked up again, we were in the upper atmosphere and Two Rivers was a distant speck on the continent below, the western ocean stretching out and around to the east.

"*Orion*, this is Alvarez, do you read me? Please come in, *Orion*."

Still nothing, damn it.

"Higher," I told Vicky. "Take us up into orbit so we can get a wider arc."

"Umm, we got company," she told me. "There are suborbital fighters heading our way."

"*Whose*?" I asked, watching the approaching threat icons on the sensor scans.

"Unknown. Ms. Frost neglected to give us the Confederation military IFF codes." She snorted. "Short-sighted of her, and of me for not asking. I guess we'll find out in about two minutes when they get into firing range."

"Can they shoot us down?"

"Maybe. If we were in an assault shuttle or even a drop-ship, I wouldn't be worried, but this thing is a glorified school bus. I don't know."

"I guess I should have brought one of those," I said. "Probably short-sighted of *me*. But I didn't want to deprive the *Orion* of a space asset just for us to use as a glorified school bus." My eyes flickered to the screen. We were still heading west, which would soon be east, and east was the Grey. We were also nearly to orbit. I touched the control again. "*Orion*, do you read me? This is Alvarez."

"Alvarez, where've you been?" That was Nance's voice, and I sighed in relief. "We've been trying to call you for a half an hour!"

"Glad to hear your voice, Captain. Or anyone's. There's basically a world war breaking out down here."

"That's we've been trying to call you about. I'm not one hundred percent on this whole situation, but there's a blue water navy fleet heading across the western ocean. And while I'm not an expert on primitive military structures, I'm thinking it's a pretty damn big one. A couple thousand ships, and I think a hell of a lot of them are missile boats. Nuclear missile boats, I'd assume."

"Yeah, and while I haven't asked, I'm pretty sure the Confederation is launching their own navy and maybe getting ready to do the same with submarines and orbital weapons if they have them. We need to do something damn quick, or there's gonna be nothing left of this place but a cinder."

"What do you suggest? You want me to blow that fleet out of the water?"

I was distracted from my thoughts on the subject by a proximity alarm from the sensors. They were in weapons range. We were running, running faster than they could pursue... but not their missiles.

"Oh, shit," Vicky snapped. "They're launching."

Two dozen, maybe more, coming in fast at twenty gravities. Coming way too fast. We were dead.

[10]

"Up!" I yelled. "Straight up at max boost!"

It was the counsel of desperation, but it was the only thing I could think of. The missiles a fighter that size could carry would burn out quickly, wouldn't be able to follow us into orbit. Or that was the only hope I could grab onto, and it was a pretty fragile one.

"Hold on," Vicky warned. "I haven't done this before!"

She shoved the throttle forward and a mastodon sat on my chest.

I couldn't breathe, couldn't speak, but I could still think. Barely, the thoughts ringed in desperate fire. The lander was no assault shuttle, but it still had a nuclear-thermal drive burning metallic hydrogen, and it was a hell of a lot faster than the fighters could match. Eight Gs. The limit of what a human could take and not black out, at least not without sophisticated G-suits that weren't standard issue for a lander. We could have gone higher if Vicky had put the lander on autopilot, which would have taken us into orbit but would also have robbed us of the ability to react to what came next.

Acceleration squeezed my vision into a narrow tunnel

ringed with darkness, and I wasn't sure if the darkness at the center of it was space or I was just blacking out. Until I heard Nance's voice again.

"Shit, Alvarez, we have spacecraft incoming from the other side of the moon. They're launching missiles."

I wanted to ask him why that worried him, since even the defensive systems before our Resscharr upgrade would have stopped their missiles, but I couldn't ask anything. I could barely keep my eyes open, and focusing on the sensor screen was a minor miracle. Those missiles might have been small but they still had enough fuel left in them to catch up with us, and the lander didn't have as much as an ECM jammer for defense. If we lived through this, I was going to have to see about fabricating some weapons and mounting them to the landers...

It didn't seem like I was going to get the chance, because those missiles were seconds out and we weren't pulling away fast enough. Searing white light bright enough to blank out the screens, close enough that the hair on my arms stood up despite the thin atmosphere up here, the static charge running through the hull of the lander.

Nuke. Had to be a nuke, maybe one of those missiles... but no, then it would be hot, the hull, the air inside the lander would have been an oven baking us all. And that was about as far as my conscious mind was going to make it after a couple minutes of eight-G acceleration. I was a heartbeat from blacking out when the boost fell away, along with the massive weight on my chest. I wasn't weightless, but Vicky had dialed back to around one gravity, and I was about to ask why when a huge silver delta roared past our nose, its tail on fire with fusion flame.

Intercept One, and I'll be damned if she wasn't a beautiful sight. The missiles had been wiped off the sensor screen by the proton cannon blast, the same one that had lit us up with static electricity, which was clearer now that my brain was getting adequate oxygen. We were out of the atmosphere now, in low orbit, and the curve of the planet below us was deceptively peaceful, picturesque, giving no clue as to the chaos unfolding below.

Behind us, either Jay or Bob or both was burbling like someone holding back rising gorge, and for once I empathized.

"You're all clear, Cam," Villanueva told me. "Get back up to the *Orion*. We got trouble."

"Thanks for the assist," Vicky replied, and anyone who didn't know her wouldn't have guessed she was scared shitless. I knew she was because *I* was too. "What's going on?"

"Beyond the enemy fleet trying to start a war?" I asked her. "And the missiles heading for the *Orion*?"

"Commander Brandano is taking care of the missiles," Nance answered for her. "The Fleet is a problem, but the Feds are already rolling out their own, and their tech is good enough to shoot down any incoming nukes. Our worry is up here. The Grey launched shuttles from their moon to the asteroid they're mining and we couldn't get assault shuttles to them before they docked. Wojtera thinks they're going to rig it up with fusion charges and use it as a weapon."

"Shit. And I bet the Confederation military doesn't have anything fast enough to get there in time."

"You'd win that bet. What do you want to do?"

"Tell Lt. Springfield to get Alpha Company suited up and ready to launch in Drop-Ship One," I told him. "We'll take care of this ourselves."

―――

"You're going along, boss?" Springfield asked, her eyebrows going up as she paused in the open chest plastron of her Vigilante.

"Yeah, sorry, I'm going to be taking the company for this one, Springfield," I told her, clambering into my suit. "Not that I don't trust you, but I want eyes on this one personally."

The rest of the company was already suited up, using gentle nudges from their jump jets to file out of the equipment bay toward the drop-ship. Moving two tons of BiPhase Carbide was easier in free fall, but still not *easy*. Once we were out of the equipment bay, we could use the magnetic anchors we all had on the bottoms of our footpads, and the drumbeat rhythm of one set of heavy, metal suit after another attaching itself to the deck was a suitable martial hymn for the war unfolding below us.

"And why am *I* not coming along?" Vicky asked, her voice coming over my earbud. She was at the other end of the bay, getting Bravo Company ready.

"Because we might need Bravo for a reserve," I explained for the third time since we'd docked with the *Orion*. "Plus, none of your people have any experience in low-grav combat, and I don't think this is the right place for them to get it."

"You're the commander of this mission. By all rights, you should be staying here on the ship and... you know, *commanding* all of us."

"I should be," I admitted, since I never lied to Vicky. The chest plastron swung upward and I tucked myself into the suit, then plugged the interface jacks into their sockets. They made a scraping, hollow sound inside my skull, and I'd have thought after all these years that I would be used to that sound, but it still grated at my nerves now and then. "But what's the point of being in charge if I can't do what I think is right?"

The interior of the suit lit up with the heads-up display, and a flick of my thumb on a control cut loose the latches that held the Vigilante in place in its cradle.

"You know what'll happen if you get yourself killed doing this shit, right? Then they're going to ask *me* to take over. If you make me do that, I will scrape pieces of you out of your suit, have you cloned, wait until the clone grows to adulthood, and then shoot it for being an asshole."

"Be ready to back me up," I said, coaxing a short, gentle burst from the jets. It took a lot of practice to keep from bouncing off the opposite bulkhead, and we had plenty of dents and scrapes as evidence of past failures. I managed to time the hop just right, the last of the outgoing suits.

Alpha was a short company, and that was putting it mildly. We had two platoons, more or less, after the losses we'd suffered against the Skrela. Every single one of them stung, and every time I thought about them a lingering flare of anger sparked in my stomach at Dwight. It was useless, counterproductive, but I could no more stop it than I could the tide. Thankfully, he'd stayed quiet since we'd come back into comms range. He did that sometimes, just stopped talking unless someone asked him a direct question. I didn't bother trying to find out why because I was grateful for it.

"Alvarez, your Marines loaded on the drop-ship yet?" Nance asked. He was mostly a faceless voice to me these last few days, a surrogate for Dwight in a way. Which was also okay. Nance was better taken in small doses, and we'd shared too much face time on this trip.

"On our way," I replied. The *click-clomp* of my boots and two dozen others did their best to drown out the words, but long practice kept me from raising my voice. The comms pickup would filter out the background noise, and if I yelled in a misguided effort to talk over it, the software would filter that out too and I'd wind up just making myself hoarse for nothing. "What's the situation at the asteroid?"

"I'm sending a feed to your helmet," he said, then murmured something aside, probably an order to Chase to link with my HUD.

I could only award half my attention to the display, but what I saw was the computer-enhanced image of the asteroid. Vaguely round with the sort of rough, pebbly surface of the kind of asteroid that had clumped together from bits of rock over millions of years, or maybe billions. Spacecraft swarmed around the thing like flies on a cow patty, though generally cow patties weren't lit up by thermonuclear explosions.

"What the hell's going on there?" I asked, nearly stumbling on the ramp up to the drop-ship, the feed distracting me. "Is the place under attack already?"

"Missile strikes from the Confederation base on the moon. But the Grey laid down a minefield around the rock. Fusion mines, and they're damned effective at keeping out missiles. And maybe your drop-ship too."

"Can you spare Intercept One to run interference for us? Or do you need her for missile interdiction?"

Springfield was standing in the door, waiting for me to board. She was a good platoon leader and fair as a company commander. Good enough to be the skipper for most companies, but I'd developed a proprietary feeling about this one, and it was probably just my own prejudice that kept me from being totally comfortable leaving her in charge.

"We're basically impregnable here in the *Orion*," Nance replied. "The question is, how far do you think we should go in stopping this thing? Once those two fleets reach the point of no return, I think it's going to kick off for real down there, and even if they can shoot down each other's nukes, that doesn't mean tens of thousands of people won't get killed."

I stepped into the drop cradle and deactivated my magnetic soles, letting the metal arms shelter me as they had so many times before. The drop-ship shuddered as maneuvering jets banged against the hull, shoving us out of the docking bay.

"What's the blast radius of an orbital strike from the energy cannons?" I asked.

"We can adjust power between a flashlight and a ship-buster missile. You make the call."

"Shit, Nance, I'm a Drop Trooper, not a Tactical officer. I want you to shoot close enough to the leading edge of the Grey fleet to scorch their paint and maybe swamp their ships but I don't want a fucking slaughter. We're trying to stop a war, not start one. Can you do that?"

I wasn't watching the camera view from the drop-ship, so it took me by surprise when the main drive cut in, kicking us in the ass. Boosting in a drop-ship wasn't the most comfortable thing in the world, and the pressure drove the breath out of me for a second. I almost missed Nance's reply.

"Yeah, I can try. Can't promise no casualties, but we'll minimize them."

"Do it. Once we take out this crew on the asteroid, I'm gonna need a direct line to the Grey, so get Chase on that and get ready to relay my transmission, okay?"

"Will do. When do you want us to fire the warning shot?"

"Right now," I said, "before they get too damned close to each other and we wind up blowing away half their fleet."

I switched my HUD to the view from the drop-ship, a wrong feeling nagging at me. Normally by this point in a drop I would have been talking to the pilot already, getting a sense of where to drop, where to ingress the target, but playing mission commander had sucked up too much time. We were close now, close enough that the asteroid filled the view from the nose cameras, close enough that Intercept One was a clearly delineated silver wedge passing across it.

A proton blast split the ever-night, and where it touched white globes of fire sprang up, the unmistakable signature of a fusion blast in a vacuum, colorless Christmas-tree ornaments hanging in space. A lot different from a blast on the ground, with an atmosphere to conduct it, to become a wave of pressure and heat that pounded flat and incinerated everything in its path. Fusion bombs weren't that effective as an offensive weapon in space, not by themselves, but they were great *defensive* weapons if you didn't have shields. One going off close to a missile could cause a radiation burst that would throw off guidance or burn out the targeting circuits.

Or cause a lethal radiation dose for us, if we got unlucky.

Villanueva was doing her best to prevent that, but I had other worries. Scrolling back through the video of the asteroid, I finally found a clear image that showed the docking ports along the north pole of the rock. There were large, globular cargo shuttles mated with three of them, big enough to carry a couple of platoons of infantry... or maybe some big-ass fusion warheads powerful enough to knock an asteroid out of orbit.

There was one open lock left, one more port than there were cargo shuttles. That was our entrance.

"Walton, you see that open lock? That's our drop zone. Get us as close as you can."

"Roger that, Cam. I don't know if they have any heavy anti-spacecraft weapons, but I'll do my best. What's your target distance?"

"Not worried about dropping too high, obviously. The problem is flying out there like big, floating bullseyes for too long if they have defensive turrets. No farther out than a klick, preferably five hundred meters."

"Get ready, then. You drop in three mikes."

"Springfield, Top," I said, knowing they'd be listening in on the exchange, "when we drop, I want a file formation. Less surface area for the enemy to target. First squad, First Platoon on point, and I'm right behind them. Blow the fucking doors out of the lock with energy cannons, and if the bad guys are stupid enough to be out of their suits, they'll get what they deserve. Leave one squad at the rear to cover our asses. Got it?"

"Copy that, sir," Springfield replied. Czarnecki grunted, falling into the role of Top in more than name only. A true top-kick never wasted a word when a grunt would do the job.

"One minute to drop," Walton called back to us, drawing my focus back to the HUD.

What had looked like pebbles from hundreds of klicks away were boulders the size of mountains from this close, unwelcoming, intimidating. Anyone who landed among them would be stranded, cut off from the port in gullies kilometers deep. But no pressure.

I had a minute, so I switched the view in my HUD back to the *Orion*, just in time to see the ship descending into low orbit over Homeworld, hovering above the western ocean. The Tactical feed zoomed in to a point somewhere about halfway between the two continents. The Grey fleet was just as huge as Nance had promised, and it was also the first time I'd seen an actual ocean-going warship in my whole life. Probably the first time anyone from Earth had seen one in over a century. They were matte-gray blobs against the deep blue sea, arrayed in a series of wedge formations like I was watching someone play an old-fashioned tabletop wargame.

The Confederation had launched their own fleet, and scrolling across the display showed them deploying out of a huge port on the western shore of the continent. Not nearly as numerous, maybe half the size. Aircraft were already clashing above them, just tiny flashes of lightning in the white clouds, barely visible, and yet every one of them was a pilot or a whole flight crew dying. They'd be the first casualties out of millions or tens of millions if this didn't work, if we couldn't stop this rock from falling.

I was about to switch back, running out of time before the

drop, resigned to missing the show, when the *Orion* fired her main gun. I'd seen it before but never like this, not firing down through an atmosphere. It was more than a lightning bolt, it was the wrath of God called down upon mortals, and when it touched the ocean it was as if a giant creature was emerging from the depths. A mushroom cloud formed out of the chaos, roiling with fire and fury, and spreading out from the base of the thing was a wave.

It didn't quite reach the Fed ships, still close to shore, but it washed through the first rank of the Grey fleet, tossing them like toy boats in a bathtub. I winced despite—or maybe because of—the fact that I'd ordered the strike. The wave abated before it could hit the next rank of ships, but at least two dozen had been swamped, capsizing. Hundreds, maybe thousands of people dead. Not humans, but people. On me, because I'd taken this fucking job.

"Ten seconds."

I shook myself free of the fugue and the suit shook with me, which must have looked strange to anyone watching.

"Drop! Drop! Drop!"

[11]

Except it wasn't exactly a drop. My stomach and inner ear wanted to argue otherwise, insisting that I was falling, but it was a lie. We didn't fall, we boosted, the thrusters built into our suits running off the small, on-board fuel supply instead of sucking in atmosphere. That was the other thing that worried me. The Resscharr had replaced our isotope reactors with something better, more powerful and efficient, but it still couldn't do anything about the fuel. It would last us plenty long enough to get down and maybe back up again, but if anyone got fired on, had to take evasive action into those boulders...

But there was no sign of anti-spacecraft weapons, which meant that for once something had gone our way. The cargo shuttles stayed where they were, bone-white blisters against the dull black of the rock, not so much as a missile launching in response to our drop. My head was spinning, trying to maintain a controllable boost, trying to figure out when to execute turnover an decelerate, trying to keep a close watch on the threat display and on the IFF transponders, making sure we were dropping in formation.

Keeping tabs on a company in combat, even a light

company, was hard enough without adding the whole boosting in free fall to the mix. There. There was the target airlock, huge, built for cargo, for hauling mining equipment in and processed ore out. Time to decelerate. Spin around, hit the jets again, just a few bursts, not enough to burn my momentum up entirely, just enough to make the landing survivable.

A couple of the Marines on the drop weren't so lucky, or maybe hadn't done enough low-grav practice, and their pained squawks echoed inside my helmet, the only sound effect accompanying their awkward tumbles onto the rock.

"Unless your Goddamned backs are broken," Czarnecki snapped, "get on your feet and take down that lock!"

Yeah, that was Top. Not just *this* Top, but all of them, all embodied by the avatar of Top, Ellen Campbell. I was impatient, and it took everything I had not to push them aside and take the door down myself. That was *Private* Alvarez talking though, or maybe *Sergeant* Alvarez. I was past that, though sometimes I thought I was stuck on platoon leader, never having really become comfortable with company commander, but at least I could let the Marine on point be someone besides me.

"Alpha team," Top said, "you blow the door. Bravo, you're in first."

The rest of the company lighted like ducks on a pond, squeezed into the flat, open area around the ports, far too clumped together for my liking, but there was no choice. I didn't need to tell their platoon leaders to get them into a defensive perimeter, though I might have done it anyway for my peace of mind if the enemy hadn't already shown they didn't have any defenses built into the rock. The massive spheres of the cargo shuttles loomed over us like the relics of an ancient civilization, blocking out the sun and the planet, shrouding us in deep shadow. They were mocking my confidence, warning me not to take our security for granted, but there wasn't much choice. We could either cluster together in the open or hover like a swarm of bees and wait for something to swat us.

"Firing!" Not Top. The voice was Mansfield, the squad leader, his announcement actually coming a half a second after the actinic blue flash of the energy cannons. There was no sound, no vibration, just a thermal spike like a warm wind in the desert and the hatch ceased to exist.

Well, it changed states, anyway. Most of it sublimated to hot gas and evacuated into the nothingness, gone before it even registered, and what was left spun away, glowing bits of debris. All of it soundless, distant, unreal. I didn't like fighting in a vacuum. It was too much like a bad simulator run, none of the emotional involvement that came with gravity and sound and vibration and heat. No warning.

The blast had scorched and blackened the inside of the lock as well, though it hadn't managed to penetrate the inner door. The lock was big enough for a full platoon, and the Alpha team had to move into the space to take out the inner door. No announcement from Mansfield this time, just another blast of energy, this one brighter, more intense, contained inside the lock, and this time the vibration was conducted through the metal of the port and up through my boots into the Vigilante, a faint, metallic ringing.

Bits of debris ricocheted off the inner walls of the lock and one of them *thunked* against my chest plastron before spinning harmless into the black. Air rushed out of the ruined door, just the slightest hint of sound, a faint whistling, and a swirl of dust lit by the interior lights. Bravo team went in, their gait awkward and waddling, Alpha right behind them, and I tapped into the feed from the Marine walking point.

The passages inside the lock were broad and tall, with rails built into the walls for cargo containers. One of the cylindrical containers had been knocked off the rails, probably by the explosion of the inner lock, partially blocking the corridor, and the squad moved carefully around the bottleneck. It was painfully slow, and sweat trickled down the small of my back, not so much fear for the enemy response to us as the fear of being too late.

I might have given in to impatience and ordered them to move in faster if it hadn't been for the ambush. As ambushes went, it wasn't much. There was little cover and the platoon of Grey soldiers hadn't had time to set up anything elaborate, but I gave them credit for guts and commitment.

No chatter of gunfire, of course. We'd put the interior into a vacuum when we'd blown the lock. I'd hoped that would take out some of the opposition, but unfortunately the Grey had been smart enough to keep their space suits on. They were faceless behind opaque visors, their space suits a dull, matte black, and they would have been nearly invisible in the dim glow of the internal lights if not for the thermal sensors in our Vigilantes. The only way to hide the thermal signature of a suit in a vacuum was to make it too insulated to bleed heat, which would cook the person inside it.

Even without the heat signatures, we would have seen the muzzle flashes of their rifles. They were nothing high-tech, not even as advanced as what the Commonwealth had used when we'd first started pushing out into space. Magazine-fed, bullet-firing gunpowder weapons, and there was no danger of those rounds penetrating our armor. Maybe if they'd brought along crew-served missile launchers or mobile anti-spacecraft cannons, they could have inflicted some casualties, but this wasn't a fair fight, and I guess they hadn't had time to get those into place, if they'd bothered to bring them along at all.

"Am I clear to fire?" Mansfield asked, calm and dispassionate, as if the bullets sparking off his chest armor were nothing but a minor annoyance, mosquitos to be brushed away.

I was tempted to say no, to ignore the Grey soldiers and just go straight for the bombs. You could always go back and kill someone later, but you couldn't bring them back to life, and these guys were just soldiers doing their duty. But they were also trying to drop an asteroid the size of cruiser on Two Rivers and wipe out millions of civilians.

The words wouldn't come on their own, and in the end I had to drag them up and spit them out before I choked on them.

"Weapons free."

If I was hesitant, First squad wasn't. Mansfield fired before I'd finished the sentence, the blue balefire ripping through the Grey soldiers, the rest of the lead fireteam opening up before the glare of the blast had faded. The walls glowed a dim yellow, the stone heated almost molten by the heat of the energy bursts, the light revealing a black smear on the floor where the enemy platoon had been.

"Keep moving," I told them, an itch in the center of my back, like I was hanging us out as a target in the open. "Recon by fire if you need to, but keep moving. If they set off those charges, there's nothing that'll stop this rock."

"Couldn't the *Orion* blow it up with their main gun, sir?" Top asked. Over our private line, of course, because top-kicks didn't ask those sort of questions in front of the troops. Top was supposed to know everything. For once, this was a science question I actually knew the answer to.

"The *Orion* could vaporize it," I explained, "but the plasma would still be traveling at the same velocity as when it was blown up, and the plasma would do even more damage than the intact rock. Physics is a bitch."

First squad hadn't waited for our scientific discussion, pressing on through the bottleneck, and I followed them with Springfield on my heels. I cut the connection to Mansfield's feed, concentrating on controlling my gait. The suits had a powerful stride and this asteroid had next to no gravity, which meant a single step could send me crashing into the ceiling. It wouldn't hurt, but it would be embarrassing as hell, though the scuffling, skating motion I had to use to avoid it wasn't much more dignified.

Stone scraped under the spiked soles of my suit's footpads, the sound conducting through the metal so much more gratingly annoying than it would have been through the air, but I fell into a rhythm quickly. More quickly than the lead squad, and I had to slow down to avoid running right into the back of the last Marine in the file.

"Pick up the pace, Mansfield," I told him. I felt a little guilty since I should have had Top give the order, but we didn't have time for those sorts of niceties, and we didn't have time for Mansfield to drag his feet. Figuratively. Literally, we were *all* dragging our feet.

"We got a T-intersection up here, sir," Mansfield told me.

It wasn't unexpected, but I hadn't been sure when we'd reach it.

"I'm coming up."

The corridor had brightened as we'd walked, which would normally have been barely noticeable given how efficient the enhanced optics were in a Vigilante, but even infrared needs some sort of light source to work with, and thermal would have been useless without heat. We were fresh out of heat, which had fled right along with the air, leaving only the sonar and laser ranging systems. I'd used them before when nothing else was available, but the results, even run through the computer enhancement software, were plasticky and unreal. There was enough unreality about this situation as it was, so I was grateful for the light.

Squeezing past First squad, the carved stone walls of the corridor terminated in an intersection, heading around the periphery of the rock.

"Which way, sir?" Springfield asked, still clinging to my shoulder like a remora on a shark.

"Both ways," I told him. "You take Second Platoon and head left, I'll go right with First. Leave Top with me, riding drag."

"Yes, sir."

This was where I missed Vicky. Despite what I'd told her, I'd *wanted* to bring her along, wanted to have her be my second-in-command to take care of Second Platoon in just this sort of circumstance, but I hadn't been making excuses. If we needed support, she had to command Bravo, because Bravo was all Vergai recruits and no one else knew them as well as she did. Or their suits, which weren't as good as Alpha's. They had the original isotope reactors rather than the Resscharr-tech power plants, and not even plasma guns for their main armament because fabricating those would have required materials we hadn't brought with us and couldn't manufacture ourselves. Instead, they had coilguns, which were nothing to sneeze at but required regular reloading and the supply train to support them. That wasn't going to be possible inside the rock, which was another reason I'd gone with Alpha.

"Mansfield," I told the squadleader, "take your people to the right and keep up your speed. We're running out of time. Top, make sure the rest of the platoon keeps up."

"Where the hell are the miners, sir?" Top asked, again on a private channel. "Is the whole damned thing automated?"

"Most of the mining machinery is automated," I told him, "but they are supposed to have a maintenance and repair crew that lives here."

"I ain't seen anything like living quarters. Hell, I haven't seen as much as a hatchway."

"They're gonna be at the center," I guessed. "To shield against cosmic rays and solar storms. And since they intend to drop this whole rock on the Confederation, they might have all evacuated to those cargo birds."

"Creeps me out," he confided, a scowl in his voice. "Like the place is haunted or something."

"If we don't get to those damned bombs, Top, it's going to be haunted by *us*."

He was right though. The corridors were bare, empty, no decoration other than the rails on either wall and the occasional cargo pod sitting empty and forlorn. No workers, no more soldiers setting up ambushes, which told me all the rest of the Grey troops would be with the bombs, guarding them while their techs got the charges into place.

The place wasn't *that* large, or at least that was what I'd told myself looking at it from the outside. A klick in diameter, maybe a little more. Which meant we had to be close, unless I'd chosen the wrong direction and Springfield was going to be the one to find the charges. That should have been okay, but it wasn't. I needed to be at the tip of the spear, and I needed almost pathologically to be in control of my own fate. It wasn't something I was proud of, but it also wasn't something I could deny anymore, not after the last couple years. As much as I'd protested that I didn't want to be command of this mission, the truth was that I'd agreed to it for one reason—not that I wanted to control everyone else, but I couldn't stand letting anyone else be in control of *me*.

That might have been why I got out of the Corps in the first place instead of taking the brigade commander's offer to stay in and go the Officer's Advance Course, claw my way up the ladder. That also might have been the real reason I'd never managed to stay in one of those group homes in Trans-Angeles. Sure, some of them had been hellish, but there'd been one or two I might have been able to endure. If I'd been willing to let someone else be in charge of determining my fate.

It was a weakness, but one I understood and couldn't change.

"Thermal signatures ahead, sir," Mansfield told me, slowing his pace. I dug my heels in and scraped to a stop. "One hundred meters, around the curve."

"That's what we're looking for," I assured him, grinning at the surge of satisfaction. Not at the battle that was coming but that I'd guessed right on which way to go. "Double-time, Sergeant. If they have too much warning, they might set the damned things off just to spite us."

"Come on, First squad," Mansfield said with the fake enthusiasm of a man who knew the war is almost over and desperately didn't want to be the last one killed. "Follow me."

He hadn't made it twenty meters before we all found out where the Grey had deployed their heavy weapons. It was an anti-armor missile. I couldn't have sworn to it in the moment, with the flash of explosives and the dull ache of impact, but I knew it within a second, even through the pain and alarm. The suit's threat display screamed it at me, as if unaware that the explosion had tossed the Vigilante up against the side wall and smacked the fleshy, vulnerable occupant into the inadequate interior padding as hard as any of those group home bullies had managed.

Yellow damage warnings flashed distraction in my HUD, making me want to find the idiot who'd designed them and slap him around a little, but I didn't wait to see if I was actually injured or even what Mansfield's condition was. *This* ambush was serious, not just a few infantry thrown into a grinder to slow us down, and there was only way to handle an ambush.

Well, there were two. One was to break contact, but that wasn't an option. The other was my favorite. Assault through.

"Jets!" I yelled and took my own advice.

If running inside the low-grav rock was tricky, flying was

doubly so. Moving forward was all well and good, merely requiring me to keep myself parallel to the deck, but the trouble was, without much gravity pulling me downward, boosting straight ahead kept trying to send me upward. It wasn't impossible to handle, just forced me to adjust my flight every couple seconds, all the while dodging incoming missiles and streaks of fire that I guessed were cannon rounds.

And firing my main gun. I aimed by instinct, lacking the time and opportunity to use the targeting systems, at least on a conscious level. Thankfully, the Grey soldiers were packed tight enough across the corridor that it didn't matter. There had to be a company of them, or whatever the local equivalent of a company *was*, laid in deep with half a dozen man-portable missile launchers and just as many heavy, crew-served cannons, maybe designed for armor, maybe for spacecraft. They weren't shy about wasting their ammo and neither were they squeamish about friendly fire, since at least two of the cannon shots aimed at me took out swathes of their own people instead.

Crackling, azure energy, the product of some sort of particle accelerator—though *what* particle had evaded the best efforts of our Fleet techs—cut a wedge through them, and I burst through it way too fast to maintain control. I took out one of the cannon crews through the simple expedient of crashing into them at sixty klicks an hour, and I didn't find the experience a whole lot more pleasant than they did, the bruising collision adding insult to injury from the earlier missile explosion.

Still out of control, my Vigilante didn't roll away from the crash as much as it bounced. Back up off the ceiling like a baseball bat to the shoulder blades, down again, and my teeth clacked together with the taste of blood in my mouth and stars filling my vision. I didn't indulge the pain, didn't wait for my vision to clear. I'd cut my jets after the impact, but now I hit them again, enough boost to get me through the first wave of troops, to get me far enough clear that I had time to think... and to see.

The cargo tunnels had given way to what I took for a dig chamber, gigantic boring machinery mounted to the ceiling, extending into the pits they'd excavated. Even Frost had to admit they were clever machines, separating the ore as they dug, the results churned out their back end for transport in the cargo pods. They took up a lot of room, but there was a lot of room in the chamber to be taken, since the excavators had scraped down the external shell to just a few centimeters thick. The *Orion* had figured that out with a long-range sensor scan, but it was also in the brief we'd received from Frost by way of Confederation Military Intelligence.

That's how I knew they'd be planting the charges here, one to blow through the thin shell, then a dozen more to send the thing out of orbit. Thirteen wasn't a guess, wasn't an intelligence report, it was the number of squat, cylindrical devices being bolted to the floor by space-suited technicians at the center of the chamber. They must have known we were coming, because none of them stopped work on the charges to look at me, which showed considerable discipline. The only ones looking my way were the weapons crews, the last-ditch defensive stand. Not just man-portable missile launchers this time though.

Drones. I don't know why they surprised me. Maybe because we didn't use them, hadn't for over a century, but they made sense. Not propellor or jet driven, not in a vacuum. Maybe they used compressed gas like the manned maneuvering unit thrusters techs and engineers used in free fall at shipyards. These weren't for repair or recon though, not with the missile tubes mounted on them, an old-fashioned pipe organ setup like the ones I'd seen in history vids. Five of them, all pointed my way.

All launching at once.

[12]

I didn't think. Thinking took precious seconds, and I'd learned that most people made their decisions on a subconscious level anyway and only rationalized them via conscious thought a half-second later. I skipped that part and just acted.

It made perfect sense in hindsight, of course. The one thing the drones wouldn't shoot would be the fusion charges. Maybe. If the Grey troops operating them were thinking clearly, which was *not* a given in these circumstances. But it was all I had and I hit the jets full blast, straight up into the ceiling, where that one charge was already affixed. This was going to hurt, but not as bad as all those missiles would have.

Killing the jets, I spun end for end and managed a half-second braking burn before my feet hit the polished stone of the ceiling, driving my knees up to my chest, pain flaring in my hips and ankles and knees. I'd strained something, maybe even torn it, but it was too hard to localize the hurt when the ache seemed to come from all over. The suit didn't need me to be intact to move it anyway. Jets again, this time down, right into the middle of the dozen silvery containers, each about the size of the old

200-liter drums that were scattered all around the ruins of Tijuana.

Missiles were impacting by the time I touched down, soundless flashes of white against the far walls of the chamber, some ripping into the boring machine, sending sprays of metal debris ricocheting in all directions. The Grey soldiers wore armored suits, bulky and black and menacing, but the technicians who'd been placing the charges didn't. Shards of white-hot metal sliced through the fabric of their space suits and air sprayed in tiny, white streams, freezing as it hit the vacuum.

Their screams were trapped inside their helmets, but their death throes were a St. Vitus dance at the end of the tethers attaching them to the floor. I wish, in that instance, I could have seen the face of the Grey commander, could have watched his expression change as he realized what he'd done. I'd seen the look before and it was universal across Tahni and human, and I was curious as to whether it was the same for the People. Whether the commander's look of horror would have been recognizable, his hesitation surely was. The missile drones froze in place, giving me the second I needed to act.

There was the chance that firing my energy cannon at the charges might set them off. It wasn't a huge risk—the beam would have had to hit the deuterium-tritium fuel pod at just the right angle—but it wasn't zero either. I'd like to say it was calculated, that I'd weighed the plan, thought it through and made a sane decision, but the truth was, I just went in blasting.

I'd aimed away from the direction the rest of the company was coming out of in an effort to avoid friendly fire, hoping they'd extend the same courtesy for me. Four of the tall, fat drums disappeared in the lighting flash of subatomic particles, leaving behind only strips of glowing casing and no fusion explosion. But that was enough for whoever was leading the

Grey troopers to decide he didn't care if the missiles hit his own people, that priority one was getting rid of *me*. The drones still hovered at the far edge of the chamber, silent sentinels, but they weren't lost from my attention, and when they turned again, trying to target me, I moved.

The recharge interval for the energy cannons was much faster than it had been for our old plasma guns, but it still wasn't zero. Even if it had been, I couldn't have gotten turned around for a shot at the rest of the fusion bombs before the missiles reached me. What I *could* do was jet right into the midst of the Grey soldiers. There was less than a platoon of them, the main body already engaged with Springfield and her Marines, but they weren't totally helpless without the drones. I found that out the hard way when a baseball bat smacked me in the chest.

Not a literal baseball bat, of course. That would have been beyond the bounds of parallel evolution or even the power and reach of the Predecessors. Baseball was uniquely human, but anti-armor cannons were ubiquitous and really annoying. The round didn't penetrate, but it slowed me down long enough for a second shot to catch my left leg just above the knee, ringing the suit like a bell and sending me tumbling forward.

The jets ignited as if on their own, but somewhere below conscious thought, I'd hit the control without realizing it to straighten out my flight, setting me down between two of the tripod-mounted cannons. They were short-barreled, fat, bulbous, fed by nautilus-shell drums, artistic in a way. I almost felt guilty smashing them to scrap metal... almost. The soldiers who'd been crewing the weapons scrambled away, but not fast enough, and a gun tube cracked into the helmet of one of them, shattering his visor. Blood froze alongside oxygen and the Grey soldier tumbled sideways in slow motion, not quite falling.

Tap-tap-tap as if someone was politely knocking on the shoulder of my suit. Bullets. Useless, impotent, but all they had left so I didn't begrudge them the attempt, though I did ignore them, turning back to the charges. There were fusion bombs to disable, and I didn't have any better way to do that than to blow the shit out of them.

Except the commander had gotten his nerve back and finally figured out that the only way to salvage this shitshow was to detonate the damned bombs now. I'd been afraid of that, and when the man grabbed a large tablet off his belt and stabbed desperately at the thing, I knew exactly what he was doing. It was overkill, but I shot him with my energy cannon.

Not just *him*, of course, not with the main gun. I don't know how, exactly, the beam killed him. It might have been the radiation, might have been the heat turning every milliliter of liquid inside his body into superheated steam, or it might have been a nuclear reaction, but the bottom line was he was gone, nothing left of him, and so were half a dozen of the soldiers behind him. If Top—the original Top—had been there, she would have used that as a teaching moment about maintaining proper separation.

"Sir, all due respect, but get the fuck out of the way."

Mansfield. I hadn't even been certain he was still alive and his suit was beat all to hell, scorched black where it wasn't sand-blasted silver, craters dug out of his chest plate, but he was still moving and still fighting, a fireteam trailing behind him. I was a captain by rank, field commander of this op, and overall commander of this mission, but I did the smart thing and got the fuck out of the sergeant's way.

The team was a firing squad, their weapons discharging as one, and everything the blue flashes touched burned with atomic fire. The rest of the fusion charges set in the floor disappeared in a haze of sublimating metal as I touched down on the edge of the boring machine's maintenance catwalk. One left, the one on the ceiling that was to breach the chamber, and I took it out myself.

The chamber filled with a haze of particulates, twinkling in what remained of the lights, a model of the stars outside these walls.

"Springfield," I said, not snapping at the woman but still making the words harsh enough to get her attention. "Casualty report."

It took a second for her to reply, but I waited patiently. Maybe the words hadn't registered or maybe she was trying to gather reports from the others, but I didn't rush her, instead scanning the chamber for further threats.

There were survivors, of course, huddled against a far wall, cradling their rifles, uncertain, frightened. I had a translation program built into my 'link for the Grey language, which was different from the tongue the Confederation spoke, and I *thought* I could communicate with them via laser line-of-sight.

Sighing, I decided to give it a shot.

"Put down your weapons and surrender," I told them. "We won't hurt you."

Actually, I was probably going to leave them here and let their own government worry about them, but they didn't need to know that. They didn't reply, looking at each other through faceless visors, probably having conversations I couldn't overhear. The first one to set aside his rifle started a chain reaction, all the others dropping theirs as well, putting their hands up. Another universal gesture, apparently.

"Sir," Springfield said, skating over to me with a shuffling motion, "we have no KIA. Several suits with minor damage, but no serious injuries. What are your orders?"

"Mansfield and his squad are coming with me," I told her. "Take the rest of First Platoon and go round up Top and the others, get them out to the lock so we can get the hell out of here."

"Where are you going, sir?" she asked me.

"I have to make a call."

"Alvarez, I wasn't sure if something had gone sideways in there," Nance said.

The *Orion* hung off the asteroid, gleaming silver in the light of the primary star, staring down at me like an elephant regarding an ant on a hill. Irrationally, I felt resentment, like they should have been down here helping me somehow.

"We took care of the bombs," I told him. "I need Intercept One to take out the cargo shuttles once we're off this rock, make sure we didn't miss any. What's the situation downstairs?"

"The orbital strike has everyone back on their heels for the moment, but no one's retreating just yet and no one's talking either. There's still air combat going on and a shitload of satellites and shuttles shooting at each other in orbit."

"Patch me into the Grey receivers on the ground. And loop the Feds into it too. We all need to be on the same page."

"Getting Chase on it. Give us a second."

Yeah, take your time. World war, maybe other asteroids out there ready to crash, but sure, I could be patient. I stared at the stars and concentrated on what I was going to say. That, and trying not to bounce off the rock into space.

"All right, Alvarez," Nance finally said. "You're up."

A green light flickered on in the comm section of my HUD, telling me the same thing. I cleared my throat.

"Leaders of the Supreme Council of the Grey," I said, "I am Captain Cameron Alvarez of the Commonwealth ship *Orion*. You've seen what we can do, seen what just one shot from our main weapon could do to your fleet. We've already taken out the team you sent to the asteroid in orbit and defeated your plan to strike the Confederation with the rock." *Jesus.* I sounded like a fucking colonel, or worse, a general. Fucking politicians in uniform. "If you attempt to launch another asteroid at your own world, we'll use our main gun against your military bases. You'll be left with nothing, at the mercy of the Confederation. We won't allow you to start a world war on this planet."

I hadn't expected an answer, not directly, but I got one almost immediately. Which told me this council of theirs was mostly one or two people calling the shots.

"This is Supreme Councilor Brand." I assumed that *Brand* was an approximation of the translation of the man's name, the same as all the others I'd heard from the Confederation, and I idly wondered what the full name was. "You say you won't permit a war lest we be destroyed, but you're already destroying us. You're giving massive power to the Confederation. They'll gain the resources they need to leave us behind, to take over everything. What difference is it if we die now, at your hands, or later at theirs? We won't be their slaves, and neither will we be yours."

And there was the rub, of course. I'd expected that response and I had an answer for it. Of a sort. The problem was, I wasn't sure how they would receive it, and more importantly, how the Confederation would.

"What if we make you the same deal?" I asked Brand. "You share with us everything you have, your best experts on mythology, legends, lore, anything that might tell us the story of the Predecessors, as well as any astronomical data that might give us an idea where they went to. In return, we give you the specs for our Transition Drive. You get the same chance as the Confederation to build it, to make your own place among the stars. If you want the deal, you need to call off your fleet, your planes, your space assets, and stand down right now. Be smart. Because if you don't take this deal, you'll leave us with no choice but to wipe your ships and your armies out. And don't think for a second we can't do it."

Silence. I closed my eyes, feeling suddenly tired. I'd just had to kill a bunch of soldiers whose only sin had been to be born under the rule of assholes, to be patriotic for their country and follow orders. If those aforementioned assholes did the stupid thing, the suicidal thing, then I'd be responsible for ordering the deaths of tens of thousands more, and likely destroying their entire society. It wasn't what I wanted, wasn't anything I ever thought I'd be willing to do, and yet I was. God help me.

Please don't put me in this position. I wasn't sure if I was begging with the Grey or begging God. Either way, there was an answer.

"Very well, Captain Alvarez," Brand said after nearly five minutes of silence. "We will accept your offer. Our fleet will be withdrawing to port. I sincerely hope for all our sakes that you're telling the truth."

"All right," I sighed. There was very little gravity here, yet somehow, a great weight had lifted off my shoulders. "I'm coming back down to the planet with a research team. We'll set up a time and place to meet with you."

There were more words, meaningless niceties, assurances, blathering that I barely registered, until finally Brand was assured that I meant what I said. I don't know how long it took, but by the time we were through, the company was emerging from the wreckage of the cargo lock.

"Did it work, sir?" Springfield asked me. There were dozens of suits shuffling around the entrance, and I didn't bother checking IFF to see which one she was. "Are they going for it?"

"They are, Lieutenant," I replied.

"Thank God," she sighed, sounding as if she'd been just as worried as I had about the possibility of taking a side in the war.

She was an intelligent woman, and as a combat vet she knew better than most what war meant.

"Well, I don't know if it isn't too early to be thanking anyone just yet. We've taken care of our enemies... now we just have to worry about our allies."

[13]

"I'm not happy about this, Cam," Frost said, living up to the name we'd given her, a winter's chill in her voice. "We had a deal. We came forward in good faith and offered you what we knew."

She was sitting, sprawled across a very comfortable-looking chair upholstered in leather, while Vicky and I stood in her private office. It was a power move, one I'd seen before from senior officers, meant to show who was in charge. The fact that we all knew now that I controlled a starship that could destroy anything on this planet didn't seem to mean anything to her, but that was an act. She was angry, true enough, but more than that, she was scared. I could read it in her eyes.

"It's not only that you're going back on the agreement we made," she went on, "it's that by offering the Transition Drive to the Grey, you're *rewarding* their military aggression." Frost made a sweeping gesture out the transparent wall on the other side of her office, at the vistas of the Two Rivers skyline, glimmering with internal light in the darkness. "Tell me honestly, both of you... do you find it so hard to believe that they'll do it again once you're gone?"

"So, you'd rather we just let them invade you?" Vicky snapped at the woman, arms crossed, anger flaring behind her dark eyes. "Because we could have done just that. We could have gotten on our ship and left this system, taken our chances finding the Predecessors without your help. God knows we had enough reason to. There's no upside for us getting involved in your conflicts."

Frost *wanted* to argue with that, I could see it in her petulant expression, but she was also damned smart, so she bit down on the words.

"We are, of course, grateful that you prevented the Grey from invading and prevented their attempt at an orbital strike." Her words were measured, controlled, disciplined. I admired her ability to control her temper because of how hard it was for me. "Our people celebrate you for your intervention."

And we'd seen that after we landed. There'd been demonstrations of support for us at the spaceport, tens of thousands of people filling the streets carrying signs and chanting slogans about how great the Commonwealth was. My cynical inner street hood wondered how much of that was genuine and how much had been engineered by Frost and her social media engineering, but it *had* felt good to finally have a parade. I'm sure there'd been a few after the War with the Tahni, but I hadn't been around for them.

"But surely you can understand," Frost went on, "how concerned we are with the Grey retaining their military potential. Perhaps it would have been better for us had they turned down the deal."

"Yeah, I can see where you might think that," I told her. I glanced around the room. She wasn't going to invite us to sit and the chairs had been removed from the office, but I didn't feel like standing. The corner of her desk was empty of the small, metallic sculptures that decorated the rest of it, and I sat on the edge there, ignoring Frost's glare. "It would have been convenient as hell for the Confederation if we'd taken out the entire Grey military all on our own. You don't suffer the negative public impact of losing your own troops, don't have to foot the bill for a war. The enemy just sort of disappears and you can move in and take over."

"As you say." At least she didn't bother to deny it. "It isn't as if you would have suffered losses. Everyone saw what your weapons can accomplish."

And here was exactly the sort of situation where I would like to have had that sort of control over my temper.

"You know, Ms. Frost, I may be making some bad assumptions about how alike our peoples are just from our physical similarities, and maybe that's a mistake. But if you think we're the sort of butchers who'd kill hundreds of thousands of people just because it would be easy for us, maybe neither of us should be making deals with the other. Because if you're right about us, what's to stop us from just taking this whole place over? And if you're wrong, well... you're kind of an asshole."

Frost's eyes widened and I thought I'd pushed her too far, that she was going to snap and throw us out, and I was okay with that. Yeah, it would have been inconvenient, but that was the great part about being in overall command—I didn't *have* to make any distasteful alliances, didn't *have* to go along with shit that made my skin crawl. If she thought we were mercenaries, her own high-tech hired killers, that was coming to an end right now.

But she demonstrated again the extent of her self-control and plastered a warm smile over her rage.

"No, Captain Alvarez, I would never think of you and your people that way." Frost pushed her chair back and stood, as if finally acknowledging the gamesmanship of denying us seats. She offered me a hand and I took it with a little hesitation, wondering what it signified in her culture. "Please, allow me the chance to apologize. I meant no offense. As you say, there are likely cultural differences neither of us understands, and we should try to put any unintended slights aside and work together for the sake of our peoples."

"Of course," Vicky said, speaking in my place, probably because she was afraid I'd say something stupid. She was likely right about that. "We all want the same thing. Peaceful cooperation and a free exchange of information."

She offered her own hand to Frost and, rather than let go of mine and take Vicky's, Frost took it with her left hand, gripping both of us at the same time. I hoped we hadn't entered into some kind of weird, alien threesome.

"Very well. I don't say that I approve, but I understand your position and we will abide by your wishes. My only wish is that we maintain our friendship and alliance. But that goes both ways. I've spent quite a bit of political capital to take your part in all this, to justify the risk we took. I'm a patriot and I have the best interests of the Confederation at heart, but I'm not completely an altruist. You offered me... *us*... a gift of great price in exchange for our cooperation, and we took a risk to help you and ourselves. It seems unfair that the Grey receive the same payment only after being forced into the bargain."

Well, at least she was honest. Annoyingly persistent and blatantly mercenary, but honest. I bit back my initial response and tried to think of something politic to say. Something Jay had mentioned tickled at the edge of my thoughts, something about how even the simplest technology we had would be worth a fortune here.

"We can work something out," I assured her.

Not the holographic projector, because I'd promised that to Jay and Bob. Probably wouldn't be enough to satisfy her, anyway. Maybe I could give her the processing details for

BiPhase Carbide. It was in nearly every piece of military equipment, yet I'd seen no indication that the Confederation had ever heard of it.

"We'll make it worth your while," Vicky added, which was a bit more direct. At first, I thought she'd been *too* direct to the point of insulting, but Frost smiled, the glint of avarice behind her eyes.

"I trust that you will. But for now, you're scheduled to meet with Confederation and Grey researchers at the Two Rivers Institute in an hour." Frost scowled. "Not that anyone's thrilled with allowing Grey aircraft to land here so soon after the attack."

"I think you'll be okay," I said. "We have one of our Intercept cutters bringing down a couple experts. They'll be flying cover, and if anyone tries anything funny, well..." I offered Frost a thin smile. "You've seen exactly what we can do."

"I have to say," the little man in the voluminous black overcoat declared, looking me up and down, "I expected different."

Spinner was every stereotype of a science nerd, filtered through the lens of the People, skinny and frail, lost in his oversized clothes, his eyes wide enough that I thought he could see distant stars without a telescope. He was an astronomer and an astrophysicist, or some combination of specialties between the two, the translation hadn't been too clear on that, and theoretically he'd brought with him all the astronomical data the Grey had collected since they'd first started recording their observations.

"What *did* you expect, Dr. Spinner?" I asked the man, covering my chuckle behind a sip from the red-tinged drink I'd been given by a server.

The whole affair was more like a corporate gala than an intelligence-gathering operation, the curved, glass walls of the amphitheater lit up by multicolored lights, tables set out on the stage where the speaker would normally be standing, addressing their equivalent of graduate students. There'd been food too, but we'd cleaned that out pretty quickly. Not just Vicky and I, of course. Jay and Bob had come along, claiming this was part of their nebulous, poorly defined job and had been stuffing their face with sandwiches the whole time. The Confederation version of Dr. Spinner was a jolly, round-faced woman who didn't seem to have missed too many meals and wasn't about to do that today either, while the historians and mythologists packed the hors d'oeuvres down like they hadn't eaten in weeks. Our own experts weren't here yet, which worried me, since they'd landed at the port half an hour ago.

"Given that the only other aliens we've had experience with are the Nova," Spinner told me, "I'm shocked you're not... more different." The little man frowned, staring at the small speaker pinned to the breast of my uniform jacket. Frost had taken some time to get used to my translated voice coming from the thing, though now she was treating it as perfectly natural, and Spinner would become as accustomed to it as I was to the delay between him speaking and the translation in my earbud.

"Yeah, our people discussed the same thing," I admitted. "We have our theories, but none of us are really qualified to do more than guess."

"I take exception to that, Captain Alvarez," Dwight complained. I tried hard not to roll my eyes lest Spinner misunderstand the expression.

"Where are they?" I murmured to the AI. "Lilandreth and the others?"

"Their aircar from the spaceport was delayed," he informed me. "The Confederation flight crew claimed it was because of a mechanical problem, but I suspect that their people wished more time to examine Lilandreth."

"Of course."

"They just set down outside the main entrance. They should be walking in any..."

"Oh my God," Spinner said, his eyes going even wider, if that was possible. "What the hell is that?"

That was Lilandreth, and if Spinner had been expecting strange, she was it. Nagarro had escorted her, and the Intelligence officer's hand rested on the butt of her holstered sidearm as if she expected the gathered Confederation military officers to try to ambush them. Yanayev was along as well, the Helm officer the closest thing we had to an astronomer on the ship, though I think Nance had sent her just because he wanted someone representing the Fleet crew. I couldn't recall ever seeing the woman off the ship, now that I thought about it. For all I knew, she was a fixture of the vessel, a holographic projection like Dwight.

"Dr. Spinner," I said, "Ms. Frost." I nodded toward the woman who wasn't goggling quite so openly at the Resscharr but was still staring. "This is Lilandreth of the Resscharr, the ones we call the Predecessors."

"I thought you said you were searching for these Predecessors," Frost said, eyes still on Lilandreth. "If you've found this one..."

"I am of a sect of my people who split off from the others thousands of years ago," Lilandreth told them, and unlike the rest of us, she didn't have to use a translator. I still didn't know how the hell she was able to do that, to pick up languages within hours and speak them perfectly despite having a voice box not designed for English and certainly not for whatever they called the language the Confederation spoke. "We were cut off from the rest, lost. I'm helping these humans so I might have the chance to reconnect with my own people and find my way among them while the humans find my way back home."

Which was *sort of* true, and the real story was far too complicated to explain to this group.

"I would very much like to examine the astronomical data you've brought," Lilandreth said, towering over the astronomers from both nations. "I believe by examining the anomalies you've discovered I may be able to detect the signature of my cousins."

"Of course!" Spinner said, unable to tear his gaze away from the Resscharr. "I've connected the drives to the overhead display here."

The astrophysicist opened a larger version of the tabs that were so ubiquitous on this world, this one twice the size and thickness and with a cable running from a port on its side to a black box just below a flatscreen display. The screen was huge, four meters across and mounted on twin columns running from either side of the speaker platform, and at Spinner's touch on the tablet controls an image flickered to life, expanding from the center of it and banishing its reflective darkness. Replacing it with more darkness, but this one filled with stars. Spinner began scrolling through images, all of them beautiful but also indecipherable to me other than that they were stars and galaxies and whatever else was out there.

"This is the first of the thermal anomalies we've discovered," Spinner said. "It's in what we call the Aether Quadrant, approximately a thousand light-years from here. As far as we can tell, it's a massive gamma ray burst which happens at predictable intervals. If you like, I can go over..."

"That will be quite all right, Dr. Spinner," Lilandreth told him, putting a long-fingered hand on his arm and urging him gently away from the tab. "I'd prefer to look at the data with unbiased eyes."

Spinner looked up at her with puppy-dog eyes like she'd

smacked him in the face, but Lilandreth ignored him, fiddling with the tab until she started scrolling at high speed through the images.

"Let me ask you something, Dr. Spinner," I said, putting an arm around his shoulder and steering him away from the screen. "I haven't had the chance to visit your nation since we arrived, and you're the first of the Grey I've talked to face-to-face." The corner of my mouth turned up, and I tried not to gloat. "Well, I *did* talk to your Supreme Councilor, a guy named Brand, but it was a short conversation. So, the only impression I have of your people has come from the Confederation, and I don't think they're an unbiased source. What do *you* think about the political systems of the two power blocs here? The Grey and the Confederation?"

Spinner glanced around furtively as if he was making sure that none of his people were close enough to overhear. When he was satisfied no one was, he leaned in close.

"Discussing politics with outsiders is discouraged," he said in an urgent whisper. "Particularly not with members of the Confederation."

"I'm not from the Confederation," I reminded him. I looked around myself. No one was paying attention to us, not even the dark-suited young man who I assumed was a Grey intelligence officer sent to keep an eye on Spinner. He'd been waylaid by Jay, who was attempting to engaging him in conversation but not having much luck. Vicky was talking with Frost, and from the exasperated expression on Vicky's face, I had to think that Frost was still chewing her ear off about how we could make up for giving the Grey the Transition Drive. "Come on, just between us."

"Our system of government is very efficient," the man said, straightening like he was pledging allegiance. "We have a huge amount of territory to administer, both here on Homeworld as well as our offworld colonies. The decisions that must be made for such an expansive empire with over two billion people in total can't be left to the whims of the masses. Individual citizens may not be adequately or accurately informed about the details of the situation."

Not a bad point, but it was obviously the well-rehearsed party line, and I wasn't going to let him off the hook that easily.

"The Confederation seems to be doing its best to keep their people informed," I countered. "They look like they're doing okay for themselves." I shrugged. "Of course, some of them think that your government tries to fuck up their process with disinformation."

Spinner's smile was thin but genuine, and even before he spoke, I knew I'd be getting his actual thoughts on the issue.

"It's not inconceivable. But Ms. Frost over there..." he nodded toward the tall woman. "She's more likely to be the one swaying votes for her own ends. Do you understand how frustrating it is to try to maintain diplomatic relations with the Confederation, Captain Alvarez? They have no actual government, and the representatives they *do* have can make no guarantees, no pledges, no treaties, because everything has to be voted on by the public. I'm a scientist, not a politician or a diplomat, but even *I* understand how impossible that is."

Another good point, and one I hadn't considered. Probably because the Earth hadn't had actual nations for a century. But I wasn't ready to give up just yet.

"You don't think it's better to let the people have a say in how they're governed? Even if the system has its flaws, isn't it better than being ruled by an unelected oligarchy?"

Spinner laughed too loud and the intelligence officer glanced over until Jay distracted him again, saying something about the differences in food between the Confederation and the Grey. Spinner watched the officer carefully before replying in a low, conspiratorial tone.

"Is being ruled by an unelected oligarchy worse than being ruled by the whims of one woman?" Spinner sneered at Frost's back. "She's a celebrity here, considered a philanthropist, a hero for all the *sacrifices* she's made to keep the public informed. Sacrifices... yet her *service* has made her one of the richest people on this planet, and any idea she pushes becomes policy. She *runs* this entire nation, controls any policy she cares to. Foreign, domestic, trade, social policies, it's all at her mercy."

"She's not the only influencer out there," I objected, though it was half-hearted. "There's opposition to her. She's always complaining about it anyway."

"And any opposition is blamed on us. Convenient."

"Cam." It took me a second to realize it was Dwight talking to me rather than Spinner, since both voices came over my earbud and there wasn't that great a difference between them. "We've found something."

I excused myself from the conversation with Spinner and turned back to the screen. Lilandreth stared at an image of a white flare among the stars, a finger tracing the edges of it on the screen as if she could feel the edges against the glass.

"This is it, Cameron," she murmured, as if talking in her sleep. "This is them. The Reconstructors. I believe we've found them, or at least something they left behind. It's less than a hundred light-years from this system."

"That's not good," Skinner said, shaking his head.

"Why not?" I asked him. "It's not impossibly far. We could make that in a few weeks."

"Maybe. But to get there, you have to go right through the Nova."

[14]

The white blob looked just as much like a white blob on the holographic display in the Operations Center as it had back in the amphitheater, though everyone seemed very excited about it.

"What the hell *is* this thing anyway?" Vicky asked. "I missed the whole revelation everyone had because I kept having to offer bigger bribes to Frost."

"This," Lilandreth told her, gesturing at the blob, "is the gamma signature of a Resscharr singularity. The artificial black holes we used to create the gravitic drives. It's a technology lost to my people on Decision since we abandoned the Cluster, something we didn't have either the resources or the knowledge to rebuild there. But someone did."

"So, the Reconstructors are taking their name seriously," I said. "They're not just rebuilding the civilization they lost, they're also rebuilding the technological base."

"That means we're damn close," Nance enthused, pounding a fist on the table, a manic glint in his eyes. "Just a hundred light-years. A few months, maybe."

"3,246 hours in Transition Space," Yanayev told him, looking up from the display of her 'link. "Not exactly a hop, skip, and a jump, but close enough we wouldn't even have to go back into stasis."

"The singularity, perhaps," Lilandreth said, "but not the Reconstructors."

"I don't get it," Nance admitted.

"The singularity is a production plant," Dwight explained, his avatar's expression long-suffering, as if Nance should have already understood this. "But it also produces very powerful gamma ray bursts, along the lines of a supernova, at regular intervals."

"Okay," I interjected, "even *I* get that. It's too dangerous for them to live near this thing."

"It would sterilize any habitable world within a few dozen light-years," Lilandreth confirmed. "It would kill anyone in an unshielded starship as well, though the *Orion* would survive due to the modifications we made to her."

"But it shows us the right direction," Dwight said. "All we have to do is go back into stasis and travel to the other side of the singularity, along the galactic ecliptic, and take readings there."

"That's over six months." Vicky didn't quite whisper the words, but I had the sense they were for me rather than general consumption. I knew what she meant. We'd already spent five years in stasis, and even though I hadn't been on board ship much in the last few days, I knew the mood on the ship.

"There's no guarantee," I said, "that we'd be able to detect them from the other side of that thing. What if it's not even an active facility anymore?"

"It would not be abandoned," Lilandreth insisted. "Producing an artificial singularity requires an enormous investment of resources, and it continues to be productive for tens of thousands of years."

"Vicky's right though." Nance must have heard her. His fevered enthusiasm had morphed into a pensive melancholy quickly enough to count as a bipolar mood swing. "This'll be a hard sell to the crew." Wojtera and Yanayev were both present in the Operations Center, and neither could meet his eyes. "We've been away from our homes, our families for seven years already. You're talking over six months just to get to a point where we might have a clue which course to set. That could mean *years* more before we get back."

"What are our other options?" Lilandreth asked. She was adroit enough at English and at human body language that I recognized the impatience behind the question. "Ignore it? Set off blindly and hope for the best?"

"The systems between here and the singularity belong to the Nova." I stood, pacing around the table to the display. I could have adjusted the view from my seat, using my 'link, but I was restless from too many meetings, too much talking. I thought better on my feet, so I used my finger instead, tracing a line through the haptic hologram of the display, carving out a swathe of stars. "These two star systems are the colonies the Nova allow the Homeworlders, but everything past that is off limits." Turning away from the screen, I scanned their faces, trying to judge how well my argument was landing. "I don't know how far this wormhole network goes, but if the Reconstructors engineered it, then there's a possibility it might go all the way around the singularity. We could skip those six months of travel and head straight for the thing through the gates." I shrugged. "But only if we talk to the Nova, find out what they know."

Nance goggled at me like I'd grown a third head.

"Are you shitting me, Alvarez?" he blurted. "You heard the same reports I did from the Confederation. Those fuckers sent a hundred ships after them when they trespassed on their territory. We're pretty badass with the shields and the energy cannon, but quantity has a quality all its own."

"I know." Well, *maybe* I did. I'd learned a lot about ship-to-ship combat in the last couple years but I was still a ground-pounder, and maybe I didn't quite grasp it like Fleet officer would. "But we're not going in looking or a fight. We just need to talk to them."

"They didn't seem very interested in talking to the Homeworlders. I mean, shit, they're like walking octopuses." Nance scowled. "Octopi. Whatever it is. They're barely humanoid, and God only knows if they think even close to how we do."

"They don't have the Transition Drive," Wojtera said, shrugging. "That gives us some advantage. If nothing else, we can run away and they can't catch us."

Nance grunted, his expression skeptical and unconvinced, and again I found myself missing Colonel Hachette. This was going to be one of those decisions that had the potential to bite me in the ass no matter which way I went, and it sure would have been nice to have someone else around to make it.

"We're going to do it," I declared, deciding the debate had gone on long enough. "We'll find out everything we can from the Homeworlders before we make the trip."

"You're the commander," Nance declared, the set of his jaw reminding me of a mule resisting the tug of the lead, "we all agreed to it and I'm not about to go back on it now. But I'm going on record that I think this is a mistake."

I was very close to saying something I'd regret, and only Vicky's hand squeezing vicelike on my leg under the table kept my mouth shut. A furnace had kindled in my belly and the heat was working its way up my chest, across the back of my neck and into my head. Vicky didn't let go, and if I'd taken my glare away from Nance to look at her, I knew she would have been staring at me with that look, the one she gave me when I was about to fuck up. When I finally had the wherewithal to speak without invective, it came out surprisingly calm, if a bit chilly.

"I'm always willing to listen to suggestions, Captain. We don't have many options here that I can see. We either ask the Nova for the map to the jumpgates, or we can go into stasis again and head straight for the singularity. Straight *past* the singularity and pray to God we find something. This place has food we can eat, resources we can trade for, but we don't know what the hell's out there, and it might take months... might take years." I tilted my head toward him. "Am I missing a possibility?"

"There's one," Nance said, anger flashing behind his eyes. "We don't need their fucking permission to use their jumpgates. They can't stop us. We just make a run through them and follow them to the end."

"That's an idea," I admitted. "And I'm prepared to keep it in reserve, but you said it yourself, Captain. They got the numbers, and I have to believe they're going to have those gates pretty well defended."

He rubbed at his eyes, then nodded.

"All right. We'll do it your way. But if these octopus things are anything like the Tahni, I don't know if reasoning with them is going to do a damn bit of good."

"You're going to do *what?*" Frost asked, pushing herself up from desk like she was about to throw herself over it and tackle me. "Do you have any concept of what a bad idea that is?"

"It's what we're going to do." I kept my voice calm, because one of us had to be and because Vicky wasn't here to keep me under control so I had to do it myself. "We're not asking your permission, and I'm telling you as a courtesy."

She'd responded to this about the way I'd expected, if I was being honest.

"Do you understand what could happen if you piss off the Nova?" Frost demanded, circling the desk to get in my face, as if she believed that would intimidate me. She was nearly as tall as I was, and her nose was only centimeters from mine. This close, I could smell a scent of something sweet, either her perfume or her natural odor. It wasn't unpleasant, but she was. "You're leaving, but I'm here dealing with the ramifications. Do you understand how much of my reputation I've staked on your people? On getting the public to accept that?"

"And I've assured you that you'll be taken care of."

"Taken care of?" She spun on her heel, arms spread as if appealing to a higher power. "If the Nova blame your interference on us and come here, the people will have me drawn and quartered! I won't be able to show my face in public! I'll lose everything I've spent the last twenty-five years building!"

Okay, that was it. Before Frost had just been irritating, a typical corporate executive. Now, she was infuriating. She was worried that we'd bring the wrath of the Nova down on her world not for the threat they'd be to her populace but for the threat they'd be to her position. I really, *really* wanted to tell her off, to tear her a new one in my best drill instructor voice, had half a mind to have the Intercept come down and blow out her picture window to pick me up off the hundredth floor of this building, but I didn't.

Instead, I thought. I thought about how to give her what she wanted.

"Okay," I said, smiling thinly. "You want something to make it worth your while, something to make sure this ends well for you, right?"

"It'll have to be something... *significant*," she told me, eyeing me doubtfully.

"It will be. I can give you one of two things, either one of which will make sure everyone considers you a hero, a *savior* even."

Frost took a step back, hands on her hips.

"You have my attention."

"We have something called an auto-doc," I said. "It uses medical nanotechnology to repair anything short of death. If we do a scan of your biology, we could program the nanites to do that for you and your people. It'll cure any disease, repair any damage, extend the lives of your people by *hundreds* of years. You study that, duplicate the tech, you'll be seen as the greatest philanthropist in the history of your world, the woman who ended all disease, gifted your people with longer lives, conquered death itself." The look on her face was intrigued but not quite convinced. "Or."

"Or?"

"Our computing power is a lot more advanced than yours. Our quantum-core computers are a century more advanced than yours, maybe more. Their predictive power could revolutionize your entire society. Whoever controlled it wouldn't just have an advantage, they'd be the ruler of this world. You could manipulate the populace, not just your own but the entire planet—*all* your planets. I could give you our replacement quantum core, the only spare we have for the ship's computer. It's worth more than anything else we could give you, even the Transition Drive. It's pure political and social power."

Frost licked her lips, pure lust and desire written across her face.

"What do you need from me?"

[15]

"Why the hell would you want to come with us?"

I hadn't expected to see Dr. Spinner here at the spaceport. One of the things I'd requested from Frost in return for the quantum core was more provisions. Their food was strange but not bad and we needed it for the rest of this trip, even if we used the stasis chambers, and she'd been happy to provide it. I'd called down a cargo shuttle to carry it up... and to bring down the computer.

Frost was all over the cargo container with the computer, caressing it like a lover while her technicians received a briefing from ours. With the help of Dwight, of course. I'd given him some special instructions for helping them install it.

I'd also ordered them to bring down the holographic projector for Jay and Bob, though the two of them were a great deal more chill about their gift than Frost. They were huddled in the shade of a pedestrian shelter with the small crate, talking quietly.

But while I'd been supervising the loading of the cargo, Spinner had showed up, alone, just walking across the spaceport pavement like a tourist.

"And where's your handler?" I added, motioning around us. Morning again. It was difficult to keep the time down here straight after so long working with the shipboard schedule. "Last time I saw you, you had that spook hanging over your shoulder watching every word you said."

"I am embarrassed to admit," Spinner said, hands clasped in front of him like a guilty child, "that I evaded Lt. Ward on the public transportation before I came here. I heard you were back in the city and needed to talk to you before you left again. Unfortunately, the lieutenant was unpersuaded by my arguments and planned on returning me home. If you refuse to take me with you, I'm afraid I'll be in no small trouble with my government."

"But why do you want to come with us?" I shook my head. The little astrophysicist had even brought a suitcase with him. "I don't know that we're coming back here. We probably aren't. Why would you want to leave your home, maybe forever?"

"I have studied the stars all my life, Captain Alvarez, with no hope of ever seeing them. I could have had a family, but instead I devoted my years and my love to science. I have no attachments here, and as you pointed out, my home isn't the most pleasant place. My field of expertise is considered too vital, and I would never be allowed to even travel to orbit, much less the star colonies. I don't know how many years I have left, but I wish to spend them searching for more knowledge than I can find here."

Which was all very moving, and I might have let it sway me before I'd become the mission commander, but there was a more important question that I was forced to ask.

"That's why you want to come with us," I said, "but why should we bring you along? Don't get me wrong, Dr. Spinner, I don't begrudge you your dream, but this is a starship with limited resources and limited space. If you don't have a use for us, I'd be derelict in my duty allowing you on board."

"That is a fair point," he admitted, raising his clasped hands in front of his chest, as if in prayer. "I am no linguist, no diplomat, but I have studied the universe around us my whole life. I know you have no such specialist on your ship, and it may be that you will need one before your journey is complete. If not, I will endeavor to be useful however I may. Surely, you are not so crowded that a willing pair of hands would not be welcome?"

"Yeah, dude, us too."

I looked up sharply, found that Jay and Bob had walked up while I'd been caught up in my conversation with Spinner. They'd left the holoprojector behind, their hands empty.

"You too, *what*?" I asked.

"We want to go along with you too," Jay announced.

I rubbed at the sudden aching in my temples.

"Your job's over," I reminded them, arguing logically to buy time because, in my short acquaintance with Jay, I still had the impression that logic wouldn't dent his optimism. "You've already been paid for it." I motioned back at the crate with the holoprojector. "You said that thing'll make you rich. Go, take it, start a family, make lives for yourselves."

Jay and Bob shared a glance. I couldn't read it, but I got the idea they were on the same page.

"Money ain't everything, dude. This whole thing has been like the coolest shit that's ever happened to us." He gestured between himself and Bob, who was nodding enthusiastically. "We want to see the universe too. And we're willing to do whatever needs doing. You guys got bathrooms that need cleaning, right?"

"You're not thinking, *any* of you," I snapped, looking from one of them to the other. "Especially not you two! You're going to be hundreds of light-years from home, the only members of your own species. The smells, the food, the customs, the furniture... all different from anything you've ever known, and that might sound exciting now, but it'll get annoying damn quick. I bet you think this is all going to be one big adventure, don't you?" I paused, waiting for an answer, but Jay just shrugged. "We have a saying in the Marines. Adventure is someone else in deep shit far from home."

Jay laughed, which wasn't the reaction I'd expected.

"Dude, we were living by ourselves, no one else around for days, in a tiny rock out in the asteroid belt, nothing between us and millions of kilometers of vacuum but a thin metal shell, every breath we took coming from decades-old air recyclers that broke down every week. Do you think we were doing that because we *liked* it? It was the only job we could find that wouldn't involve us doing some mind-numbingly boring shit for ten or twelve hours a day for years, with an asshole for a boss and no chance of getting anywhere. My dad did that until he finally died of cancer, and my sister is *still* doing it." Another laugh, this one even more bitter and cynical. "As for families. Well man, neither of us is single on purpose. We're kind of what you might call losers."

"I ain't a loser," Bob muttered, though without much conviction. "I'm just shy."

"Either way," Jay went on, rolling his eyes at his friend, "the likelihood that either of us is going to settle down and raise kids isn't good. The way we see it, we got a better chance of doing something cool and meaningful going with you." He shrugged. "Anyway, since from what your people said, no one's ever come across a real alien they could talk to before, I figure if we make it back to your home, we'll be, like, celebrities."

Bob nodded eagerly.

"Besides, Earth girls are cute."

"Yeah, man," Jay agreed, grinning. "Your wife's a stone-cold fox." I must have been glaring, because he blanched to an almost human color. "No offense."

What I should have done, by all rights, was throw all three of them out on their ear. I had no obligation to take them with me and every reason not to. If they did anything stupid, it would be my responsibility. If Spinner was a plant by the Grey and was playing us, trying to get a better line on our technology or worse, sabotage us, that would be on me.

On the other hand, they were all three of them right about one thing. We didn't have enough working hands. The ship had been on an intelligence mission, which meant it was overstocked with analysts and Marines and had just the bare minimum of Fleet crewmembers. We got by, mostly because there were a lot of things that could be done through automation and robotics, but that also meant we had crucial, highly trained technicians doing grunt work like shifting cargo and cleaning out filters, shit that anyone could do after a few days of training. We'd put some of the Vergai Marines on it just to give them even more of a taste of a technological society and the work they could expect to do in one, but they were Marines and already had their fair share of busywork to be done.

And the bottom line was, I *liked* Jay and Bob. They reminded me of some of the other street kids I'd met in the Underground, cruising by without much of a plan, just living one day to the next. I didn't know about Spinner, but he wasn't wrong about us lacking anyone with a background in astrophysics. Dwight and Lilandreth were as close as we came, and if we wound up needing one before we reached home...

"If I do this... *if*," I emphasized when I saw hope flaring in Jay and Bob's expressions, "then you need to know how it's going to work. You do exactly as you're told. No one's going to make slave labor of you, but I can't have any of you telling my people that you just *won't* do something just because it's unpleasant. This is a military ship, and we all do unpleasant and dangerous things. Get that through your head. You don't work, you don't eat. You cause trouble, I will dump you on the first habitable planet we come to and, if you're lucky, I'll leave you with some food and basic supplies. If any of you do anything that causes harm to my ship or my people, that's it. That's the end. Don't want to hear excuses, not interested in whether it was an accident. You hurt my people or damage my ship, you're out the airlock without a suit."

Jay's throat bobbed like he'd just swallowed the lump in it, and Bob's shoulders heaved with heavy breath. Spinner said nothing, looking unperturbed as if he'd expected this.

"Am I clear?" I asked them. "Because this is the first, last, and only warning you get. Once we're out of this system, it's too late for do-overs, too late to turn back, too late to realize you've made a huge mistake. I want all three of you to think about this before you make a decision. This cargo bird..." I jerked a thumb behind me at the tubby, bulbous lines of the shuttle. "... will be taking off in two hours. You two, if you want to come, you need to go grab some clothes and whatever else you need to take care of yourselves *for the rest of your lives* and get back here."

That took them back. I figured it would. The idea that they'd be leaving forever had to hit hard, despite the fact that they'd already been living offworld. Hell, it had hit *us* hard when we thought we'd be stuck out at Yfingam forever, never able to get back to the Commonwealth. It had made us desperate enough to try *this*, which was crazy enough that I almost hadn't been willing to lead us into it. Hell, I didn't even *have* a home to go back to, had everything and everyone I loved along with me on the *Orion*, and I still felt the same sort of desperation.

"Okay, man," Jay said. "But we're coming back." They did take the holoprojector with them though.

Spinner didn't move, feet set as if he were getting ready to weather a hurricane wind.

"As I've said," he told me, "I have nowhere to go and no other alternative than to leaving with you." Spinner toed his suitcase, resting at his feet. "And I have everything I need already. Might I hide inside your shuttle before Lt. Ward finds me?"

Shit. There wasn't any talking this one out of it. Did I really want to?

"Okay," I sighed. If all else failed, we'd be passing through those two Homeworld colonies and I knew there was a Grey presence on both of them. We could leave him—or Jay and Bob—there, despite what I'd told them about this being their last chance to decide. "Get on board. It's not going to be the most comfortable thing in the world waiting in there for two whole hours, but I guess it's better than standing around in the open waiting for the secret police to come arrest you."

Skinner smiled.

"I knew you'd understand."

"I don't understand," Vicky admitted, arms folded as she watched Jay, Bob, and Spinner disembarking from the cargo shuttle, hauling themselves along the railing into the docking bay. Jay and Bob moved with practiced ease, having spent the last year or so in free fall and low gravity, but Spinner nearly rammed headlong into the bulkhead, looking like he was close to puking. "Why the hell did you bring them along?"

"A moment of weakness, I guess," I admitted, glancing back and forth between the Homeworlders and the cargo being hauled out of the boat by the freight-loading machinery.

The resupply of food was a weight lifted off my shoulders.

I'd been worrying about that since we left Yfingam, even with the stasis chambers. We could recycle water and oxygen, but food had to be grown, and we didn't have the capacity to do that. What Frost had given us would last months for the entire crew, years if we rotated in and out of hibernation. Though I certainly hoped it didn't come to that.

"The scientist'll come in handy," I elaborated. "And as for Jay and Bob, well... yeah, that's the weakness part. But on the bright side, when we get home, we'll have definitive proof of everywhere we've been and everything we've seen. A living Resscharr and members of the only race we've met beside the Skrela that didn't originate from Earth life." I snorted a laugh. "That's gotta be worth something. Maybe enough for them to not court-martial all of us for desertion."

"That's what I love about you, Alvarez," Vicky said, hand resting on my shoulder. "Always looking on the bright side. You sure about this plan though? It seems kind of... well, it seems like we're just going to blunder right through the wormhole into the Nova system and hope they decide to come talk to us."

"That's pretty much the plan." I waved an arm demonstratively, though the motion was oddly ephemeral in free fall, my only connection to the deck the magnetic soles of my ship boots. "I mean, the Confederation and the Grey have both tried communicating with them through the gate but there's never been any response. The only time the Nova have ever talked to any Homeworlders was when they breached that gate, so it's what we're going to do." I smiled aside at her. "Though like I told Nance, if you have a better idea, I'm all ears."

She elbowed me in the ribs, and I grunted reflexively even though it hadn't been that hard.

"Don't you go comparing me to Nance. He's only thinking about his ship. Sometimes I think if she was a woman, he'd marry her. But what happens if they just start shooting? I mean, we could take them as long as they don't have a hundred ships but that sort of defeats the whole purpose of getting their help. What if they won't talk to us?"

"We have to hope they're smart enough to realize we're not the same as the Homeworlders and that they try to communicate with us." I shrugged. "I mean, they're obviously pretty sophisticated."

"You think we'll be able to understand them? I mean, it took us a while to translate the Confederation language, and we had a couple of willing..." She shrugged. "Okay, *semi*-willing participants cooperating with us. The Nova might not want to sit around and yammer at us until Dwight figures it out."

"The last time the Homeworlders encountered them, the Nova beamed a laser straight to them in their own language. Frost and Spinner told me they had no idea how the Nova learned to speak it, but they do. I guess we just have to hope they'll do the same thing again."

Vicky cocked an eyebrow at me.

"You know what Top would have said about that, right?"

Unfortunately, I did.

"Hope in one hand, shit in the other. See which one fills up first."

[16]

"Been a long fucking time since I took a ship through a jumpgate," Nance said, settled back into his acceleration couch comfortably, probably enjoying the boost gravity. I know I was. We'd spent too much time recently flailing around in free fall.

The gate loomed in front of us on the viewscreen, a hole in space ringed by a spectral rainbow. The station the Homeworlders used to keep it open wasn't that different from the ones the Commonwealth had constructed over a hundred years ago, a fusion reactor mated to a huge laser, pumping energy into the wormhole to enlarge it. We couldn't see it from this angle since the gate blocked the station from view. The only thing visible on the front screen were the stars as viewed from another system, light-years away.

Off to the side, in the ship's peripheral cameras, Confederation and Grey space stations watched in prurient curiosity, waiting to see whether we'd get destroyed. I wondered if Frost cared one way or the other. She had what she wanted. Or so she thought.

"Passing through the gate in three," Yanayev chanted,

fingers tracing lines through her station controls, "two, one... transitioning."

Theoretically, there were no physical effects from passing through the gate. I mean, EM signals could run through the transition without distortion so there *couldn't* be anything that a human could feel. And yet I did. Every time I'd passed through one, I'd felt it, a stretching out not of my physical form but somehow of my spirit, like my soul was in two universes at once. Not quite the same as the discomforting sensation of a Transition, yet somehow worse.

It lasted an eternity, but then we were somewhere else and it was over.

The star here was a little different, not appreciably bigger but perhaps a shade brighter, and the gate had deposited us just beyond the orbit of the moon of the habitable planet. The world wasn't that different than most other habitable worlds, a beautiful, blue marble, though the distribution and ratio of the greens and browns and whites were skewed from Earth.

"We call this system Sanctuary," Spinner said. I'd invited him to the bridge for the passage, which Nance hadn't been very happy about, but I figured he'd know these systems better than we did. "The habitable world is known as The Glen by my nation, though I believe the Confederation calls it something different."

"Don't you both live in the same settlement down there?" Vicky asked, her eyebrow shooting upward. "How's that work when you call the planet different names?"

"How often do any of us mention the name of the planet we're standing on?" I countered with a shrug.

"The next gate should be four hundred thousand kilometers out," Spinner went on, "at the edge of the outer asteroid belt. I believe you have the coordinates."

"We do," Nance confirmed. "Helm, plot a micro-Transition as close as you can to the outward gate."

"Sir," Lt. Chase said, looking up from his station, raising a hand like a schoolchild asking to go to the bathroom. "We're getting a transmission from the planet. It's from the Confederation outpost there."

Nance was about to snap an order at the Communications officer, but for once he looked to me first.

"Put it on the main screen?" he asked. I nodded and he passed the command along to Chase.

The image that appeared on the holographic projection was of a Homeworlder female, though I couldn't have sworn to her age. They didn't have our anti-agathic treatments, but neither did they seem to wrinkle and shrivel like humans did without the advanced medical care that had become available after the Sino-Russian War. Not everyone got it, certainly not the refugees who'd settled into Tijuana and the other ruined cities, and I remembered old people from my time there as a young child. None of them looked like this woman. Her feathery hair was cut short and she wore some kind of uniform, though not one I'd seen back on Homeworld.

"Commonwealth vessel *Orion*," she said, the translation software giving her a deep, almost seductive voice, which seemed an odd choice to me. "I'm Colonel Banner of the Confederation Space Forces. I've been briefed on your mission and I need to ask a favor of you in the name of Ms. Frost."

"This is Captain Alvarez of the Commonwealth Marine Corps," I replied, counting on Lt. Chase to make sure the audio and video pickups centered on me. I was out of my seat, standing beside Nance rather than strapped in since we didn't anticipate combat maneuvering anytime soon and I hated being belted into the acceleration couch. "What can we do for you?"

"We know you're going to speak to the Nova. It's something

we've attempted to do many times and have always been ignored. Ms. Frost was of the opinion that you'll have more success than we did and she wondered if we might send a shuttle up to tag along, perhaps to take advantage of the situation and see if the Nova are interested in negotiations."

My brow furled and I realized how deeply I was frowning, tried to force my expression into neutrality.

"Colonel, there's an obvious problem with that. We're not coming back here. How would you get home?"

The woman shrugged, offering me a thin smile.

"We presume you're going to make your attempt at communication in the breach system. If things don't work out, we'll simply launch our shuttle back through the wormhole and have a rescue ship waiting on the other side of the gate to pick us up."

Heartburn roiled my gut, and I couldn't even blame it on free fall since we were still under boost. I didn't much want any of Frost's people on my ship, but I couldn't think of a good reason to turn them down, and this would be easier with their help than without it. Plus, if any of our Homeworlder volunteers changed their mind, or I changed it for them, it would be very handy to have a shuttle heading back to their colonies to dump them off.

I might have been standing there, silent, for minutes, but I knew it was probably just a second or two.

"Two conditions," I told Banner, making the decision as I spoke, the words coming in the echo of my thoughts. "One, no weapons. Your ship has to be unarmed and none of you will be allowed to carry any weapons on board ours." Her nod was delayed because of the translation, but I had the sense that it was immediate and unhesitating, as if she'd expected it. "Second, all your people stay in our Operations Room and you don't interfere. You don't touch anything, you don't try to communicate with anyone else without asking us first. Whatever you want to say to the Nova, you run it by us first, and you wait until we've cut our deal before you try to make yours."

That might have been harsh, but I wasn't feeling particularly generous at the moment. This time it took longer, and the consternation in her expression was plain, even for an alien. She didn't really have any choice, and we both knew it.

"Of course. If you can make orbit around the planet, we'll have the shuttle up to you in two hours. If that's acceptable."

"We've waited this long," I told her with a shrug. "I suppose a couple more hours couldn't hurt."

"Are you Captain Alvarez?"

The woman was younger than Colonel Banner, less severe, her hair longer and softer, her attitude less that of an officious chairborne ranger and more that of a field soldier. Her uniform was the same but it lacked the spotless, starched precision of the senior officer, looking more like a woman who actually worked for a living. She also used a set of magnetic ship boots like she was accustomed to moving around in free fall, though the rest of her team not so much. There were ten of them in all, and even though none of them were armed, in accordance with our agreement, it was obvious who would have been if they could.

"That's me," I told her, offering a hand. "Welcome to the *Orion*."

"I'm Captain Singer," she said. "Chief of Security for the Confederation colony at Otherside."

"*Otherside*, huh?" I repeated. "Now I understand why the Grey call the place by a different name."

She surprised me by smiling broadly.

"Don't blame me. The ship's captain who found the place got to name it, and I'm afraid he wasn't an imaginative fellow."

"We have the same problem where I'm from," I told her, chuckling. "Every star and planet has to be named after some ancient god or hero, but there's only so many to choose from, so we wind up reusing them."

"Hello, I'm Councilor Raft." The guy was a prick. I could tell immediately, cultural differences be damned, by the way he inserted himself between Singer and I, jamming a hand at me and grabbing mine before I had a chance to accept it. His clothes were along the same fashion as Frost's, though not as expensive, and he had *politician* written all over him. "I'm the official delegate of the Confederation government on Otherside. It's nice to meet you, Captain. I want to personally thank you for allowing us to accompany you on this voyage, as well as conveying the gratitude of the free, voting citizens of the Confederation and that of Ms. Frost."

Funny, that. Everyone had a title, a job, but not Frost. She just *was*, like God.

"Of course, Councilor," I said, pulling my hand out of his soggy, flaccid grasp. "I assume you're here to negotiate with the Nova for your government."

"And to advise you on your own negotiations, if you need it," he confirmed, straightening the collar of his jacket, then smoothing down his hair. "After all, we have more experience with them than you do."

"True," I allowed, matching his insincere smile with one of my own. "However, since that experience is almost exclusively the Nova refusing to speak with you and ordering your ships out of their system at gunpoint, I'm not certain it'll be of much use to us." He was sputtering a reply, but I interrupted before my 'link could even attempt a translation, waving behind me to the half-dozen armored Fleet Security personnel lined up in the docking bay behind me. "This is Lt. Stillwell, our head of ship's security. She's going to escort your people to the Operations

Center. From there, you'll be able to monitor everything that's happening, but I'm afraid you'll have to go through me if you want to contribute to the situation. I don't want to piss off the Nova needlessly, and they already have a negative opinion of you Homeworlders."

With the natural, deep-bronze complexion of the Homeworlders, it was hard for me to tell if Raft's face was flush, but if his deep scowl and the twitching of the muscles in his cheek were any indication, I decided that, had he shared my own coloration, his cheeks would have been bright red.

"You're making a mistake here, Captain," he told me in that scolding, solicitous-sounding tone I'd heard from many other politicians, some of them pretending to be military officers. "We have valuable insight that could only help you in your endeavor."

"And I'm very willing to listen to it," I assured him. "From the Ops Center, directly to my private line. And after we get a chance to talk to the Nova, I'll be sure to let them know that you're on deck. If you need anything to eat or drink or have to use the facilities, just tell Lt. Stillwell and she'll see to it."

"Yeah," Stillwell said, eyeing me sidelong as she put a hand on Raft's shoulder and pushed him toward the hatchway out of the docking bay, "that's exactly why I attended the Commonwealth Military Academy, to play flight attendant to a bunch of politicians."

"Thank you, Stillwell," I said, smiling sweetly, then pretended not to notice the bird she shot me behind her back. She still wasn't happy with me as commander even though she accepted it. She was an Academy grad, and one who was happiest when everything went by the book. A Marine captain being in charge of a Fleet Intelligence mission with several officers higher ranking than him on board was *not* by the book.

Raft kept grumbling as Stillwell led him away, but the

others followed silently. Three of them were clearly Raft's civilian toadies, but the other five were military and they were the ones who would have been armed if they could. Singer hung back from the rest, catching my eye.

"Captain Alvarez, could I speak with you for a moment privately?"

Stillwell looked a question back at me and I waved her off.

"Sure. I'll take the captain to the Ops Center in a moment, Lt. Stillwell."

The Security officer shrugged and kept chivying the others through the hatch.

"This isn't the ideal place for a conversation, Captain," I told Singer, gesturing around us.

The docking bay was a busy place, with crew hauling maintenance gear from one ship to the next. They only had an hour until we broke orbit, and they were taking advantage of the free fall to get the heavy work done. Metallic bangs and creaks echoed off the deck, the overhead, the bulkheads, assaulting our senses on the catwalk to the umbilical that hugged the Confederation shuttle close into its docking niche.

"Actually, it's perfect for it," the woman said, eyes flickering around. "If you get my meaning."

"Ah." I still wasn't much of a spy, despite Hachette's best efforts, but I also wasn't an idiot. "In that case, let me show you one of our assault shuttles."

Assault One just happened to be the spacecraft the crew was working on, doing their best to get a replacement turret weapon installed in the portside wing. We'd long ago run out of ammo for the Gatling laser that had been the craft's secondary weapon, but we'd fabricated a coilgun turret to take its place. We *could* fabricate replacement ammo for the lasers if we had a source of raw materials to make hyperexplosives, but we didn't. Coilgun slugs were easy to make and we could fab them out of any ferrous metal, though tungsten was preferred.

This close to the crew closing up the wing panels on the dagger-shaped shuttle, the whining of machine tools and the clanging of metal on metal were nearly deafening, and Singer had to lean close to my shoulder to make herself heard.

"I'm a soldier, Captain Alvarez," she told me by way of preamble, "not a politician."

"I'd guessed that," I said, then spread my hands invitingly. "I assume you wanted to talk someplace we wouldn't be overheard, not even by whatever listening device that Raft guy has planted on you, and this is as good as it gets. The EM scatter from all the BiPhase Carbide in the bay should be enough to block anything microwave."

There was a hint of bitterness to her smile.

"It's simpler than that, I'm afraid. It simply records everything and he downloads it later. But this should be enough. Captain..."

"Call me Cam. There are too many damn captains running around this boat."

"Very well. *Cam.* I assume you know we're not simply here to try to negotiate with the Nova."

"I was born at night," I told her. "I wasn't born *last* night. Yes, I figured that out. You're here to spy on us, maybe try to figure out what of our tech you can copy."

Singer's brow furled at the joke, and I suppose the translation wasn't exact. She shook her shoulders like she was shedding water and pressed on.

"Yes, that's certainly part of it. Those civilians with Councilor Raft aren't just his entourage, they're trained engineers. They're supposed to take photographs and thermal scans of every piece of equipment they come across. That's what's out in the open, what they're not trying to hide from me." She shrugged. "And I wouldn't be talking to you if that was the only thing. I *am* a soldier and, being honest, I *do* want your technology for my nation."

"Fair enough. So, what's the secret part?"

"There's no evidence of this," she warned me. "Nothing I can point to except an impression I got speaking to Raft." She paused as if waiting for me to respond to that, but I just cocked my head to the side, waiting. "Raft is Frost's pet. He wasn't stationed out here before you came. In fact, he only beat you here by *hours*, him and his people. He marched in and showed me my new orders, putting me under his command, demanding I offer him whatever he needs for this mission."

"That makes sense." I shrugged. "Frost doesn't strike me as a woman who leaves anything to chance. I'm not surprised she wanted one of her own people on this. If she can make an agreement with the Nova to open more systems for your people, she'll be even more popular than she is already."

"She may want Raft to reach an agreement with the Nova," Singer acknowledged, "but more than that, I believe she wishes to make sure *you* do not."

I blinked. Nothing she'd said before had surprised me, but this had.

"Why the hell not?" I blurted. "What motive could she have for sabotaging our mission?"

"You're an asset. Ms. Frost is not one to let an asset get away. If the Nova allow you to pass through their jumpgates unopposed, you're gone. If they deny you access, perhaps you'll leave anyway, but you'll more likely come back and she can find some new way to exploit you. Even if your technology is too advanced for her to do anything drastic, like seize your ship, simply your presence might be useful for her purposes."

I nodded slowly, the idea sinking in.

"That is a depressingly persuasive argument, Captain Singer. What would you suggest I do about it?"

"Whatever you do, Cam, you can't allow Raft access to communications. Not just while you're trying to talk to the Nova, but even after you leave. Your best bet might be to simply kick us all off the ship now."

"There's only one problem with that. What if the Nova turn us down? Frost is right about that. We're going to press on either way, but we'll likely need to come back to Homeworld first. Alienating her would be a bad idea."

Singer shrugged.

"Then my only suggestion would be to watch Raft carefully. Don't trust a word he says."

"That's not gonna be a problem," I told her. "I'm not the trusting type."

[17]

"Wow," Dr. Spinner breathed, his eyes wide. "I'd seen the pictures and video that the expedition took of this place, but they didn't do it justice."

It was impressive. A hell of a lot more impressive than the last system, the second Homeworlder colony. The Feds and the Grey shared a name for that one—Wasteland. That was a translation to English, of course, and I was sure their own word carried more nuance, but the description was apt. The planet had been more desert than anything else. Some high desert, some low desert, and small bands of green at the poles, a couple larger, lush islands where the population was settled, but not much chance of expansion without extensive planetary engineering. Which was centuries beyond these people.

We'd passed through the jumpgate with hardly a look backward, our attention and our worries all focused ahead. Duty stations were on high alert, Intercepts and assault shuttles were prepped for launch and, just in case, I even had Vicky ready with a platoon to repel boarders. No, that wasn't likely, but part of being the commander meant preparing for *every* scenario, not just the likely ones.

"It seems like such a waste," Dwight said and Spinner started, goggling up at the AI's avatar at the side of the main display. "Two habitable planets, the third and fourth worlds out, plus the largest moon of the gas giant shows signs of being habitable as well, depending on the radiation exposure. And not a soul living here."

The worlds were beautiful, both of them. Having two habitables wasn't unheard of. 82 Eridani had both Eden and Inferno, and it wasn't the only system like that. But generally, only one of the living worlds was *hospitable*. Eden was exactly as advertised, a world with huge temperate zones and a moderate climate, while Inferno was a hellhole, barely livable in summer and then only near the poles. That wasn't the case here. These planets were twin sisters, each wreathed in blues and greens.

Even the moon of the closest gas giant to the primary star wasn't bad, at least seen from a distance.

"We're not picking up anything?" I asked Wojtera. The Tactical officer shook his head.

"Not around the habitables. No signs of ships, stations, satellites, and absolutely no energy signatures on the planets. There's at least plant life there, but if there's anything sentient on either of them, it hasn't built anything hotter than a campfire."

"That doesn't make any sense," Nance grumbled. "Why would they chase everyone out of here if they didn't plan on taking advantage of the place themselves? This system is a gem. If it was in the Commonwealth, there'd be a billion people living in it, minimum."

"You have a billion people living in your colonies?" Spinner asked me, disbelief strong in his stare.

"A lot more than that now," I confirmed. "There's at least as many people off Earth as on it nowadays."

This time, I *was* strapped into the commander's chair. We

were decelerating at a comfortable one gravity at the moment, but God alone knew what we'd be facing on this side of the jumpgate. Spinner occupied the seat I'd usually chosen back when Hachette had been in command, and having him up here for the jump had been... well, controversial was an understatement. But I'd wanted a local present, and the choices were him or Singer. While the captain had been the one to warn me about Raft, that didn't mean I automatically trusted her.

But I did need her right now.

"Chase," I said to the Comms officer, "connect me with the Ops Center. Straight to my earbud." The man gave me a nod. "Captain Singer, can you hear me in there?"

"Yes, Cam," she said.

"We *all* can, Captain Alvarez," Raft added helpfully. I grimaced, but there was nothing for it. Their tabs weren't connected to the internal communications net and, what's more, I didn't *want* them to be, so there was nothing other than to use the PA speakers in the compartment.

"Good to know, Councilor," I said. "Captain, are you familiar with the records from your attempt to explore this system?"

"I am, sir," she said. "They're required study for any officer stationed in the colonies."

"How long after your ships arrived did the Nova come through their gate to contact them?"

"It wasn't immediate," Singer replied. "If I recall correctly, it was nearly sixty hours."

Great.

"Thanks." I signaled to Chase and he cut the connection.

The faint rumble of the ship's main drive was the only sound for a moment, different now than it had been before Decision. The Resscharr there had given us a new drive, something Nance and the engineering crew called a photon drive, though all I knew about it was that it used a different type of fusion than the engine it had replaced. I kind of missed the old drive, the familiarity of its vibration through the hull. It had been white noise that had helped me to shut everything out and think. I needed that even more now.

"Captain Nance, we may be waiting here a couple days before the Nova show up. Tell you what, let's go into orbit around the third planet and take a closer look." I shook my head. "I just can't help but think there's some *reason* the Nova don't have colonies here, not even an outpost. Let's find out."

"That's it, right there," Wojtera declared, tapping his finger against the haptic hologram at his station, the action reflected by a red dot on the main screen. "It's not much, but it's the only sign of habitation on either world."

The third planet had been a bust. I mean, it had been pretty and full of life, and if our mission had been to find a nice place to live, it would definitely have ranked up there with anything we'd seen during our forays out from Yfingam. There was complex animal life, totally different from anything back in the Cluster, and if we'd had any xenobiologists along they would have had a field day. But we'd seen nothing that could explain the Nova interdiction of this system, and we'd wasted nearly twenty hours figuring that out, starting with orbital scans, working our way down to drones, and then finally sending out one of the assault shuttles for a low-level flight.

The fourth hadn't seemed much more promising at first. Three orbits slicing the orange with the sensor scans, running everything through Dwight because he was more efficient at coming up with algorithms for that sort of thing than any of us would have been, and nothing. The drones had provided no results either, and this time I'd ordered both assault shuttles down to save time.

That had done the trick. Barely.

"You're sure it's metallic?" I asked, staring at the screen as if I could somehow make the distant lump of faded gray cohere into something more recognizable. "It looks like a rock."

"The albedo confirms it. Definitely metal and angular enough it can't be natural. I don't think we're gonna be able to tell much more without landing and taking a look though."

"Couldn't one of the drones get closer?" Vicky asked, leaning over my shoulder to peer at the display. I'd had Springfield spell her as the watch officer for the ready platoon once it had become clear there was no immediate threat.

"Maybe if we still had the factory models we started the mission with," Nance commented, chin resting on his fist. We'd gone through three bridge crew shifts since we'd started this, but Nance and I had remained, only leaving long enough to clean up and grab quick meals. Certainly no sleep, and weariness dragged at me but I was used to it. Nance looked like he was about to start snoring in his captain's chair. "But all we have left now are the cheap copies we've been able to fab from local resources. They're fragile and underpowered and they're not going to get through the tree canopy intact."

"What about the assault shuttles?" Vicky suggested, waving a hand as if she was exasperated by the excuses. "They're still suborbital. Have one of them land and take a look around."

"Not a bad idea," I admitted, "but I want to take a look at this myself."

"Why?" Nance demanded, gaping at me. "Jesus Christ, Alvarez, what's it going to take to get it through your head that you've got people to do this shit for you? You need to learn to trust them to do their jobs."

Sigh. Count to ten. *Don't* smash Nance in the face. This

shouldn't have been a conversation we had in front of the bridge crew, but Nance didn't seem capable of getting that through his head.

"I do trust them. To be Marines and pilots and bridge crew, and..." I gestured toward him. "... ship's captains. If I trusted any of them to be the commander, well... I'd let *them* be commander instead of me, because God knows I didn't want this job. I'd send Captain Sandoval because I trust her implicitly, but then I'd be left as the company commander of the Marines when I'm trying to make decisions that affect all of us." I tapped my chest. "*I* am the one who's going to have to live with the ramifications of every decision I make, and I'm not going to make them blind. I need to see what's down there." Something else that didn't need to be said in front of the crew, but it had to be said. "Captain Nance, if you want overall command of this mission, you have the rank for it. I won't oppose it. You say the word and it's yours. But if I'm in charge, then we do things my way. That's the choice."

Every eye on the bridge was staring at us, including Spinner. I wondered how this was going over with him, given the authoritarian regime he lived under. They probably didn't have too many debates like this in front of the proletariat there. Heat filled my face, an instinctive reluctance to be the center of attention that came from all those years avoiding bullies in the group homes. I didn't look away though, just met every single one of their gazes until they turned away.

I thought for a second that Nance might take me up on it. It might have worked, if we'd done it from the beginning, with him as the figurehead and me as the right hand, making the decisions for the Marines, but that ship had sailed. In the end, he shrugged his surrender.

"It's your call. But if you *do* get yourself killed, no one's foisting that damned job off on me."

Revealingly, Vicky hadn't bothered to try to talk me out of it. She simply regarded me with a look of consternation.

"I'll take Intercept One," I promised her. "And Campea, and one of his squads. But I doubt there's anything down there that we're going to need to shoot at."

She grunted, unconvinced, but didn't bother arguing.

"I suppose I'll go get a drop-ship ready just in case the worst-case scenario raises its ugly head yet again."

"Thank you, Captain Sandoval," I said, smiling sweetly. "Chase, could you call down and ask Lt. Villanueva to prep Intercept One for launch? Oh, and tell Lilandreth to meet me in the docking bay as well, if you please."

"Yes, sir."

"Lilandreth?" Nance asked, eyebrow going up.

"She's as close as we have to an expert in alien archaeology and technology. She's a hell of a lot more likely to know what she's looking at than I am."

"Well, that's as sensible as anything you've said today."

"Captain, I'd like to go along." Spinner was out of his seat, though he held onto it with one hand, like he was afraid he'd get thrown around suddenly by some unexpected, violent maneuver... or maybe like he thought he was breaking some rule by standing up and wanted to be ready to sit back down if I yelled at him.

"All due respect, Dr. Spinner," I said, "but you're an astrophysicist. This doesn't seem like it would be in your wheelhouse."

I'd used the idiom without thinking, but I idly wondered how it would translate, if there was some equivalent phrase in his language or if Dwight's program would change it into something more literal.

"You're correct about that," Spinner admitted. His eyes were cast downward as if in embarrassment. "I don't know that my specialty will be of any use to you. But I'd still like to come. As you say, this likely won't be dangerous and, to be honest..." he looked back up, smiling. "I've never set foot on another planet."

It was silly, of course. There was no reason to take him along to the planet and this wasn't a vacation tour. Just bringing him on the mission in the first place had been silly, been a stupid decision on my part, but there was something about the little man... for some reason, I wanted to believe him. It was strange. I hadn't been lying to Captain Singer when I told her I wasn't a trusting person, so why did I want to trust this guy? That, in itself, made me mistrust *myself*.

"Sure," I told him. Not because I trusted him but because, suddenly, I had doubts. "Come with me, I'll get you suited up."

The little scientist was practically dancing as he followed me off the bridge. He seemed so genuine, so enthusiastic. Spinner made it very hard to believe he was an enemy, but that could also make him the worst sort of enemy.

And the best place to keep your enemies was close.

[18]

"This place reminds me of Hermes," Campea said, sniffing the air.

His visor was up, which was probably un-tactical of him, but there was obviously nothing getting ready to attack us and I couldn't blame him. The air in Two Rivers hadn't been exactly filthy, but you could tell it was a city in an industrialized society. Here... it was pristine, cleaner than anything I'd ever smelled before. Well, except for the smoke. We'd tried to aim for bare dirt, but on the landing zone there'd been a few stray patches of whatever passed for grass in this ecosystem, and they'd burned up quickly beneath the cutter's belly jets. Curls of white smoke disappeared into the crystal-blue morning sky, the light of the primary star glinting off the silver of the cutter's skin.

The rest of the Force Recon Marines who'd come along didn't indulge in Campea's sightseeing, always well-disciplined, their Gauss rifles pointed outward as they clomped down the ramp of the Intercept. The squad leader had been scandalized when two officers had disembarked before them, but she'd have to live with it. Just because we'd had bars pinned on didn't mean we weren't combat Marines.

"Yeah," I agreed, taking in the distant mountains, the great swathes of forest. Green. Theoretically, there were other chemical combinations that could take the place of chlorophyll, other colors that could signify plant life, but we hadn't found them anywhere except the Skrela worlds. "I never spent a lot of time there, but yeah, it definitely reminds me of the mountains outside Hesperides."

"Oh, man, you missed out then," Campea said. "Hermes is a great place to live. I was born in a little town about thirty klicks outside of Hesperides." He nudged my arm. "You and Vicky don't have any ties anywhere... you should think about settling there once we get back." He shook his head. "I'm going back home. I've had enough of this shit. No more bouncing around from one battle to another. I'm gonna use my seven years' worth of back pay to buy a little ranch, settle down. Find some nice girl and have a family."

"You sure about that, Camp?" I teased him, grinning sidelong at the lieutenant. "They'll probably bump you up to major just for time served, pin a bunch of medals on your chest for being part of the op that got rid of Zan-Thint and discovered the truth about the Predecessors. After this, you could name your posting, make general in ten years or so."

"You should know better than me," he said, sliding down his visor, "that you can only throw sixes so many times before the dice come up snake eyes."

The Marines had spread out into a small perimeter around the rear of the Intercept, and I realized the others were waiting for my okay to disembark.

"It's clear," I called back up into the shadowed interior of the utility bay. "Come on down."

Lilandreth was first, maybe because she'd been through so much shit a forest glen didn't scare her, or maybe because was armed, one of the Resscharr energy pistols affixed to her hip.

She hadn't asked my permission to carry it and maybe that should have bothered me, but of everyone on the ship, she and Dwight were the ones who could most easily fuck everything up for us if they wanted to, and neither would need a sidearm to do it.

Behind her, emerging from her shadow like a groundhog about to predict the length of the winter, was Dr. Spinner. His mouth dropped open, and he gawked openly at the vistas surrounding the valley as if he'd never seen the like before. I hadn't had the chance to visit his country, just looked at a few videos that might have been Fed propaganda, but they'd all leaned pretty heavily into skies blackened by industrial pollution, endless urbanization, and twisting streets clogged with traffic. Even if they were exaggerations, there had to be some truth to them, or Spinner wouldn't have been so awestruck at the sight.

At the foot of the ramp, he paused, kneeling down to touch a clump of stringy grass, running the blades between his fingers.

"Another world," he mused. "I'm actually on another world."

Which could have been genuine appreciation of the experience or might have been overacting. He looked up, noting my expression.

"Is it so old to you now?" he wondered. "So commonplace that you don't even think about it?"

"I don't recall ever feeling that way about it," I said, seeing no reason not to be honest with the man. "Of course, the first time I set foot on another planet it was a humid, muggy hellhole and I went there to train to fight in a war that seemed pretty much like suicide." I shrugged. "That might have colored my impressions."

Getting impatient, I took a step back up the ramp, looking for the last two passengers to come out.

"What the hell's the problem?" I asked.

Councilor Raft stood at the head of the ramp, arms crossed, jaw set stubbornly while Captain Singer leaned in toward him, whispering urgently. She looked up at my approach, a flash of embarrassment in her expression.

"I do not see, Captain Alvarez," Raft announced, glaring at me, "why my military escort can't be allowed a weapon to defend me on an unexplored alien world."

"I didn't have to bring you at all, Councilor," I reminded him. "You being here is a courtesy to your employer, Ms. Frost. You insisted on being involved in these matters, that you had valuable input. This is your chance. If you'd rather stay on board the cutter, I can inform the crew..."

"No," he snapped. Raft blew out a breath and straightened his jacket collar, smoothed down the front of his suit, and stalked down the ramp.

"What are you doing?" Singer hissed aside at me, pausing beside me. "I told you to keep him contained on the ship, not to take him with you on some wild goose chase down to Nova territory!"

And suddenly she didn't seem so concerned about being spied upon by her tab. Interesting.

"I don't trust him," I told her. "And I don't trust you either. It seems to me that the safest place for the both of you is right in front of me where I can keep an eye on you. Not on my ship where you can cause trouble."

Again with the honesty. There'd been a day when the question wasn't whether I was going to lie but how elaborately. I wasn't sure if the Corps had remade me into what I was now or if it had been Vicky. Or maybe it was just that lying was too much fucking work.

Singer shot me one last glare before she followed the politician down to the packed dirt of the clearing.

"Dwight," I said, "how far are we from the thing?"

"The site that your shuttle spotted," the AI replied, "is two and a half kilometers due south of your position, Cam. I've taken the liberty of dropping a location pin in the dead-reckoning nav systems of your Marines' helmets."

"Thanks." I motioned to Campea. "Move it out."

Campea didn't walk point himself, leaving that honor to the squad leader, but I think that was mostly because he wanted to be with me behind the arrowhead wedge of the squad. Not to bullshit or try to convince me to move to Hermes but because that was where the aliens were gathered and Campea wanted to help me keep an eye on them. I appreciated the thought, though the three of them were unarmed and I had a pulse carbine slung around my neck and a service pistol at my hip. Maybe Singer was a ninja.

"We picking up anything from the outer jumpgate?" I asked Dwight. I could have directed the question to Villanueva back in the cutter, but she'd have to relay it upstairs and I'd be waiting minutes for an answer, while the omnipresent AI would just *know*.

"Nothing yet." Dwight didn't let me down. The only thing limiting his connection with the *Orion* was the lightspeed limit on the comms, and that could be measured in fractions of a second. "Are you certain this detour was wise? If the Nova come through the gate, it will take the *Orion* perhaps as much as an hour to reach minimum safe distance for Transition."

"It's always better to negotiate from a position of knowledge. If we don't know *why* they don't want anyone in this system, we don't know how to convince them otherwise."

The Force Recon squad would be keeping a hard watch, and doing a better job of it with their helmet sensors than I could with my Mark-1 eyeball, but instinct and ingrained habit kept my head on a swivel and my carbine at the ready as we entered the woods. There was no sound except the crunch of boots on dry leaves and twigs, and if the trees of this world weren't exactly like the ones back in the Cluster, neither were they so totally strange that I couldn't recognize them. Physics and biology being what they were, there were only so many ways plant life could efficiently turn sunlight and water into food while protecting itself from the weather and the fauna. Surrounding themselves with rough bark and growing toward the sun must be an easy solution.

I liked the trees. I hadn't had too many around growing up and none at all in the Underground, but after the Hausos and Yfingam, I was growing attached to the idea of the forest, the sheltering boughs, the embrace of nature. They say converts are the worst sort of fanatics, and that's the only excuse I can give for not noticing the animal before it burst through the brush only twenty meters away and galloped right through the middle of our formation.

"What the fuck!" I didn't know which of the Marines had blurted out the exclamation and didn't have time to find out because Campea's order overwhelmed all the other gabble.

"Hold fire! Hold fire! It's just a fucking deer!"

Well, it wasn't *actually* a deer. The fact that it had *six* legs should have been his first clue. I only caught a fleeting glimpse of the thing as it retreated from us at top speed, but its hide was scaly and covered with spines, a fan-shaped tail waggling with each leaping step. Then it was gone, and I let out the breath I'd been holding and lowered the muzzle of my pulse carbine.

"What if that thing had attacked us?" Raft squawked, pointing after the animal, sweat pouring down his face despite the cool breeze filtering through the trees. "That could have been a predator! And it would have gone right for me because I'm not wearing armor and don't have a gun!"

"In general," I told him, keeping my voice low and calm,

"predatory animals aren't familiar with body armor and firearms. If it wanted to hunt one of us, it would have gone for the smallest, which would be Dr. Spinner." Spinner's face paled, and I fought to suppress a laugh. "But if it had attacked, the Marines would have shot it. You're our guests, and we're not going to let anything happen to you."

I doubt I convinced anyone, but when the squadleader set out again they all followed her, though their eyes were wide and scanning back and forth. The game trail through the forest led eventually to a dry creek bed curving through to the left, and I blinked in surprise when the Marines stepped into it.

"I thought you said south," I told Dwight. "Are you sure this is the right way?"

"You're not far now," he assured me. "I would caution you to watch for snakes, however. Or the local equivalent."

I decided not to pass that warning on to the Homeworlders, figuring they were nervous enough and would probably be better off just walking blindly by any snakes we did come across. I didn't see any, though I was so busy looking out for them that I didn't notice the banks of the moribund creek rising higher around us until they'd blocked out the trees on either side of us.

"I don't like this shit," Campea confided over our private net. "Yeah, there's supposed to be nothing here, but down in this depression I feel like ducks in the water."

"Shouldn't be too much longer..." I started to say, but the squadleader interrupted me.

"Lt. Campea, Captain Alvarez! Come on up here. I think we've found it."

I didn't tell Spinner, Raft, and Singer to come with me, but I guess they felt like I was the only one who cared whether they lived or died, so they tagged along. We had to squeeze through a narrow point in the old creek bed where the banks had caved in, but on the other side of the bottleneck was the... artifact. I didn't know what to call it. Not a sculpture, there wasn't enough of a shape to it for that. A monolith, perhaps, although it was low to the ground, broad and sprawling and squared off at the edges.

I didn't understand how big it was until we approached closer and I realized that this creek bed was dry because the monolith had been dropped across it. Twenty meters long, ten meters wide, and massing at least a hundred tons, it had sunk a meter into soft earth that had, at some point, hardened around it. The surface of the thing had once been silvery and still was where rain or wind had cleared off the silt and dirt, but without the sharp, angular edges, I could have mistaken the artifact for a glacial boulder.

It seemed random, like someone had dumped the thing out of the back of a spaceship to drop weight for takeoff, yet I knew it had to be purposeful.

"Why here?" I didn't know who I was asking, but Dwight answered.

"The riverbed. You can't see the other side of it from where you are, but it's like an arrow pointing to the artifact. It was put here so someone would find it."

"What the hell is this thing?" Campea murmured, then seemed to realize we weren't out of the woods yet. Literally and figuratively. "Sgt. Lovell, get the squad into a perimeter around this thing. We don't need anything sneaking up on us."

Lovell scrambled to obey, but I was too enthralled by the size of the monolith to check up on them. The surface seemed rough, but when I traced a line across it dirt came free and below that it was slick, frictionless, almost like it wasn't really there.

"There's gotta be an opening somewhere," I decided. "Lilandreth, help me look for an opening."

Getting out of the collapsed creek bed wasn't easy, not with what was left of the bank crumbling under my boots, but the

Force Recon squad had done it while wearing heavy combat armor, and I wasn't about to admit they could do something a Drop Trooper couldn't. Sand and dirt worked their way beneath my fingernails as I dug into the side of the bank, my carbine slung over my shoulder, and pulled myself up. Loose, sandy soil gave way with each push of my boots against it, but a final surge got me up far enough to grab an exposed tree root and haul myself over the top.

I looked back to see if Lilandreth needed any help, but she simply leapt up the two meters to the crest of the rise, springing on backwards-canted knees like a kangaroo. It was easy to forget how powerful the Resscharr were. If she wanted to, she could snap my neck like a twig, and I missed my Vigilante. She loped around the other side of the monolith, and I had to force myself to look away from her curious, inhuman gait. Another detail I could forget until something emphasized the differences again.

Turning my attention back to the monolith, I ran my left hand across its surface, walking slowly, trying not to stare at one part of the thing, just letting my eyes take in the whole so I wouldn't miss any details. Yet I saw nothing. No hint of a seam, no doors, no gaps in the metal block at all. Yet what was the purpose of the damned thing if it didn't have anything inside it, or if there was no way to get inside to look?

"Cam," Lilandreth called from around the next corner of the block, from the side facing out in a direct line with the dried-up creek bed. "You must see this."

Where the monolith had blocked the stream, a lake had grown up however many thousands of years ago that had been, and what remained were beds of clay, overgrown in places by the saw-bladed grass. My boots sank a few centimeters into the soft clay with each step, leaving caked, brown stains on them, trying to suck me down, drag me into the past. I got a look at that past when I rounded the corner and saw Lilandreth standing like a statue of some medieval gargoyle, staring at the face of the monolith.

It wasn't visible from the air because of the tree canopy overhanging it, a trick of fate and botany, because it was meant to be seen. The rest of the metallic block was coated with centuries of dirt, sap, bird feces, most of the color camouflaged under the refuse. But not the glittering, golden plate that took up the entire side of the block.

I was frozen, speechless, not from the strangeness of the thing but from its familiarity. I'd seen its like before in the history vids, mounted on the side of a cliff in the Edge Mountains on Hermes. Stylized stars connected by deeply etched lines, a map not of space but of hyperdimensional transitions. Of wormholes.

"Well, that clinches it," I said once I finally found my voice. "The Reconstructors definitely built the wormhole system here. And I think I understand why the Nova don't want anyone trespassing in this system. Anyone who gets this map controls this section of the galaxy."

"More than that," Lilandreth said, and though her people didn't smile, I recognized the expression that passed for one on her long, striated face. "Do you see where this leads?"

A long, slender finger traced a line from one end of the huge panel to the other, the whole hand spreading out at a system on the far end.

"The Reconstructors. This map will take us straight to them."

[19]

"How long?" Nance asked, tapping a finger on the center table in the Ops Center. "How long will it take to get to this Reconstructor system through the jumpgates?"

"Well, sir," Yanayev said with a shrug, "I'm having to guess on some of it because we don't know the exact distances between gates in the systems on the map. But assuming the distances aren't any greater than those in this system and using that as an average, I'd say we're looking at about seven hundred hours of realspace travel. Maybe under two thirds of that if we can micro-Transition between gates and cut off some of the distance."

"Commander Yanayev is correct," Dwight declared. His avatar was hopping from virtual foot to virtual foot, looking as if he had to pee. "This is perfect. If the Northwest Passage exists, this place will be where we can find it."

"You seem very happy about that," Lilandreth noted, a hint of disdain in her voice. The two of them had made peace before we'd left Yfingam, but that didn't mean they liked each other.

"Of course I am," Dwight assured her. "While I don't regret the actions I've taken, I do know that they've resulted in hardships for our human allies. They didn't deserve this, and I'm gratified to be able to play some small part in making things right."

And I could believe that as much as I wanted to. I was working with the AI because there was no other choice. He was part of the ship now and the ship was our only way home, and frankly, out here, we needed him.

"I must admit," Raft said, clearing his throat, "I'm confused by some of this, but if I gather correctly, the map of the jump-gates we found will allow you to return home?"

We found. That was rich. When we'd returned to the ship and brought Singer and Raft back to the Ops Center, the politician had started preening like a peacock, bragging to his aides and Singer's soldiers what a daring and dangerous expedition it had been and how well he'd represented the Confederation. Singer had kept quiet, though as tight as her jaw had clenched, I'd been sure she was about to break a tooth.

"Yes, Councilor," I replied, since it was fairly obvious no one else would. I would really have liked to kick the Homeworlders out of the Ops Center, but the only alternative was to stick them in the brig and that would have been... rude. We'd even brought in cots for them to sleep here while they were on board and took them to the head in shifts, under guard. "That's why we're here, to find the passage back to the Cluster, the collection of star systems we call home."

"I have an idea then," the man said, leaning forward conspiratorially. "This isn't an *official* proposal, but I have the feeling that Ms. Frost would be receptive to it if I brought it to her as a fait accompli."

"Oh, good," Vicky murmured from beside me.

"You have the superior technology of course," Raft went on, talking with his hands like one of the peddlers in the open-air kiosks at the Trans-Angeles mercados trying to push black-market fabricator codes. "Superior to us and even to the Nova. What you lack is numbers. Come back to Homeworld and help us to set up shipyards, factories, teach us your methods of production, and we can build our own fleet. And in return, we'll support you in your quest to take control of the Nova jump-gates, get you to this system you need to reach in order to get home." A grin split his face like he believed he'd just come up with the greatest idea ever.

"And I suppose," Dr. Spinner commented drily, "that it would only be a coincidence that this arrangement would give you total domination over the Grey."

"If your country wasn't intent on stealing our secrets and dominating the system," Raft ground out at the scientist, "then we wouldn't *need* the humans to overcome the Nova! We'd have accomplished it already, working together!"

"Gentlemen," I said, standing and slapping a palm on the table, "bickering isn't going to accomplish anything."

Oh, my God, I *was* turning into Hachette! It was like turning into my father except so much worse.... Shaking my shoulders to try to cleanse myself of the sensation of channeling the late Intelligence colonel, I tried again.

"We're not committing to a *war* with the Nova just because it's mutually beneficial," I told Raft, the words thick with strained patience. "I have enough experience with war to know that it's not the easy solution to anything. We came out here to *talk* to them, to negotiate, and that's what we're going to do, if the fuckers ever show up. You said it was sixty hours last time, Singer?" The Confederation captain nodded. "Well, it's been damned close to seventy-two and we haven't seen a thing from them."

We were still in orbit around the fourth planet, just because I wanted the assault shuttles to run one, last, comprehensive scan of the place to make sure we hadn't missed anything. The map *seemed* like the big prize here, but like the Skipper once told me, being thorough never cost anything but time.

"What happens if they don't show?" Nance asked. "Maybe their surveillance drones or satellites or whatever stopped working. I mean, we didn't even detect any in the system, so maybe there *aren't* any. They could have just happened to be running a patrol in this system last time, stumbled onto the Homeworlder ships."

"That doesn't feel right," I told him. "Not with that map down there. Unless there's another one closer to their home system, I gotta think they found it here and they obviously want to keep it for themselves."

"We can't stay in this room much longer," Singer spoke up for the first time since we'd returned from the surface. The woman didn't look like she'd slept since then. "We've been here for three days. Surely there are some quarters for us somewhere."

There *were*, surely, but I didn't want to tell *them* that and I really wanted to keep them in one place where they'd be easier to watch, but it wasn't an unreasonable request. I was about to give into it when the alarm sounded, drawing all eyes to the Op Center's main projector. The view there had been a split screen of the planet as seen through the ship's external cameras and a shifting, zooming image from the assault shuttles still patrolling. Now, it had switched to a telescopic view enhanced with gravimetic sensors and computer simulations based on the footage we'd taken earlier.

It was the outer gate, between the fourth planet and the asteroid belt that served as a barricade between it and the inner of the two gas giants. A red halo surrounded it on the screen, and I knew what the announcement would be even before Wojtera's strained voice called down to us from the bridge.

"Sir, we have ships transiting the gate. Four so far and more coming. They don't match the drive signatures of the Confederation or the Grey. They have to be Nova."

They weren't visible on optical cameras yet, of course. The outer gate was hundreds of thousands of klicks away. But the computer did a wonderful job of piecing together a sim of the things based on the gravimetic sensors. They were of a sort with every other fusion-drive spaceship I'd ever seen because form followed function, but distinctly different in many ways, certainly from the Feds and the Grey. Fusion drive bells, cylindrical fuel tanks masked under armored skirts, comm antennae extended out on long gantries to clear the drive flare, a silvery skin over the hull to reflect light—and heat—back outward, and cooling vanes sticking out from the sides to keep the ships from cooking in their own juices.

Such were the accoutrements of any pre-Transition Drive long-range spaceship, but these weren't just for exploration or scouting. Weapons pods jutted out on either side of the ship's waist, just in front of the armored skirts that protected the fuel stores. I wasn't sure what sort of armament they carried, but I could guess from their shapes. Railguns, missile launchers. Maybe lasers, though I didn't see the focusing mirrors.

The distinction between these ships and ours, even ours from fifty or sixty years ago, was in the nonfunctional aspects, the aesthetics, the things that were ingrained in a species. Human ships just looked *right* to me, the correct ratio of length to width, the right amount of bilateral symmetry. These things... they seemed elongated, stretched out to the absurd, some abstract art project given a multibillion-dollar budget.

They were here. We'd come here to draw them out and it had worked, and it shouldn't have been a shock, yet it was. Like peeking out of my covers at night, waiting to see the boogeyman come out of the closet and then actually having the closet door open. When I spoke, it was with a mouth gone cotton-dry.

"Recall the assault shuttles and tell both Intercepts to prep for launch. Captain Nance, get back to the bridge and call up your primary crew. Vicky, get both companies suited up and in the drop-ships, and tell Campea to have his platoon armed up and ready to deploy. Double-time... we have to break orbit and get to minimum safe Transition distance before they get close enough to hit us with anything."

For once, Nance didn't question or second-guess me, just moved, Yanayev following in a sprint for the lift cars and the bridge. Vicky stood but paused to give my hand a squeeze before she left the Ops Center.

"Good luck."

I took one last look at the screen, trying to judge how many ships were coming through and how hard they were boosting. Tactical readouts floated beside the projection, answering my questions. Six ships so far, three of them boosting our way at just over five gravities, the other three hanging back, coming out from the gate at under a single G, probably heading for a defensive position.

Good. That meant they might listen. If they'd sent all six ships after us with their tails on fire, I doubt they'd give us a chance to talk. The three burning for us could achieve a flyby in maybe twelve or fifteen hours if they just stayed on their current boost pattern, but the likelihood was they'd do a turnover and a braking burn. Twenty-four hours to reach the planet, but we wouldn't be here. We'd be meeting them halfway.

"Captain Alvarez," Raft said, jumping to his feet. He moved around the table, coming uncomfortably close to me. Different societies had different ideas about personal space, but I'd already seen that the Homeworlders generally stayed even farther away during casual conversation than people from Earth. But not this guy. He was close enough that the stale rank of his breath wrinkled my nose. "Let me go up on the bridge with you. I know I can help. This affects my people as well."

"No can do," I said, not even considering it. "The only chance we have to get them talking is to make it clear we're not interested in staying here, that we're *not* connected with you. Like I agreed, we'll let you talk to them after we've made our deal—*if* we can make one. You being part of this can only screw it up."

He was still protesting as I pulled free and headed for the hatch. Singer said nothing, just stared at me, her expression unreadable.

"I suppose I should stay here as well then," Spinner reasoned, "since you don't want to complicate things by having Homeworlders present on the bridge when you speak to the Nova."

"Yeah, that would probably be for the best." I offered him a grateful nod, then swept a look across all of them. "You'll be able to see what's going on over the display. I'll make sure it's left on and linked to the bridge. But please remain here in the Ops Center and stay strapped into your acceleration couches." I gestured at the seats in the back of the compartment. "If there's any high-G maneuvering, you're gonna want to be belted up."

Raft looked like he was going to keep arguing, but I ducked out of the hatch and closed it behind me, then took a moment to check the security settings. It was locked from the outside and could only be opened by someone with crew access. I'd have to remember to send someone down to take them to the head if there was an opportunity.

The lift bank had a line for it already, but rank—or at least command structure position—had its privileges, and I cut to the front. Everyone was trying to get out of the rotational drum and to their duty stations before we cut the spin and fixed the thing in position. Which would be shortly after the assault shuttles docked.

I could feel every eye on me in the queue for the elevators, feel all the unasked questions behind them.

Go ahead, damn it, I wanted to yell at them. *Ask me.* I hadn't changed any just because they'd pushed this job off on me. Finally, one of them did. I couldn't remember her name, but her face was familiar. She was a reactor tech, one who'd had to learn her job all over when our ship's power core had been replaced by the Resscharr.

"Sir," she asked, "I heard there was a jumpgate map on that planet."

Yeah, I should have sent out a shipwide briefing on that, and would when there was a chance. I'd wanted to meet with the leadership first, and the arrival of the Nova had interrupted that.

"There was," I confirmed, and a murmuring spread through the gathered Fleet personnel like I'd thrown a stone into a pond. "It confirms what we thought. The Resscharr engineered these gates and they're out here, at the end of the line."

"How much longer will it be, Captain Alvarez?" Not the woman this time, a younger man. No one I'd encountered one-on-one before. "Before we get there?"

"Before we get back to the Cluster?" I clarified. "I have no idea. But *if* we're right about where the Reconstructors went and *if* we can use the gates, then it'll take us about a month to get to our destination."

"What would happen if we can't use the gates?" Same guy, more petulant tone, like a child running through worst-case scenarios with their parent. "If we have to go through T-space?"

He *should* have known this already. They all should. I *had* put out a notice to everyone's 'links when we'd received the information from Spinner about the singularity factory. I guess that was just a heads-up for me about how little attention people paid to those notices.

"Minimum of a year. We'd have to go back into stasis again." Well, technically we wouldn't *have* to, not with the supplies we'd taken in at Homeworld, but that would be taking the risk that we could resupply again... plus, the ship was just pretty damned crowded with everyone awake and no place for shore leave.

The talk of a year hit them between the eyes and stunned expressions met the words. I knew what they were thinking. Another year. Another year away from their friends and family and loved ones. It wasn't an estimate to them, it was a sentence... or rather, an extension of the seven-year sentence they'd already served.

I was saved from any more questions by the car arriving. I took a spot in a corner and hoped they'd forget I was there, but the younger man was chivvied next to me, and as the car lurched into motion he shot me a look and I knew he wasn't finished.

"What do we do, sir?" he asked, and there was a tremor to his voice that he tried to hide by speaking softly so no one else would hear. "I mean, if you can't talk them into it? Are we going to fight them? Go through the gates anyway?"

"Let's not borrow trouble."

The car left the rotational hub and we were left in free fall again. I grabbed a handle set in the wall of the car, then grabbed the kid's shoulder when it seemed he'd float off toward the overhead. I wanted to leave things there, but I was the commander. Part of my responsibility was assuaging the fears of the crew, no matter how little I cared for it. I kept my hand on the young crewman's shoulder and squeezed.

"We're going to get back. I can't promise whether it'll be a month or a year or three years, but we're going to get back. And then you'll have a bunch of retroactive promotions and a shit-load of back pay waiting for you."

He chuckled and a small relief lightened the load on my shoulders. I'd gotten them to believe in me.

Now all I had to do was not fuck up.

[20]

"Are you certain we should do this?" Dwight wondered.

My eyes flickered upward to his avatar, a useless instinct but one I couldn't fight.

"What?" I asked. "Contact the Nova? What's the alternative?"

"There are a few," he allowed, shrugging expressively for an AI pretending to be human. But then he'd told us his brain patterns had been adapted from a human subject, so maybe he wasn't pretending. "But what I was referring to is the micro-Transition you're preparing for."

Yanayev glanced up from her controls at the reference to the maneuver. We were an hour out from breaking orbit around the fourth planet and three hours from when we'd first detected the Nova ships coming through the jumpgate and finally at minimum safe jump distance. We would have micro-Transitioned already, except that I'd instructed the Helm officer to calculate a jump distance that would give the Nova ships time to decelerate before they reached us, which was trickier.

"It'll take us six hours otherwise," I pointed out.

"You're giving away your advantage. They don't know you

have the Transition Drive. Once they find out, they'll adjust their tactics."

It wasn't a bad point. I half-expected Lilandreth to argue against it out of reflex, but I'd sent her to the auxiliary control room. Just as I hadn't wanted the Homeworlders on the bridge, I didn't want her showing up in our first communications with the Nova either. Keep it simple. Just us humans looking for a peaceful passage through their gates. Unless it was necessary, I didn't even want to let them know we'd found the wormhole map.

"You're right," I admitted. "We are giving up a tactical advantage, but they're going to find out about the Transition Drive soon enough, and I'm thinking maybe seeing it in action will make them think twice about trying to attack us. Besides, I'd be willing to bet the first time they see it, they'll think their instruments are fucked." I nodded to Yanayev. "We ready?"

"Whenever you give the word." Her hand was hovering over the control.

I could have given the order myself, but instead I looked over to Nance and his fragile, ship-captain's ego.

"Helm," he said crisply, "micro-Transition now."

I dug my fingers into the armrest, and when the twin existential crises came only seconds apart, the connection to something material helped me fight back against the disorientation. It was never fun, but it had saved us hours. On the screen, the three Nova starships were tens of thousands of kilometers closer, their drives already facing back toward us, drives burning like miniature stars as they decelerated.

"If we transmit now," I asked, turning to Lt. Chase, "will they be able to receive it through their drive flares?"

"They got those extended comm antennae," Chase said, shrugging. "If we do a tight beam right at one of them, then sure."

I almost elected to wait. It felt weird talking to someone who was facing the other direction, whether they were in a starship or not.

"All right. Set for translation to the Confederation language and let me know when you're ready."

Chase's brows knitted, and he looked at his control station with an expression of consternation, fingers moving feverishly through the menus.

"Is there a problem?" I wondered. "Are we not able to get a transmission through?"

"No, sir." He frowned. "I mean, yes, we can get a transmission through. And so can they. They're hailing us."

I sniffed. That hadn't taken long.

"Is the signal something we can decode?"

"Aye, sir. It's the same configuration as the Confederation uses. In their language too. We got video and audio."

"Put it on the main screen," I decided.

I knew what to expect. I'd seen the photos and videos. Yet, somehow the sight of the alien still sent cold tendrils up my spine. The hairless, rubbery skin didn't bother me and neither did the bulging eyes or the lack of a nose. No, it was the mouth. There's something familiar about the mouth of any mammal, an arrangement of jaw and tooth that isn't entirely different whether it's Resscharr or Tahni or human, or even Homeworlder. Not the Nova though. They'd evolved from something very much an octopus or squid, and their mouths were lower into their head, almost part of their necks, with no chin to speak of. No teeth either, or at least nothing that I recognized as teeth.

At least I couldn't see those wormlike fingers in the view on the screen.

"Who are you and what do you want here?"

It was short and to the point, totally lacking in the fake civility a human would have included in such a message. I suppose I appreciated the straightforward attitude, and I decided to take the same approach in my response.

"I'm Cameron Alvarez," I replied, trusting Chase to translate the message and send it through. "Our ship came here from a distant part of the galaxy, from a place called the Commonwealth. We need to get back home, and we'd hoped we might be able to negotiate with you to use your jumpgate system to get us there faster. Our intentions are peaceful, and we have no designs on any of your worlds. We just want permission to pass through."

It was about as brief a message as I could come up with and still be truthful and accurate and I waited for them to ask for more details. They did not.

"Your request is denied. You are not welcome here." The thing's face had next to no expression, its voice no inflection, so I couldn't tell if the Nova on the screen was pissed, bored, or even afraid. "Either turn back and exit this system, or you'll be destroyed immediately."

"Well, that's rude," Yanayev said sotto voce.

I gestured to Chase to kill the audio pickup and turned to Wojtera.

"You getting any readings from their weapons pods? They carrying anything in there that could touch us?"

"Each of their ships is powered by a fusion reactor," the Tactical officer told me. "There're thermal signatures from power conduits running from the reactor to the pods, but that's about as exact as I can be without taking a shuttle on over there and taking a look." He snorted. "Or letting them shoot at us."

A signal to Chase and I was back on.

"There's no reason for us to be enemies. We don't want to hurt you, and I'm not certain you're capable of hurting *us*." I leaned forward and spoke softly to Yanayev. "Micro-Transition as short as you can, jump to the other side of their ships."

"Transitioning now," she confirmed.

No opportunity to steel myself for this one. The *whip-snap* sensation traveled from my head to my toes and took my consciousness along for the ride. When it was over, an eternity later, we were on the other side of the triangular formation of Nova ships, nose to nose, facing them from only a few thousand kilometers away.

"Our technology is superior to yours," I said, wanting to wave my hands demonstrably but refraining, unsure how the body language would look to creatures this alien. "We don't want to fight you. We're here to negotiate."

The creature stared at me in silence for seconds that seemed to creep on into hours, then it made a gesture with one of its tentacle arms, something I couldn't interpret.

"We must discuss this." And the screen went blank.

"Dwight," I said, "are you getting any sort of impression of that thing? Because he's just freaking the hell out of me."

"I'd need more time and exposure to them," the AI confessed. "Until the Homeworlders, I'd never encountered a sentient being not related to Earth life." His avatar shrugged. "Well, except the Skrela, and I'm not comfortable calling them sentient."

Uncomfortable grimaces echoed on several faces across the bridge, and I thought I should have a talk with Dwight about not reminding people that he'd been responsible for the Skrela. Later.

"I get the impression though," he went on, "that they have no concept of human—or even *humanoid*—sensibilities. Communicating with them is going to be difficult."

"They're back," Chase warned, just a half second before the screen went back to the bald octopus guy.

"The language you speak," the Nova representative said, "is

that of the Homeworlders who call themselves the Confederation. Are you allied with these people?"

"No." I said it quickly. Maybe a little *too* quickly, and I hoped these guys didn't have the insight to read human emotions and inflection. "We encountered the People of Homeworld when we entered the spiral arm and we traded with them for supplies and information. That's how we found out about the jumpgates, and about you."

"You say you're from this place you call Earth." If a human had said the words, I would have expected a skeptical, suspicious tone, but the octopus or whatever translation software they were using spat the words out flat and neutral, with no inflection. "You came here. Why would you need our help returning?"

Well, I'd been trying to keep things simple, but now things were about to get complicated.

"Back where we live," I said, feeling like I was telling a bedtime story to a child, "there's a system of artificial wormholes like the one you have here. It was engineered by a civilization we call the Predecessors, tens of thousands of years ago. All we have left of them back home is a map of the wormholes, carved into a plate on the side of a mountain on a planet of the system closest to ours. Our ship was... scouting, trying to find anything else the Predecessors might have left behind, and we came across another gateway, one that led us out here. But it was one-way, with no portal back to our home. We've been searching for any sign of the Predecessors out here for some time now, and these gates are clearly their work. We think at the end of it we might find them and maybe a way back."

A muscle twitched beside my eye, the nagging of a guilty conscience. What I'd said hadn't *quite* been an outright lie, but I'd left out enough context to fill a twelve-book volume. I tried to assuage my guilt by reasoning that the whole story of our journey wouldn't mean anything to these guys and would just confuse them.

"With our Transition Drive, the device we just demonstrated, we *could* make it to the Predecessors on our own, but it would take years. If you allow us to use your jumpgates, we could cut that down to a month. It would save us time and resources, and we'd be happy to work out some sort of trade with you to make it worth your while."

I was also feeling a little guilty about *that* part, because the only thing we could trade these guys would be the design of the Transition Drive, the exact same thing we'd given to the Homeworlders.

The Nova on the screen was silent, those bug eyes just staring at me through the screen. Was this normal for them? Did they spend most of their conversations just staring wordless at each other? Was I missing some important nonverbal cue? Was this guy male or female? Did they even *have* just two sexes? I couldn't be sure, and I was trying to negotiate with a culture we knew next to nothing about.

"I'm not empowered to make such an arrangement," the Nova said after an intensely uncomfortable twenty seconds. "It will take some time to speak to my superiors, perhaps hours, but I will grant you the leave to remain here while I undertake that. Maintain your present course and speed and don't approach the gate or you will be fired upon."

The screen went dark and the breath blew out of me in a long sigh. I felt wrung out like a dishrag.

"Tactical, let me know if any of them make any sign of breaking formation," I told Wojtera. "Keep the shields up. Helm, station keeping. Try to maintain our position relative to their formation."

"Those damned things give me the creeps," Nance admitted. "Tell me you don't actually intend to give them the Transition Drive?"

"I'll give them as little as I can get away with," I assured the man. "But if that's what it takes, then yes. What other choice do we have?"

As if in answer to my question, an alarm sounded. It was one I hadn't heard before except in drills, one I never expected to. It was the internal security alert, and it meant a threat... on board the ship. It took me a second to find the right control on the command station.

"Stillwell," I yelled over the whoop of the klaxon, "what's going on?"

"Sir!" That was the junior Flight Ops officer, Lt. Prada. I doubt I'd spoken two words to him the entire time I'd been on board this ship, mostly because he usually wasn't on the main bridge shift and I didn't spend much time up here without Nance and the main crew. "We have an unauthorized launch!"

"What?" I blurted, leaning forward and coming up against my harness. "What's launching?"

"Captain Alvarez!" The pained cry seemed to come from nowhere, and I looked around helplessly, the hits coming from every direction. "Captain Alvarez, it's me, Dr. Spinner..."

"The call is coming from the Ops Center intercom," Chase supplied, bless him.

"Spinner, what is it?"

"Alvarez, we have a problem." Stillwell. Of course, because I didn't have enough people talking at me. "There's been an incursion in the docking bay, and the bastards injured one of my security people pretty bad."

"Who?" I demanded, yanking at my quick release and getting ready to bolt... somewhere. "Who did?"

"The Confederation contingent," Spinner told me. There was stress and pain in his voice. "I tried to stop them, but they overpowered me. Someone opened the door for them and they ran out..."

"The Confederation shuttle," Prada interrupted. "They overrode our safeties... it's launching."

Shit. How the hell... *no.* No time to think about that right now. Just do it.

"Get an assault shuttle out after them right now," I told Prada, jabbing a finger at him.

"Shoot to disable if possible, but take them out whatever you have to do."

"Aye, sir," he said, nodding, but I was already turning my attention to Stillwell.

"Lt. Stillwell, get a security detail down to the Ops Center and get Dr. Spinner medical attention and find out what the fuck happened! Find out if we have any other injuries and make sure none of the Fed contingent stayed behind!"

"Oh, son of a bitch," Prada breathed, his eyes going wide. He turned to me. "Sir, I don't know how, but those fuckers managed to corrupt the software in the docking umbilicals. None of our spacecraft can disconnect from the lock until we reboot... which is going to take another ten minutes."

What. The. Fuck.

They'd been confined to the Ops Center and not a one of them had the experience with our software to do something like that, much less the access. Hell, their computer technology was decades behind ours, maybe a century. There was just no way.

"The shuttle has cleared the docking bay," Prada warned. "It's accelerating in the direction of the Nova ships."

No assault shuttles. No Intercept cutters. What did that leave?

"The coilgun turrets," I said, pushing myself over to Wojtera's station. "Can you depress them far enough to get target the shuttle?"

"Not yet," he told me, shaking his head. "They're not designed to shoot at spacecraft launching from our ship. It'll have to be at least another twenty kilometers out before we can get a lock on it."

"Nance?" I asked. It felt like a failing having to ask for his advice. I knew it wasn't, knew it was the smart thing to do, that this was his ship and he knew it better than anyone, but knowing in my head and knowing in my gut were two different things.

"We could micro-Transition," he said, infuriatingly calm. "The gravitational tidal forces would rip them apart."

"Do it, Helm!" I snapped, anger roiling in my stomach, not just at the betrayal but at my own hesitation.

"Minimum shift," Nance added, not afraid to kibbutz me.

"Transitioning," she confirmed, but even as she hit the control, Wojtera's eyes were going wide, mouth opening to warn us about something... until he was interrupted by the Transition.

I was out of my restraints, and even though that shouldn't have mattered since there was no acceleration, the lack of an anchoring point made the micro-Transition even more jarring, and I clenched my teeth at the gut-wrenching sensation.

"Missile!" Wojtera yelled, gulping in the middle of the word as if he was about to throw up. The Tactical officer slammed his fist down on his console, helpless rage in his expression. "They launched a missile!"

For a terrifying, humiliating moment, I was lost, the lights of the displays a kaleidoscope blur, a haze over my thoughts from the micro-Transition, but then the Tactical screen came into focus and everything became horribly clear.

We were tens of thousands of kilometers out from where we had been, nearly twenty thousand from the formation of Nova ships, and the shuttle was gone. Where it had been was a cloud of burning gas, the spacecraft torn to pieces by the tidal forces from the Transition... but not soon enough. The missile was traveling at close to thirty gravities according to the readout, and it had moved away from our position too quickly for the field to catch it.

Too fast for the Nova to stop it at that range, and I had the terrible thought our micro-Transition had caused too much distortion for them to notice it. Whatever the cause, the missile struck home, not on the heavily armored nose of the ship but into the juncture of the main body with the fuel tanks. It was a fusion warhead, because what would have been the point if it weren't?

A sphere of thermonuclear destruction expanded at the shoulder of the ship, swallowing it up... but the thing was pretty heavily armored, built for combat, and I held out the hope for a long second that the Nova vessel would survive. Until the blast reached the fuel stores. I don't know if the explosion was a fusion chain reaction or if it was simply the fuel pellets heating up and cooking off, but the result was the same. One moment the ship was there and the next it was a nebula, not one speck of debris large enough to be recognizable.

Wojtera spoke for all of us, the only voice breaking the stunned silence on the bridge.

"Oh, shit."

[21]

What the fuck are we gonna do now?

Everyone was thinking it, but no one was asking it. They wanted to, I could see it in their eyes, all of them. They didn't stare at me because they were professionals and paid attention to their own stations, but the sideways glances out of the corner of their eyes were plain. I was thinking it too, and I very nearly froze up.

It wasn't the danger, wasn't the confusion, it was the knowledge that I'd fucked up. I didn't know what had happened, but I was the commander and, whatever happened, it was my responsibility. That was what hit me like a sucker punch, threw me off. The only thing that pulled me out of it was a memory of something the Skipper had told me. Not in combat but sitting on empty ration crates in the wreckage of a Tahni outpost.

"You ever play soccer, Alvarez?" he'd asked, eyes focused on a pouch of chili-mac. I envied him since I had the beef patty and macaroni, which sucked.

"When I was a kid," I'd replied, only half paying attention because I was wondering if I could trade the meal to Scotty for his spaghetti and meatballs. "I've watched the World Cup a few times."

"I played keeper at the Academy. The thing my coach always told me about playing keeper is, you gotta have a short memory. You're gonna let goals in, and there's not a damned thing you can do about it. If you keep thinking about it afterward, though, you're going to be so preoccupied you'll let the next one in too. You have to forget the last goal and concentrate on not letting the next one in."

I'd looked up at Covington, suddenly sensing this wasn't a casual conversation about sports.

"Being a platoon leader—or a company commander—is a lot like being a keeper." His eyes had bored into me. "When you lose, you get all the blame, and when you win, someone else usually gets the credit. But if you get hung up on the goals you let in, you're sure to let the next one by the exact same way."

I was the keeper. I'd let a goal by and I had to forget it.

"Chase, get me a line to the Nova ships." I winced. "The surviving ones."

The Communications officer looked as shaken as I was, but he nodded and gave me the signal that the transmission was going out.

"Attention Nova vessels, the attack on your ship was not by us. It was carried out by spies from the Confederation..."

I knew it was an exercise in futility, that they'd never listen, but I had to try. I hadn't even finished the attempt before alarms sounded and warning lights flashed.

"That was a railgun round," Wojtera announced. "No damage... shields took it." Red flashes again and the Tactical officer winced. "Another one."

"Cease fire," I said, still transmitting. "Cease fire, we do *not* want to fight you. I repeat, the attack was not from us."

"They're not gonna listen," Nance declared. He shrugged.

"I wouldn't either. To them, it's pretty fucking obvious we *did* attack them, and nothing you say is gonna change their mind."

"You're right," I admitted, rubbing at my eyes. "But I had to try."

Another flash, another jangling klaxon, but this time it wasn't an invisible slug of metal going too fast to be seen. The white fury of a star erupted from the weapons pod on the port side of one of the Nova ships and washed over our shields like a wave crashing on the rocks. The *Orion* shook. I grabbed at the arm of my acceleration couch and pulled myself back into it, the vibration ringing off the hull and coming up through my seat.

"What the *hell* was that?" Prada blurted.

"Helm, micro-Transition," I ordered. I tried to sound calm and, to my surprise, it wasn't that hard. Everything had already gone to hell. "Back to the gate."

"Not happening," Yanayev said tightly, shaking her head. "Getting a fault."

"We have damage to one of the main power conduits for the Teller-Fox warp unit," the junior damage control officer, Lt. Uranga, barked urgently. He was an intense, dark-eyed tornado of a man who looked like he was in constant motion even when strapped into his acceleration couch. "Feedback through the shields caused an overload in Conduit A. Minor injuries in the Engineering compartment."

Oh, that was so not good.

"Helm," Nance jumped in, knowing when it was his show to run, "sound alarm for high-gravity burn and take us to six Gs."

"They're firing again!" Wojtera said.

It was, I saw, paying closer attention this time, a white fireball traveling slower than light, but not by much. When it struck, it shook us harder this time and red and yellow warnings flashed everywhere.

"Goddammit!" Uranga said. "We've lost another conduit. We lose one more, we're dead."

And now I knew exactly what we had to do, though I didn't like it.

"Helm, belay high-G burn," I said. "Slave Helm control to Tactical and return fire." The words were a sigh of regret.

There'd been, I thought, a chance to salvage this, if we could have just held them off long enough to explain what had happened, get them to review their recordings and figure out we were telling the truth. It wasn't *much* of a hope, but it was all we had. With this one order, it was dead. And so were they.

"Targeting lead ship," Wojtera said, sounding more relieved than anything else. "Firing main gun."

If their energy weapon had the threatening air of mystery to it, ours had the funeral tinge of finality. Where the blue tendril of the energy cannon touched, the Nova ship's armor shredded on the molecular level, the lance of azure fire spearing through the guts of the thing and out the other side. The beam wasn't wide enough to cut the ship in half, but the stress on what remained finished that job, and the habitational section of the Nova cruiser tumbled away from the drives and fuel, leaving them to continue on blindly into the darkness, a *Flying Dutchman* fated never to touch land again.

The third and last of the formation of ships could have saved herself, could have turned and run. We'd have let her go. But I guess the captain of that ship couldn't know that and wanted to go down swinging. She was out of position to line up her weapons pods with us and maneuvering thrusters flared on her nose, but it was already too late. Ours had started sooner and had a shorter arc to describe, though the jackhammer pounding of the steering jets against the hull was echoed by my racing heartbeat as I watched and wondered who would win this quickdraw and if I'd made yet another mistake.

Not this time.

"Target locked," Wojtera declared. "Firing main gun."

This time, we took her head on. The actinic surge of accelerated particles sliced through the armored nose of the Nova ship and cored her like an apple, blowing flaming gas and debris out cracks in the side until the entire ship came apart, its death throes hidden behind a shroud of glowing, white gas. The nebula of her destruction merged with that of the other two ships, lingering in the vacuum for long moments before it had dispersed enough for the light to fade inside those clouds.

"Are the other three ships attacking?" I asked, trying to find them on the tactical display that covered the main screen, shoving aside all else.

"No," Wojtera replied, tracing lines in his controls until an image of the far-off Nova vessels took up half the view. "They're turning. I think they're heading back through the outer gate."

He was right, and it took only minutes before they vanished through the discontinuity, their fusion drive flames disappearing as if God had leaned down and snuffed them out. Leaving us here with one hell of a mess to clean up.

"Damage control," I said, my own voice sounding dull and lifeless in my ears, "can we replace the power conduits?"

"We have spares," Uranga told me, calmer now that we were out of immediate danger. The man *did* take affront to his ship personally, which I suppose was an asset in a damage control officer. "It's not gonna be fast. Maybe twelve hours if we run all three shifts on it."

"Twelve hours," Nance mused. "I'm not a tactical genius or anything, but I feel like the Nova aren't going to give us that much time if we stick around here."

He wasn't exactly sneering at me or rubbing my nose in the disaster, it was more subtle than that, but I felt the knife go in.

"Yeah. Uranga, get Engineering on the repairs. Helm, turn

the *Orion* back to the near gate and start us on a one-G burn back through it."

"We're going back?" Nance asked, sounding surprised. "To Homeworld? They're the ones who got us into this shit to begin with."

"*They* didn't," I corrected him, rage burning away the pain and uncertainty. "Frost did. And I'd very much like to have a talk with her about it."

———

"Tell me what the fuck happened here."

Stillwell glared aside at me from where she stood by the security lock to the Ops Center, her 'link plugged into it via a physical cable. We were still at one gravity burn and the Ops Center, along with the rest of the habitation drum, had been locked into place, which basically cut the usable space in half in this section, but the Ops Center was always lined up with our functional gravity, whether it came from acceleration, spin, or the ship's gravity during Transition.

"I wish I fucking knew," Lt. Stillwell said, not showing a bit of deference. "*Someone* opened the compartment hatch from the outside, someone with clearance, someone who knew what they were doing."

I looked around the corridor, frowning.

"Hold on a second. Are you telling me that you don't know who it was? What about 'link IDs? What about security scanners?"

Stillwell took a deep breath, and I got the impression she was holding back rage, knowing it wasn't properly focused on me.

"The security scanners and the 'link IDs worked fine. That's how I know that the person whose 'link was recorded opening this hatch was Technician Second Class April Herrera, an Engineering tech. The only problem with that is, Technician Second Class April Herrera was *in* Engineering at the time the hatch opened." Stillwell turned her 'link around and showed me a video feed that I guessed was a record of the Engineering compartment at the time of the breakout. I didn't know the woman from Adam and was about to tell her that, but she turned the thing back away from me. "She claims not to know her 'link had been taken. Not just taken but *replaced*. Someone slipped a clean 'link onto her belt, one that hadn't been personalized yet."

"What about cameras though?" The ship wasn't a prison and we didn't have cameras in the living quarters, but there were scanners in every passageway. One of them winked down at me from inside a polarized dome affixed to the overhead. "Didn't they see who opened the compartment?"

Her lip curled in a sneer and she tapped at her 'link again, turning it around to show me.

"Sure."

I sighed. Whoever had opened the hatchway was dressed in a full radiation hazard suit, helmet, gloves, and all. They held their 'link up to the security panel and the hatch slid aside, with Singer and Raft leading the way out. Singer. Boy, had she played me with that act. The guy in the suit didn't stick around, didn't speak to the others, just loped away as fast as they could in the heavy getup.

"And we don't have any footage of them before or after that?" I demanded. "I mean, they had to get the suit in Engineering and they had to dump it somewhere."

"They did. They dumped it in a storage closet next to the access hub."

Disconnecting from the security lock, Stillwell waved at me to follow her. She led me on an uphill curve from the Ops

Center, what would have been flat if the drum had been rotating, until it became steep enough that we had to use the steps built into the deck on the sides. I'd never seen an arrangement like this before I'd boarded the *Orion*, and it only served as an object lesson as to why most military ships didn't bother with rotational gravity.

After a five-minute climb that would have taken about thirty seconds in other circumstances, Stillwell yanked open a narrow hatch set in the bulkhead, revealing a storage bin packed with cleaning supplies and a bulbous, insectoid cleaning robot. Something else they had no use for on most military ships, since enlisted crew were ubiquitous and needed busy work. Tossed in beside the robot was the suit.

"And there's the access hub," Stillwell told me, pointing across the passage at the rounded hatch leading to the central hub. It was useful for getting around in free fall and a necessary emergency access in case we lost power, but not accessible when the drum was spinning. "There's no cameras here." She shrugged. "Not by design, just how the thing wound up being built. A blind spot."

"Son of a bitch."

The door was locked down, but I had an override code, and I tapped it in and yanked the hatch open. The hub went down the whole way from Engineering to the docking bay, and looking down it while under way was like staring off the top of one of those Two River skyscrapers. It helped that I wasn't looking at the opposite end—I was concentrating on the bulkhead, looking for the nearest camera. It wasn't until thirty meters or so down before the next one showed up... and unfortunately there was another exit just ten meters down, out of the line of sight.

"What's that level?" I asked. I should have known after all this time, but it wasn't an exit I ever took.

"It's the air recycling plant." Stillwell's perpetual scowl

deepened, and I began to wonder if the woman had ever smiled in her life. "Only one fucking camera on the whole level, but there's maintenance crawlways that would've let them come out two levels up or down." She shrugged. "I can go over the footage from each level and see if anything sticks out, but that's going to take a while. It's not like we can just figure out who did it from the people walking around. I'm gonna have to track every one of them back to where they came from and where they went."

"You'd think," I mused not without bitterness, "that a Fleet Intelligence ship would have software routines that did that kind of thing automatically."

"Well, until we got our asses hauled way out here," she shot back, not giving a centimeter, "we never had to worry about anyone on the ship sabotaging us." *Point.* But she wasn't through. "We got those two idiots we pulled out of the asteroid. I should check into them."

"Go ahead. But it had to be someone who knows how this ship works." I took one last look down the hub, then shut the hatch. "Someone who knows where the cameras are, knows about the air recycling level. Someone who knew enough to steal a 'link and a radiation suit."

"Yeah," she admitted with obvious reluctance. "There's that."

"Let me know if you find anything out," I told her, knowing how little she'd appreciate me giving her orders and not caring.

"And what are you going to be doing?"

"I'm going to go talk to Spinner." I shrugged. "He was there. Maybe he saw something."

If not, there was a traitor on board this ship and we had no way of knowing who.

[22]

"He's going to be fine," Doc Hallonen assured me, pointing to the display above the clinic bed as if I could read any of the medical mumbo-jumbo there. "Slight concussion, cut over his eye, and a little bruising."

Spinner didn't *look* fine. The little Homeworlder sat with his legs hanging off the bed, head in his hands, and from the miserable, shocked look on his face, I doubted the little man had ever been hit before.

"You give him anything for the pain?" I asked.

"I was *about* to," Hallonen told me with a shrug. She peeled the backing off a drug patch and slapped it onto the back of Spinner's neck.

The little man jerked away, looking back at her, eyes wide with alarm. She probably didn't have a translation program on her 'link and definitely wasn't wearing the stick-on speaker on the uniform to allow it to work.

"It's a painkiller, Dr. Spinner," I told him. "You'll feel better in a few minutes. You want some water?" I'd had concussions before, and one of the worst symptoms was a dry mouth.

"Yes, I would very much like some," he said, starting to nod then stopping with a wince.

"Water bottles in the cabinet," Hallonen told me, waving dismissively. "And you can take him out of here. I have to get back to the engineers." She clucked. "Bad burns. Gonna take a couple days in the auto-doc."

She didn't wait for my acknowledgement, just headed out of the little examination compartment, leaving us there. I found the refrigerated cabinet and grabbed a bottle, twisted off the cap, and handed it to Spinner. The little man downed half of it in one long gulp, gasping for air afterward.

"Can you tell me exactly what happened?" I asked him, sitting down beside him on the bed. "Before you called up to the bridge?"

"Yes. I was there and the man, Raft, he was suspicious of me. Kept asking me who I really worked for, whether I was an intelligence agent. I was trying to tell him I was a scientist when the door opened. I didn't expect it, but they did. The one who opened it was in some kind of protective suit. He never took the helmet off, just waved at them to go. I didn't see his face." Spinner chuckled, looked as if he expected it to hurt and was surprised when it didn't. "I made the mistake of trying to get in their way and one of Captain Singer's people hit me." He touched the bandage above his brow. "Very hard. I don't know if I passed out, but when I opened my eyes and got my wits about me, they were gone and I called you."

"And that's it?" I prompted. "They didn't say anything at all?"

"Perhaps." He turned up a hand. "It was all in their own language and they were speaking fast. I know it a little, but not enough to be fluent. I believe it was something about... suicide? I don't know the word that well, but I think I recognized it."

"Well, suicide it was," I said, letting out a breath. "Not a one of those assholes lived through it."

"What do you think will happen now?" he wondered. "Where will we go now that you can't use their gates?"

We. Spinner had definitely adopted us. And I guess he would be worried, since whatever I decided was going to seal his fate. I didn't get the chance to answer his question though.

"Alvarez, you hear me?" It was Nance, calling over my 'link. "Where you at?"

"Sick bay. What's wrong?"

"We're coming to the jumpgate. You need to get back to the bridge."

"Be right there," I told him. I looked aside at Spinner and clapped him on the shoulder. "Come on. I gotta get back to work. I'll walk you to your quarters, okay?"

"You're not going to lock me up?" he asked, raising an eyebrow.

I laughed at his surprise.

"No, I'm not going to lock you up. We're all in the same boat now."

The outer gate was hundreds of thousands of kilometers away, too far to see anything in the optical telescopes. Even if we'd had an astronomical model like the ones that used to be out at the asteroid belt before they'd discovered the jumpgate there, the ships would have been little more than specks of light.

Thank God for gravimetic sensors though. They worked on the same principle as the Transition Drive, detecting gravitational disturbances. Like ships transiting a wormhole. One after another, each a red delta on the Tactical display, dozens of them. Hundreds.

"Shit," Vicky hissed. "I guess that answers the question of what the Nova are going to do about the attack."

"I count three hundred and seventy," Wojtera said, voice grim. The man had a long face at the best of times, and right now it practically dragged down to the deck. "Maybe more... there's a lot of interference. They're sending through a whole fucking fleet."

"What the hell was that weapon they used on us back there?" I asked him. "Anyone figure that out yet?"

"I believe," Dwight said, "that it was some sort of plasma weapon, though how they manage to avoid beam scatter in a vacuum, I couldn't say. I believe the weapons must be relatively short-ranged, however."

"That's some comfort," Nance said drily. "Maybe if we have the fucking Transition Drive back by the time they catch up with us, we can actually do something about it." He hit a control at his station. "Engineering, what's our status?"

"We're close, Captain," Commander Salas reported. "Making the final hookups. Maybe another hour or two."

"Another hour or two," Nance muttered. "Well, we can sure keep ahead of *those* guys." He pointed at the screen indicating the Nova fleet. "But who the hell knows what's waiting for us on the other side of this jumpgate?"

"You want to wait here for them to finish the repairs?" I asked Nance. "I'm no Helm officer, but we've been burning at one gravity for ten hours? Eleven? We'd have to change course, bypass the gate, and come back around."

Nance's smile was as condescending as any spacer dealing with a groundpounder.

"Yes, that would likely be the case, Alvarez. It's your call, but my advice would be to continue through. I'm fairly certain the *Orion* could take on whatever the Confederation might have waiting for us, but we've already had one surprise from the

Nova. I'd rather not stick around and see what else they might pull."

Yeah, it was my call, but I'd already fucked up once. I looked over to Vicky. We weren't heading for any possible ground fighting, so there was no reason for her to be back with the Marines. I almost wished there had been, because I'd rather have been in my suit than making these sorts of decisions.

Vicky didn't say anything, but her expression gave me the answer. Nance was a very good ship's captain and I was a very good Marine. Better to take his advice.

"Take us through, Captain."

"We'll transit the gate in two minutes," Yanayev piped up immediately, as if she'd figured I'd make the right decision.

I didn't know if that should have bothered me, but it didn't. The whole bridge crew had been serving under Nance for a lot longer than they'd been under my command, and one of the first things they'd told me in OCS was to never give any order you knew wasn't going to be followed.

"Tactical," Nance directed, "arm weapons and prepare to target any ships. Our shields are down until those conduits are back up. A good offense is our only defense. Sound battle stations."

The klaxon was distant. No one on the bridge needed the warning.

"Stillwell figure out anything yet?" Vicky asked me, pitching her voice low.

I glanced around, checking to see if anyone had overheard, but they were all concentrating on their workstations. Even Nance seemed absorbed with the backlit ring of the wormhole, like he was trying to see what was on the other side.

"It's bad," I confided. "Whoever it was knew this ship's routines inside and out. They not only managed to get the

Confederation crew out of the Ops Center, they did it without getting caught."

"Shit. We were only at Homeworld for a few days. For them to turn somebody, it would have to be one of the cargo crews."

I nodded. That was a possibility.

"Stillwell thinks it has to be Jay and Bob," I told her. "They have the most connection to the Confederation. And they were down there with us."

"What do *you* think?" she asked.

"I think I *want* to believe they're not guilty." It was a confession, to myself as well as her.

"For it to be them," she pointed out, "they'd have to be pretty damned smart. A lot smarter than either of them look."

"There's that," I admitted. "I need to talk to them, but I've been running around like a chicken with its head cut off."

Vicky's eyebrow shot up.

"You know, I farmed with you for a whole year and I never once saw a chicken running around with its head cut off."

"I have. It wasn't fun to watch. Stillwell's gonna keep an eye on them for the time being, but I think whoever did it is probably going to keep their head down and try not to get noticed until they have a chance to run."

"Transiting the wormhole," Yanayev snapped.

We were through the gate in a heartbeat, and I'd been too preoccupied with the discussion to anticipate the sensation. Not that my inattention made it any less discomfiting, but at least it removed the anticipation. Instead of worrying and clenching for ten seconds before the jump, I was just there in the moment, staring at a half a dozen Confederation gunboats.

"Six bogies at between ten and fifteen thousand klicks," Wojtera announced, "holding station keeping with quarter-G burns. Thousand-klick separation in the formation."

"Raft said there'd be ships waiting for him," Vicky reminded me. "Asshole didn't say how many."

The Confederation ships had a kludged-together look, primitive compared to the *Orion* but also anemic beside the Nova ships we'd encountered a few hours ago. They reminded me of the lighters we'd seen out in the Pirate Worlds and the Periphery, commercial ships at their core with armor and weapons strapped on as afterthoughts.

"We're running hot, Captain," Yanayev pointed out, looking at Nance when she said it. "This acceleration, we're going to be past them in a few minutes. You want me to perform a turnover and decelerate?"

Nance, to his credit, checked with me, despite the fact that he undoubtedly had a shitload more experience at this. It wasn't a situation I'd run across before, or even been present to watch Hachette encounter. With the Transition Drive, we could make a micro-jump and lose all our forward momentum in the process, saving us hours of deceleration and making these sorts of decisions much easier.

"Hell, no," I replied. "They just royally screwed us. If they want to talk, they have our number. Keep going for the next gate. We're not stopping until we're back at Homeworld."

I thought for a second that Nance would scoff at my choice, that he'd tell me I was being petty and juvenile, because that's how the words had felt. But he grinned tightly and nodded instead, like he heartily approved.

"You heard the man, Helm," Nance said, motioning ahead with a knife hand that would have done a Marine colonel proud. "Damn the torpedoes, full steam ahead."

"I don't know what the hell that means," Yanayev admitted, snorting amusement, "but copy that, maintaining course and acceleration."

"And any minute now..." Vicky predicted.

"We got a transmission from one of those ships," Chase piped up, confirming her suspicions. "Audio and video."

"Put it up on the screen," I ordered. I wanted to unstrap and stand up for dramatic effect, to project strength, but there was always the possibility that one of those idiots would take a shot at us, and I'd already made that mistake once.

An image of a Homeworlder male snapped into existence at the center of the holographic projection, and this guy apparently didn't share my concerns about possible violent maneuvering because he was standing bolt-straight, hands clasped behind his back. I hadn't seen a Confederation... Navy? Space Force? Whatever they called their outer-space military arm, I hadn't seen the uniform until now. It was utilitarian, a singlet that looked to be optimized for use in a vacuum, the sort of skin-suit we wore under our vacuum armor for EVA. Just pull-on gloves and a helmet with an air supply and you're good to go in case someone shoots a hole in your ship and all the atmosphere rushes out. Not without a hint of style though. Red, yellow, and blue designs that matched the colors of the Confederation flag stretched across the chest and symbols that I thought represented the man's rank were splashed across one shoulder.

The officer was stiff-necked, his chest puffed out like a strutting peacock, his hair dark and slicked back. He had the look of an admiral or a general, unless I was projecting our military organization and stereotypes onto another society.

"Commonwealth ship *Orion*," he said, "I am General Patton of the Confederation Space Force."

I couldn't help it. I looked over at Dwight's avatar, which appeared to be leaning across the top of the transmission from the Feds, and rolled my eyes.

"General *Patton*?" I repeated. "Seriously?"

The AI's virtual representation affected a shrug.

"His name translates directly to *Straight Path Along the*

Mountain Stream. There's only so many colloquial equivalents I came come up with in your language. He's a general, he thinks highly of himself, dresses fashionably, and I picked an example at random from your history."

I sighed and made a motion at Chase to put me back on the call.

"Greetings, General *Patton*," I told the man. "This is Captain Alvarez. I assume you're here to apologize profusely for the backstabbing, underhanded betrayal by your people?"

Patton blinked as if he hadn't expected me to be that direct, and when he spoke I saw genuine puzzlement in his expression.

"I'm here because I was ordered to pick up a delegation from our government that was expected to return from the other side of the gate after negotiating with the Nova." A snarl crept into his voice, his lip curling. "Where are my people, and what are you talking about?"

"Assuming you're not lying to me," I replied without the slightest hint of apology, "then you've been left in the dark even more than us. Your delegation's version of *negotiating* was to attack our security personnel, launch their shuttle without authorization while we were in the middle of a complex discussion with the Nova, and then *attack* one of the Nova ships without provocation. They destroyed the ship and left *us* to take the blame."

Patton rocked backward like he'd been slapped.

"What? Why would they... where *are* they?"

"Dead." I didn't try to sugarcoat it. "The Nova opened fire after the attack and the shuttle was destroyed in the exchange." Which wasn't exactly what happened but close enough, and I wasn't going to write him an AAR.

"I'm going to need you to provide us the recordings of the incident," Patton said gravely, as if he was the final arbiter of our actions. "I'll also need to send people aboard your ship to check and make sure you're not holding any of them prisoner."

"Oh, you'll need to do that, will you?" I asked, wishing I *had* stood up. Actually, I wished the asshole was on the bridge in front of me so I could get in his face, but that was the instinct of the NCO I'd once been. "Well, you're gonna have to turn and burn to keep up then. We're heading back to Homeworld, and I'd recommend you do the same thing. As fast as you fucking can."

[23]

"Hey, Cam," Jay said, stepping through the hatch into my office —what had once been Hachette's office—with Bob at his heels. "You wanted to see us?"

"Yeah, I do," I said, motioning them inside. "Have a seat, you guys."

Vicky was already there, leaning against the edge of the desk. Hachette's desk. I couldn't bring myself to call it mine since I'd been in the compartment a grand total of twice since he'd died and used the desk never. Admin work was sort of irrelevant when there were no reports to file, no pay incoming, no nothing except the decisions that had to be made and the only one deciding whether or not they were justified was God.

Jay and Bob settled into the chairs on the other side of the desk, Jay sprawling across his, while Bob was tighter, knees pressed together, hands on the armrests. I didn't know either of them as well as I should have, but I did know that Bob wasn't normally that tense. He wasn't as loose and floppy as his friend, wasn't the talkative type, but I thought he was smarter, more observant.

"What's up?" Jay asked, hands spread, reminding me of the small-time drug dealers who came down to the Underground to buy Spindle and take it back to the Surface. They were always chill, always acting as if nothing bad could happen to them, as if the gangsters they were buying from would never double-cross them and take their Tradenotes, as if none of those crazy bastards wouldn't kill them just for fun. "I heard we're heading back to Homeworld. I thought you wanted to follow those Predecessors things?"

I pushed the hatch shut, hiding a frown from them. We didn't have much time. The *Orion* would be hitting the gate back to the Homeworld system in a few hours, and by then the Transition Drive would be operational. This was my last chance to talk to them.

"We need to know where you were during the battle," I said. "Both of you."

"You mean when it felt like the whole damn ship was gonna rattle itself to pieces?" Jay asked, laughing. "Man, I was right there in our compartment, strapped in just like you told us. Bob was too, except when he had to go to the bathroom."

Vicky's head snapped around, though I tried not to act as if the words had any significance.

"Damn, Bob," Jay went on, still chuckling. "You sure picked the wrong time to have to take a shit. Must have taken you an hour to get back to the compartment."

Bob said nothing for several seconds, staring at the bulkhead, and I thought he was going to stay that way, unresponsive. Until his lower lip quivered and he looked up at me, fear in his eyes.

"Someone told me," he said, "that there are a shitload of Nova ships heading for the Homeworld. Is that true?"

Maybe I should have said something tough and harsh, like

Hachette would have, told him that I was the one asking the questions. Instead, I nodded.

"And they're coming because of what those Feds did, right? Because they attacked the Nova ship?"

It was the most I'd heard him talk since I'd met him.

"Yeah. They pretty much started a war."

"Can you guys beat them? With this ship, I mean? Can you stop them?" It was hard to tell if it was his own voice or the translator, but he sounded desperate.

"I don't know," I told him honestly. "I know we can keep them from killing us, but I don't know if we can keep them from your world."

"My mom is still down there. My sisters." He shrugged. "Not that we're that close anymore, but y'know... they're family." A tear trickled out of his eye, down the side of his nose as if undetected. "I didn't know they were gonna do this. Ms. Frost, she came to me before we left, told me that if I did what she asked, that she'd take care of my family. Said that if I had to come back here, she would set me up with a good job and a place to live. I..." he sobbed, head going into his hands. "They just told me that they wanted a chance to talk to the Nova, to try to work out some way to share the jumpgates. They said you weren't going to help them unless they made you."

"Bud..." Jay gasped, staring at his friend aghast. "Why didn't you tell me?"

Bob eyed the other man sidelong with a skeptical sneer.

"You can't keep your mouth shut, Jay."

"How did you get the 'link?" Vicky demanded, harsher than I'd been. "How did you know about the security and the cameras?"

"I kept my eyes open." He shrugged. "The cameras aren't hard to spot. It's not like you guys try to hide them. The 'link and the suit were the hardest part. That was Jay, though he didn't know it. He talks to everyone. Including this chick in the Engineering section. He was talking to her, and I just started looking around where she worked. No one tried to keep us out of anywhere, so I just replaced her 'link with one of the ones you gave us and grabbed the radiation suit." He gave Jay a pleading look. "I'm sorry, man. I was just thinking about my family."

"Well," Vicky sighed, shoulders sagging, "at least we know that one of the crew wasn't turned."

Jay looked like he'd been poleaxed, his eyes wide and unseeing, while Bob stared at him miserably, racked with sobs, and I just stood there. My stomach had dropped out from beneath me, and I wondered if the drive had cut off without warning, but it was just the knowledge that this was my fault. I'd brought them on board. All of them.

"Are you..." Bob licked his lips and tried again. "Are you gonna kill us?"

"God knows I should." I blurted the words out before I even thought about them, and the abject fear in Bob's eyes might have made me feel guilty if I wasn't so Goddamned furious with him. I poked a finger into his chest. "If you'd gotten any of my people killed, I sure as hell would. But now... I'm just going to leave both of you right back in Two Rivers." I sneered at Bob. "You did your part, and now I guess you'll get paid for it."

"Oh, dude," Jay moaned, shaking his head. "What the hell have you gotten me into?"

"Are we sure we want to go in like this?" Vicky asked.

I couldn't see her, of course, just heard her voice in my helmet headphones. It felt good to have the suit around me again, comforting. It felt even better to shove it right down Frost's throat.

"She's expecting our shuttle," I replied. "They're not gonna try to shoot us down."

"They couldn't even if they tried. But how far are we prepared to press this? Do we want to kill any soldiers or security who get in our way?"

"Not unless it looks like they have something that'll scratch our paint."

"You guys ready back there?" Walton asked. "Because we're at one thousand meters and on approach to the spaceport and if you want to drop near the city, you've got maybe two mikes before you'll have to circle right back through their defenses."

I checked the feed from the drop-ship's nose cameras and confirmed the pilot's report. We'd come in from the opposite side of the city than we had the first time we'd landed here, by design, the high-reaching peaks of Two Rivers glittering in the noonday light. We weren't alone, of course. Frost wasn't stupid, and if she wasn't technically the government of the Confederation, she was close enough that a few words to the right ears would put the military in her pocket.

And there they were. Fighter jets. Nothing that could have kept up with one of our assault shuttles, just atmospheric aircraft, and I was fairly certain the missiles they carried wouldn't get by the drop-ship's ECM. What they'd do to one of our suits, well... I hoped not to find out.

"Copy that," I replied. One thousand meters. It was easy to forget that these new suits didn't need to drop as low as the old ones. "Get us down another two hundred meters. First Platoon, get ready to drop."

"Hold on, gonna be a steep drop."

He wasn't kidding. The jets cut out and the bottom fell out of my stomach, two hundred meters passing by in what might have been five seconds before the belly jets roared to life, braking our descent and shoving my spine up through my skull... or at least, that's what it felt like.

"Drop! Drop! Drop!" I gave the command instinctively, thank God, because my brain wasn't quite working yet after the fall and the sudden stop.

Grey metal and plastic gave way to blue sky and blue steel and I was falling. Drops were second nature to me by now, a part of life as normal as breathing, though my instincts and training were to hit the jets immediately. I didn't do that because of those fighter jets. None of us did, and watching Vicky and the rest of the platoon plummet out of the sky churned my guts more than my own descent.

I shut out my surroundings, the blur of architecture and the glare of reflected sunlight and even the threat warnings my suit's computer was shouting at me about the approaching fighter jets, and concentrated on the target. I'd seen the office building before, been up its transparent elevators, marveled at how high the thing seemed, even though I'd grown up in a city that towered hundreds of meters taller, as well as deeper. I hadn't considered the possibility of flying by the outside of it, but then if I had a Tradenote for everything I'd done that hadn't seemed likely, I'd have been one rich Marine.

I didn't hit the jump-jets until we dropped even with the roof. It would have been suicide in the old model suits, would have left me without the lift to halt my fall, and if I'd tried to push the turbines harder, the whole unit would have overheated and torn itself apart right there on my back. Then it would have been a race to see what killed me first, the shrapnel of the internal explosion or the fall. Thankfully, Resscharr alloys weren't as fragile as our own, making BiPhase Carbide look like tissue paper.

The deceleration was far from pleasant, of course, physics being the unforgiving, unyielding bitch she was. Every muscle in my body clenched, and I bit down on my mouthpiece hard enough to send spikes of pain up through my jaw. Unpleasant, but hardly a novel experience, and I was used enough to it that I was still able to spot the target floor.

"We still got SIGINT confirmation that she's in the building?" I asked. The question could have been meant for Chase, but Dwight jumped in to answer it. Sometimes I thought the AI got bored and just wanted to be involved.

"She's in there," Dwight told me. "Northwest corner office. There are six other Homeworlders either in the room with her or just outside the doors. Impossible to determine if they're armed."

"Not gonna make a difference," I declared. "Springfield, take Second squad and set up an overwatch on the roof. Vicky, you have Third and Fourth at the ground-level entrance. First squad, with me."

The fighters were circling around, one of the bright boys or girls in the planes finally noticing that the drop-ship they'd been tailing had expelled a load of smaller objects that might have been bombs but weren't. I didn't worry about them. By the time they returned close enough to be a threat, none of us would be in the air.

"First squad, file behind me. We're all going through the same entrance."

"I don't see any entrance, sir," Mansfield said.

"You will in a second."

There was, I was pretty sure from the thermal readout in my HUD, no one on the other side of the wall. If I was wrong, well, they wouldn't be enjoying life in a second. A touch of my thumb on the trigger and the energy cannon affixed to my Vigilante's right arm blasted an entire panel out of the wall, the tempered glass vaporizing into a fountain of steam while the ones around it on all four sides splintered and spiderwebbed, bits of it tumbling to the ground below.

A nagging worry that some innocent person on the ground might get hit by one of the falling pieces had to be pushed aside so I could concentrate on fitting through the hole I'd just made. Leaning forward just a few degrees, I gave the jets one last shot of thrust, then powered down just as my head cleared the ceiling. Momentum took me the rest of the way, the floor shaking beneath the impact of my boots.

Smoke billowed through the corridor, hiding details, but the thermal sensors told me that I'd at least avoided any unintended casualties. The hallway was empty except for broken sculptures and shattered glass from the frames of fallen paintings. Frost must really have a thing for art, I decided... or, more likely, it was all expensive and she used it to show off how much money she had.

Debris crunched under my footsteps as I rumbled forward, making room for the rest of the squad to touch down behind me. IFF transponders told me they'd all made it, though I hadn't been too worried. Top had hand-picked the original Drop Trooper company on the *Orion*, and anyone too clumsy for this maneuver wouldn't have made the cut.

"We're all in, sir," Mansfield informed me, bringing up the rear. It must gall him, since I knew he preferred point. And if we expected any real opposition, I might have let him up here.

There was the office, a halo over my vision provided by Dwight, the next door down the hallway. She might have a safe room or an emergency elevator and I didn't want to give her the chance to use it, so I hit the jets again. Trickier even than squeezing through the entrance. I had to almost fall forward before triggering thrust, just enough to keep the weight of my suit off the floor without smashing through the ceiling. I couldn't have kept it up too long, but I didn't have to.

The double doors to Frost's office were thick, cherry wood, beautifully carved and polished, probably by hand, and they splintered like so much kindling against my shoulder. I stumbled into the office, nearly going down into a crouch to keep my balance, almost as if I was kneeling in obeisance to Ms. Frost. She sat at her desk, hands flat on the surface, eyes wide, and if the half-dozen men and women in business attire gathered in her office were bodyguards, they didn't do much guarding at the moment. The ones who weren't throwing themselves to the floor, diving for cover, had their hands raised, some with palms pushed out like they could ward me off, the others with their arms straight over their heads in surrender.

I straightened and stepped to within a meter of Frost's desk.

"Everyone out," I said, the external speakers booming the words off the walls.

It was as if I'd flipped a switch, sending the others in the office from frozen statues of shock into sudden motion, and they tripped over themselves and each other trying to exit the room. A few screeches told me they'd seen the other Drop Troopers in the hallway, but no one came back inside. Frost started to get up, but I slammed the metal palm of my suit's articulated left hand against the surface of her desk.

"Not you. You stay right there. We need to have a talk."

Frost was scared shitless, there was no mistaking it, but she was also a consummate professional who'd been running this nation for years from behind the scenes, and she was used to thinking on her feet.

"Captain Alvarez," she said, stuttering the first couple syllables, but smoothing it over as she went, as long-practiced instincts kicked in, "I'm sure there's been some sort of misunderstanding. Perhaps if we could relax and discuss this peacefully…"

"Sorry, this is as peaceful as it's going to get." I had the volume on my external speakers turned up, and the woman shrank back from the sheer volume. "You used us, you abused our goodwill, and you were too fucking smart for your own good, you manipulative bitch. You didn't just fuck up our chances for an agreement with the Nova, you started a war. Not between us and them, between *you* and them." I pointed back behind me with my energy gun. Its muzzle was still glowing red from the shot that had taken down the window. "There's a *fleet* of them heading this way, and if they aren't here in a few hours, that's only because they've wasted time blowing the shit out of your colonies."

She *should* still have been afraid. That last bit of news was the kicker, the one I thought sure would panic Frost, would at least make her confess to what she'd done and beg for help. Instead, her expression solidified and the corner of her mouth turned up just a millimeter.

"I doubt you will allow that to happen, Captain Alvarez."

"Oh, do you?" I stared at her through the eyes of my helmet cameras, and it wasn't enough. She was too damned calm, too impersonal. The desk was real wood, just like the door, and just like the door, it smashed very satisfyingly under my fist.

This time, she jumped back, crying out in surprise. Cursing under my breath, I yanked out my 'face jacks and broke the seal on the chest plastron, pushing it open. The smashed desk was a barrier between us, splinters from its demise turning under my feet. Heat still radiated off the Vigilante from the jump-jets, but I felt as if it was coming off of me, a tangible sign of my fury.

"Why the *fuck*," I demanded, the translation of my voice still thundering out of my suit speakers, "would you think I'd lift a finger to help you or your people after the shit you just pulled? Tell me why I shouldn't just turn around and jump out of this system and forget I ever saw any of you."

Frost didn't shrink back this time. She stepped over the wreckage of her desk and looked me hard in the eye.

"Because you're still here. You didn't come back all this way to smash my damned desk. You came here because you're a good man, and you wouldn't allow me to bring destruction down on the heads of all those *innocent* people. You came here because you plan to save us all." She smiled and cocked an eyebrow. "And I plan to let you."

[24]

"Tell me we're not really doing this," Nance pleaded with me, shaking his head. "We can just take off, Alvarez. We'll go back into stasis, head out and find this place on our own, even if it takes a fucking year, or another *five* years. It's just time... we can do it. We can talk the crew into it."

We were back in the office again. Hachette's old office. Damn it, it seemed like only bad things happened here, another reason I didn't want to use the place for anything. I pushed away from the desk and yanked open the bottom right draw, moving aside the folded Commonwealth flag to get the bottle underneath it. Hachette's preferred brand wasn't mine, but at the moment I'd make do with anything.

"You better be pouring one of those for me too," Nance warned, leaning his elbows against the front of the desk.

I wished Vicky were here to share in the drink, but I'd left her downstairs to coordinate with General Patton—and God knows, we both felt very stupid calling him that. But there were only two glasses in the drawer and only the two of us to use them. I filled each to the brim with vodka and handed one to Nance.

"You know that's not true, Captain," I told him, then downed half the glass in one burning gulp. It seared its way down my throat and into my gut, spreading a welcome warmth through my head and chest. "You've heard the crew talking. They're at the ragged edge, and maybe I am too."

"Oh, bullshit," Nance scoffed. His laugh was interrupted by the vodka and by his gasp in the wake of its passage. "If there is *anybody* on this ship who couldn't care less about getting back to the Cluster, it's you." He tilted his glass toward me as if he was toasting what he'd said. "You didn't leave anything back there. Your wife is here, no kids, no parents, no siblings."

"Thanks for cataloguing the list of my tragedies," I said, returning the toast and taking another sip.

"Sorry." He winced, and I thought he meant it. "But you know what I mean. You're not on any sort of ragged edge, you're right in your element. Doing what you were destined to do."

Now it was my turn to scoff.

"Are you shitting me, Nance?" I shook my head. "I never commanded anything larger than a Marine company, and I sure as hell didn't want to be the guy everyone on this ship was looking to for salvation."

"Again, bullshit," he insisted. "You can't stand to have anyone else in charge. You want to be the final arbiter of your own fate. You want to be the one who makes the life-or-death decision."

"Maybe," I acknowledged. I didn't *really* believe it, but it wasn't worth arguing about. "Assuming you're right, then you must know what I'm thinking." I eyed him over the top of my glass and he sighed, shoulders sagging.

"I do. You're thinking this whole situation is your fault, that you should have seen this shit coming, and you're going to make things right."

I nodded. Maybe he *did* know me better than I thought. He at least knew enough to stop arguing.

"Okay, tell me what the plan is."

"Frost has agreed to turn over command and control of her defenses to us. She's *working*, so she claims, on getting the Grey to do the same."

"And you believe that?" He eyed me skeptically.

"I wouldn't believe her if she told me the sky was blue," I said with a snort, setting the glass down on the desk. "But honestly, I don't care. None of their shit is going to do much against the Nova fleet. I doubt they'd even be speed bumps."

"And you expect me to destroy three *hundred* ships all by myself?" Nance shook his head. "I mean, this ship is dangerous, but that's some serious numbers. There's no fucking way."

"You don't need to destroy them all," I said, then swallowed the lump in my throat. "I *hope*. Unless these guys are total fanatics, they aren't going to accept the sort of casualties you're gonna be inflicting. I mean, they can't have unlimited ships available."

"The Tahni got pretty damn fanatical," Nance reminded me. "We put a hurting on them late in the war and they still threw everything they had left at us."

"We were invading their home planets. And they'd already attacked us in our solar system. Tell me something... if the Tahni had never hit the Martian shipyards, if they'd kept things about trading hit for hit out in the Periphery, how many losses do you think we'd have taken before we started trying to negotiate for peace?" I pointed a finger at the map of the Cluster on the wall, the wormhole jumpgates highlighted in red. "Remember the First War with the Tahni? We had them where we wanted them but we agreed to the truce because the whole damn thing was costing too much."

"Okay," Nance sighed. He emptied his glass, then grabbed the bottle and poured himself another. "And what are you gonna be doing while I dance with these eight-legged freaks? Playing around with your Marines, I assume."

"Vicky's going to be in charge on the ground in case any of them get through. I'm gonna take a command team and ride shotgun in Intercept One with Villanueva. That way, I can keep an eye on things up top and if they go to shit downstairs, I can provide support and jump in to fill any gaps. We're leaving the assault shuttles and drop-ships down here too, just in case the Nova try to do an end-around."

Nance grunted, obviously unconvinced but unwilling to try hard enough to change my mind.

"Look, I'm not going to tell you how to do your job," I began.

"Since when?" he snorted, but I ignored it and kept going.

"Don't become decisively engaged. Hit and run and use the Transition Drive. And..." My mouth went dry. I poured another two fingers of vodka and drank it. "And if it comes to it, if you think there's no way to beat them, tell me. I'll pull our Marines out and we'll withdraw."

Nance appeared shocked and I shrugged.

"My main responsibility is to our people. I can't look myself in the mirror if I don't try to stop the Nova from massacring the Homeworlders, but I'm not sacrificing the *Orion* to do it."

"Well, glory halleluiah." He sat back in the chair and regarded me with narrowed eyes. "Tell me the truth though. The real reason we're here is that you feel responsible for all this, isn't it?" Nance shook his head. "It's not your fault. If I'd been in charge, I'd have probably done the same thing. We thought Frost was an ally. And those two kids... they'd done nothing but help us since we picked them up."

"It was my responsibility," I insisted, unable to meet his eyes. "Hachette wouldn't have trusted any of them."

"You're not Hachette. Don't try to be, or you'll just fuck up again."

I laughed softly.

"I'll keep that in mind." I collected the bottle and the glasses and stowed the away. "According to the latest reports, the Nova fleet should be transiting the gate in a few hours. We *could* try to hit the on the other side, but I'd rather give the Confederation forces enough time to arrange their defense in depth... such as it is. I have to make one more trip downstairs before the show kicks off, so I'll be taking the Intercept to the planet." I grinned. "I promise to have her home by midnight though."

"I have good news," Frost told me, spreading her arms like a Periphery revivalist preaching the gospel.

"You got a new desk?" I guessed, lacking the patience to deal with the woman.

At least I hadn't had to meet with her in her office, which had always seemed far too Corporate Council for me. We were in an underground bunker just outside the city, tucked beneath the foothills, shrouded by forest, and it had been a five-klick drive in a groundcar to get here from the landing zone. No aircars could get through the trees, which I think was part of the idea.

Inside the command post, I felt like I'd stepped back in time a hundred years. It wasn't just the flat screens and the lack of holoprojectors or haptic controls either. The entire command structure seemed to be based on having as many surplus bodies around as possible, scurrying from one place to another, carrying messages that could have been sent via text or voice, busy at tasks that should have been carried out automatically by computers.

They even had their battlespace laid out on a table with physical icons that had to be moved around magnetically, something I'd never seen before outside of a history vid. The only similarity between their setup and ours was the ubiquitous presence of superfluous senior officers and the occasional politician... or in this case, Frost.

To the credit of those senior officers, none of them seemed too happy to have Frost there either.

"The desk will have to wait," she said, seemingly unfazed by the sarcastic remark. "No, the news is that the Grey have agreed to commit their space forces to our effort."

"Well, that's something." I sighed. "We don't have much time for them to get into position. The Nova fleet is going to be here in maybe four or five hours."

"It'll take them a minimum of fifty hours to reach orbit," General Patton declared, walking up behind Frost, looking just as stiff and self-important as the last time I'd seen him on the main screen of the *Orion*. "Perhaps more, since they'll be engaging with your ship as well as our defenses. That should give the Grey space forces plenty of time to deploy."

My head hurt from trying not to roll my eyes. The general sounded like he was giving a press briefing.

"How much good do you think they're going to do us?" I asked him flatly. "According to all of you Confederation types, the Grey just copies your technology and doesn't do a great job of it."

Patton scowled, looking as if he resented my plain-spoken assessment.

"True. But they have a numbers advantage over us, and not just in terms of the sheer population size. Their production capacity is twice what ours is, and a lot of something fifty percent as good is sometimes better than not that much of something better."

For a stiff-necked martinet, Patton wasn't stupid.

"What do they have?" I asked.

"Mostly fusion mines. Mass drivers on the lunar surface, and a shitload of basic orbital transfer vehicles up-armored and fitted with missiles launchers and rotary cannons. But a shitload of them... we're talking hundreds. Maybe a thousand." Patton shrugged. "Those little ships are basically suicide, but they've got the pilots who'll fly them, the crazy bastards."

"And what do *you* have up there?" I wondered. "I assume the ships you met us in on the other side of the gate. But how many?"

Patton's gaze flickered downward as if in shame.

"Twenty. There were twenty-four up until yesterday. We left four of them at Otherside to try to slow down the Nova, give our colonists time to evacuate." He shook his head. "Not one of them survived. We don't know what happened to the colonists, but every single spacecraft in that system, ours or the Grey's, is gone."

I closed my eyes for a second, trying to think.

"Our main advantage," I finally said, "is mobility. Our ships can jump in and out of T-space and not get pinned down. We're gonna engage the enemy at the gate and back to just outside lunar orbit. Can I speak to the Grey commander from here?"

Patton nodded, then motioned at one of the enlisted troopers scurrying around the command center.

"Get me Admiral Nimitz immediately!"

I turned away from him, grabbing my 'link and shutting off the translation circuit.

"Admiral *Nimitz*, Dwight?"

"You try coming up with the English equivalent of all these poetic names, Cam," the AI said plaintively. "I get bored."

"Well, thank you for having fun with our misfortune."

"I do my best."

I grunted and turned the translator back on. By the time I turned back to Patton, the communications tech was handing him a wireless headset. He passed it over to me and I sighed, sliding it on over my head. This was gonna be awkward, since I had to put it on top of my earbuds. I hoped there wouldn't be any feedback.

"Hello?" I said, unsure of how else to address whoever was on the other end. "This is Captain Alvarez."

"Good day to you, Captain." I don't know what Nimitz's actual voice sounded like, but Dwight's translation program gave him the gentle, patient cadence of a teacher or maybe a psych counsellor. "I understand that you are in command of our defenses. I hope this is the case, because it's a non-negotiable condition of our agreement to cooperate in this operation."

"Yes, sir. My thoughts were that, since the Grey have an armed installation on your moon, you'll be responsible for lunar orbit all the way back to high orbit around the planet. I want that area mined, and I want direct observation on those mines by your manned vessels so they can target any Nova ship that's damaged by the mines. Is that agreeable to you?"

"Of course. I will give the order immediately. If you need us to adjust position, I will await your communication."

"Thank you for your cooperation, sir." I wasn't sure if Nimitz had ended the call, but I pulled the headset off anyway and handed it back to the technician.

"What about our forces?" Patton asked, and I had the impression his nose was out of joint because I'd spoken to the Grey about their disposition first. "Where should we deploy them?"

I looked around the cramped and overcrowded room for a map or a chart that showed the space around the planet rather than the surface and finally found one attached to a clear display board at the center of the place.

"Look here," I told them, tapping the map. "Here's the gate." It was circled in green on the map, which was the only reason I found it so quickly. "We're gonna be fighting them from here..." I tapped the screen at the gate symbol. "... all the way to here." It was an estimate since I wasn't a hyperdimensional physicist, but it looked about the right place for minimum jump distance. "We're not coming closer than that except in an emergency, not with the *Orion*. We're going to have a couple assault shuttles and our drop-ships running from orbit down into the atmosphere, but that's it. Everything else, from high orbit down, is your responsibility. You take those twenty ships of yours and keep them in high orbit and coordinate between them and any armed orbital shuttles you have, and with your fighter jets. Anything that gets by us, you have to stop them."

"What if they get by us?" Patton wondered, and I cocked my head at him in the same sort of look Top used to give us enlisted back in the day.

"Well, I don't fucking know. You've dealt with these freaks a lot longer than we have. Do you think they'll nuke your cities?"

"I don't believe...," Frost began, but I interrupted her.

"No." I raised a finger. "You're not a soldier. You're a politician pretending to be a business leader. General, what do you know about the Nova?"

Patton looked between Frost and me, eyebrows raised as if the whole exchange had scandalized him. It was probably something like going up to the president of the Commonwealth and telling him to fuck off.

"They didn't use nuclear weapons against the settlers when they kicked them off the planet," Patton told me. "They fired those energy weapons from orbit to take down the defenses, then they... they landed troops. Not *just* soldiers. They had these things with them, heavy armor except they walk on legs."

"Mecha," I spat and the general blinked.

"You know the things?"

"Not this particular kind, but the enemy we fought in the

war I told you about had them. Heavy artillery on legs. We call them mecha."

"These weren't just artillery," Patton explained. "They're like main battle tanks, except more mobile." He nodded toward me. "Can those suits your people wear take them on?"

"We're going to find out." I nodded to the man. "I'll be monitoring the situation down here, but my wife, Captain Sandoval, will be in command of our Marines. I'd appreciate if you could tell the head of your own ground forces to coordinate with her."

"Of course." Patton cleared his throat, unable to meet my eyes. "Thank you. For helping us."

Something about his words struck me, and it took me a second to reply.

"Of course." I looked to Frost and saw a glint in her eye like she knew exactly what I was thinking. "Ms. Frost, would you walk out with me?"

She didn't say anything snarky the entire way up the elevator, which was my first hint that I was right. There were soldiers in the lift car with us, and whatever we had to say, she didn't want them hearing it. It was late afternoon outside, almost uncomfortably warm when we reached the surface and stepped through the thick, metal doors to the parking area.

"You've used the quantum core," I assumed. "It's the only way you could have sold everyone on this so quickly."

"Why would I sit on a resource like that?" she asked, not bothering to deny it. "But how could you be so sure?"

"Simple." I stopped halfway to the car and faced her. "There's only two people you can blame this on. You or me. I don't see you taking the hit on this, and if you'd blamed it on us, there's no way in hell the general would have been so grateful. Which means you sold everyone a story about how this was all the Nova's fault. And the only way you could push that line of bullshit is if you used the quantum core to predict how everyone would react and what propaganda to feed them."

"You're a bright boy," she admitted, moving toward the car, not waiting to see if I'd follow. "I best take care not underestimate you."

"You think you're going to come out of this smelling like a rose." The driver was waiting for us in the vehicle, the rear doors hanging open, and I slid in one side while Frost settled into the other. "You think we're going to beat the Nova for you, then you're going to talk us into staying and you'll be the big hero who unites the planet and takes your people to the stars."

"Yes," she agreed, smiling. "And there's not a damned thing you can do about it."

[25]

"You ready to get out of here and let me do my job?" Vicky said, hopping down from her open Vigilante.

The company was formed up on the tarmac at the spaceport in the shadow of the drop-ships, the massive aerospacecraft bigger than anything the Confederation could put in the air. I hadn't seen them all together like this since we'd left Yfingam, which only seemed like a few months ago to me, even though it was actually five years.

Intercept One was nestled in beside them, her belly ramp open, Villanueva standing at the top of it, arms folded, tapping her foot in obvious impatience.

"You that eager to get rid of me, Sandoval?" I asked Vicky, taking her hand and pulling her to me. "You think if I stick around, I'll wind up walking point?"

"Hell, I *know* you will, Alvarez," she told me, leaning in to kiss me. "You best take care of yourself up there. You're a groundpounder, not a spacer. If you get killed, it has to be in a Vigilante or else you won't get to go to Valhalla."

"Is that how that works?" I asked her, teasing. I should have been tense, should have been scared shitless, but I wasn't, not with Vicky here. "You just remember that if we go down, we go down together. So no getting killed without me here, all right?"

"Always trying to be the boss." She shook her head.

"Hey, you can't come through here!"

I looked over to the side, saw one of the Confederation soldiers holding back two people trying to get through the metal gate at the edge of the landing field. Jay and Bob. I frowned, jogged over to them, and touched the Confederation soldier on the arm.

"It's okay," I told him. "I'll talk to them."

"What do you two want?" Vicky asked, anger tinging her voice. She held a grudge longer than I did.

"We wanted to tell you how sorry we are," Jay said. He looked like someone had killed his dog and, if anything, Bob was even more crestfallen. "We didn't mean for any of this to happen."

"We wanted to know if there was anything we could do to make it up to you," Bob added. "Like, if you want to give us guns, we'll stand here and fight with you."

"Even if we get killed."

Vicky closed her eyes, rubbing her temple.

"Listen, you two, it's great you feel bad about what you did, but we don't have time for this and there's nothing you can do to make up for it."

"Wait," I said, raising a hand before they could turn to leave. Their eyes both lit up with hope, and I actually felt bad for the both of them. "Tell me something... did Frost come through for you? Did she give you the jobs, the money?"

"I haven't had the chance to talk to her," Bob admitted. That was fair. We'd only dropped them in the city a few hours ago. "I haven't called. I... don't think I want it anymore."

"How'd you like to give it all up then?" I asked him. "How'd you like to throw that chance away?"

"If it would make things right between us," Bob said, nodding emphatically.

"It would make up for what you did. I can't promise I'll be able to trust you enough to take you with us. Would you still do it, even if it left you here with nothing?"

"Yeah, man," Bob said, and Jay nodded, uncharacteristically quiet. "Anything."

I grinned.

"All right then." I pulled my 'link off my belt and handed it to him. "You're gonna need this."

"So, boss," Francesca Villanueva said, as casually as if three gravities of thrust weren't pressing us all back into our acceleration couches, "this bringing back fond memories for you?"

"You weren't around for the good old days, Francesca," I reminded her, straining the words out. "Back then, you were flying an assault shuttle, and I think you gave me air support a grand total of twice in the two years we served together."

"Oh, I know... I was doing the dirty work no one cared about," she said, laughing softly. "Taking out those enemy assault shuttles that would have wiped you out. Dunstan got to have all the fun." She shook her head so slightly I almost missed it. "I still can't believe he and Beckett hooked up... and they were having a *kid*!"

"The kid's going to be almost five years old now. I miss Dunstan, but I think sometimes he made the right decision. I think if I didn't have the whole crew to think about, Vicky and I would have stayed too."

"You wanted to fish for a living?" she teased. On the main screen, the deep blues of early evening were turning to black as the cutter reached the upper atmosphere. Twinkling stars formed neat rows above us, defense satellites strung out in preparation for what was coming. "Pop out some kids of your own?"

"The kids, sure. Not so much the fishing. If we'd stayed, it would only have been because the whole crew voted to stay, which would have meant we'd have had the *Orion* with us. I would have tried to set up some kind of trade agreement with all those other civilizations we found. Since we would have had the highest level of technology around and the only warship with Resscharr weapons, we'd have likely wound up as the rulers of a trade empire. Which is why I'm glad we left."

"What? Didn't wanna play kingmaker?"

"Didn't want to fight in any more wars." I chuckled. "Ironic, huh?"

"Y'know, I just got engaged before this mission." The pilot sighed. "It was stupid. I knew the assignment was going to have me out of contact for months. I told Drake that and he didn't care. Said he wanted to be sure I knew how he felt before I left."

"Sorry," I told her, wincing as I realized how many others in the crew might have the same story to tell.

"I just hope he didn't wait for me. The poor bastard's a big enough romantic that he might have." We were out of the atmosphere now, leaving orbit, and Villanueva backed the acceleration down to one gravity. "That'd be a shame. He's a good man. He deserves to be happy."

"I didn't even have a girlfriend," the copilot, Lt. Awori, lamented with equal pathos. "I broke up with her right before we shipped out. Figured it wouldn't work. My parents died in the war. There's probably nobody back home who even misses me." He shrugged. "Catching fish on the Islands sounds pretty good to me. I got outvoted." He glanced aside, then leaned back over to me. "We're receiving data from the Grey, sir. It's their deployment positions."

"Put it on the screen." I would have asked for it on my 'link, but I'd given that to Bob.

The computer displayed their ships as green icons scattered from just past lunar orbit all the way back to near our current position, though none were close enough for me to make out their actual lines.

"There's a shitload of them," Villanueva muttered. "If numbers won the fight, we'd already be moving on." She eyed me sidelong. "They contributing any troops on the ground, if it comes to that?"

"Depends on where the enemy lands. The Feds and the Grey both agreed they'd handle their own territories. Captain Sandoval will get the Marines in their drop-ships and be ready to respond though."

"Intercept One, this is *Orion*. You copy?" Chase. I leaned in and touched the comm control, hoping Villanueva wouldn't mind me messing with her ship.

"This is Alvarez," I replied. The response didn't come for a good thirty seconds, the speed of light being as it was.

"Alvarez, this is Nance. Our drones on the other side of the gate just went dead. The Nova are coming through. We're going to engage and I'll be too busy for chit-chat. Good luck. If you need me, you'll know where to find me."

I didn't bother to echo the wish, knowing it would take fifteen or twenty seconds to get there and they'd be busy by then. It probably meant the last I'd hear from Dwight too, considering the main part of the AI's cognitive abilities were embedded in the ship's computer. Except there'd been times when he'd downloaded smaller fractions of himself to the assault shuttles or Intercepts...

"Dwight?" I asked, softly, tentatively, as I didn't especially want Villanueva overhearing. "You there?"

"Some of me," the AI said into my earbud. "What I could fit

into the onboard computer systems of Intercept One. I won't have my full capacity until we're closer to the *Orion*, but I do have the last reports to come through from the drones. The Confederation vessels left defending Otherside were indeed destroyed, but indications are they took two of the Nova ships with them. Not that the lack of those two warships will hinder the enemy's invasion plan, but at least it shows the Confederation technology *can* penetrate their defenses without the benefit of a surprise attack."

"Thank God for small favors," I said, snorting humorlessly. "Since the Confederation has a grand total of twenty of those ships, I guess we can count on them taking out a whole *ten* of the enemy."

"It's better than nine."

I blinked, looking around as if I could see Dwight there in the cockpit. Awori was staring at me now but I didn't care.

"Is that a joke?"

"I'm afraid Kyler Dunstan left some of his personality and his sense of humor ingrained into the systems on this ship. The more time I spend here, the more it rubs off on me."

"What about that other slice of you? Is it going to have enough space and power to do the job?"

"More than enough." Amusement was rich in his voice, and I wondered if that came from Dunstan as well. "I must admit, your idea was well thought out, and the last-second addition was the icing on the cake."

"There they are," Villanueva said, pointing to the tactical display at the corner of the main screen.

This wasn't the bridge of the *Orion*, where even a quarter of the display was huge, and I had to squint to see the details of the computer simulation. Hundreds of Nova ships streamed through the jumpgate, a swarm of fat, deadly hornets, each with a stinger that was powerful enough to take out the *Orion* with two or three shots.

She was alone out there, a single Spartan standing at this alien Thermopylae, though I hoped we wouldn't share the fates of those ancient defenders. Flares of energy shone like fireflies in the blackness, though we were too far away to tell whether it was our weapons firing or theirs.

"We need to get in there," I told Villanueva. "How long until we're at the minimum safe jump distance?"

"Another hour," she replied. Then she shot me a grin and a sidelong glance. "Or we could do that little, highly illegal, against-regulations trick Dunstan always loved and try to Transition at the Lagrangian point."

I winced. Dunstan might have liked it, but it had always scared the shit out of me. Probably because I didn't have anywhere close to the level of understanding of how the Transition Drive worked as he did, or Villanueva. I knew the basics, that the temporary wormhole formed by the Teller-Fox warp unit could only stabilize at a certain distance from a planet's gravity well, usually beyond the orbit of its farthest moon, and that any attempt to Transition closer than that would atomize the ship that tried it. Except for one perfect spot where the gravitational pull of the moon countered that of the planet, the Lagrangian points.

It worked. We'd done it, more than once, but all it took was one, tiny error and that would be it. We'd be scattered between two realities, and no one would ever be able to figure out what happened.

I sighed, leaning my head back against the chair's rest, giving into the acceleration.

"How long till we reach the Lagrangian point?"

"Two minutes." The woman smiled broadly, clearly looking forward to this, not so much because she had any more of a death wish than I did, but because she was a combat pilot and this was the sort of shit they lived for. "Awori, start the calculations."

Great. He had a whole two minutes to figure it out.

"Don't worry, Cam," Dwight assured me. "To quote your Bible, *lo, I am with you always, even unto the end of the world*."

"Is that supposed to be a comfort?"

"I'm in the computer he's using to calculate the jump. I won't let him screw up."

I didn't say it out loud, but having a computer that single-handedly destroyed an entire civilization tell me he'd take care of everything didn't exactly fill me with confidence.

"Ten seconds," Villanueva said, as calm as if this was a train ride from her housing block to the shopping district. "We got those numbers, Chad?"

"They're in," Awori told her. "Transitioning in five."

"Four," she took up the count. "Three, two, one..."

It shouldn't have felt different than any other Transition, but it did, just like it had the other times we'd attempted it. The universe screamed as if we'd stabbed a hole through it and the scream echoed inside my head.

Into the darkness.

[26]

I was still alive.

I was never sure if I would be from jump to jump. Maybe that's the reason I'd never grown completely accustomed to the Transitions, why it always felt as if the next one might be the last. Maybe that's why relief flooded through me despite the carnage and destruction we dropped out into.

The last time I'd seen this many ships in a single battle had been during the war, and even then only in the last few, decisive engagements of the conflict. A lot of people back on Earth and the core colonies had an action-movie, Virtual-Reality-gaming idea of how many warships a government could afford to build and the sheer number of star systems between which they had to be divided. There'd never been more than ten cruisers in the Commonwealth Fleet the entire war, and even the Tahni, who had a centralized economy and a theocratic dictatorship and had been pouring money into Transition-Drive destroyers since the day after they'd stolen the design, never had in excess of a hundred of the things. The bigger a Transition Drive was, the more exotic matter it required, and the costs went up exponentially with the size.

The Nova didn't have the Transition Drive, of course, but even building something with heavy enough armor and weapons to force a crossing through a jumpgate cost a significant portion of a star system's wealth. Every ship that got built was nickel iron from an asteroid mine that didn't go into constructing gas scoops, space colonies, cargo haulers, or a hundred other things necessary to the operation of an interstellar society. Every load of hydrogen and helium from a gas giant that was processed into fuel for warships was one that wasn't sent to commercial reactors, and if the gas was cheap and plentiful, it still cost something to mine it.

Three hundred of the Nova ships, identical to the ones we'd encountered back in the system with the wormhole map, the *Orion*, twenty Confederation cruisers, and upward of a thousand of various sorts and sizes of Grey military ships. They ranged in type from barely armored minelayers to the tiny gunships Nimitz had told me about—and they *were* tiny, barely as large as an assault shuttle. I thought about the guts it would take to fly one of those little things out in cislunar space, hundreds of thousands of klicks from help, and my respect for the Grey as a people went up.

Then there were the shuttles and dual-environment fighters from both nations prowling the orbit of the planet from high to low and, between them all, it felt as if I could have walked back from here to Two Rivers on metal. It took a moment for me to pick the *Orion* out from the glowing, glittering cloud of Nova ships, each of them backlit by the light of a captive sun. She was at the edge of them, far out of optical range, coming in from relative north, off the ecliptic, coming straight down at a globular cluster of eight of the enemy, guns blazing.

"Nice move," Villanueva murmured, and I had to agree.

Ships coming through the gate were oriented to the ecliptic, the rotational plane of planets around their star, and with nothing but a reaction drive, even the powerful fusion drives the Nova had, it would take a shitload of thrust to leave that course and angle to relative north or south. That made them sitting ducks, unable to do anything except rotate their weapons toward the *Orion* and blast away... and even that adjustment took time.

Too much time for three of the ships. They went up like a chain explosion, the scintillating blue lance of power from the *Orion*'s main gun ripping through them as if their armor wasn't there. A fourth was nearly lined up for a shot at Nance's ship when Intercept Two flashed out of T-space only a thousand klicks off her port. The cutter's proton cannon was a pocket torch beside the flood light of the *Orion*'s energy cannon, not enough to core the enemy ship but certainly a damaging blow, and the thermal sensors showed a spray of burning metal coming off the armor plating near the vessel's prow.

"There," I told Villanueva. "Jump in. Hit that one again."

I grabbed the armrest just in time to avoid jerking against the shock of the micro-Transition, and within a second we weren't hanging off the entire fleet from fifty thousand klicks. Instead, we were only a thousand kilometers off the starboard prow of the injured Nova cruiser, close enough that I could see the last puff of burning atmosphere flare from the gap in her hull before it was sealed off by internal pressure doors.

She was a sterling silver mountain moving far too fast with velocity built up from hours of acceleration, and Villanueva only had a second to fire on her before she passed. If it had been Dunstan, I would have had no doubts, but I didn't know Villanueva as well, hadn't fought alongside her before. She didn't let me down, the magnetic thrum of the proton cannon discharging reverberating through the cutter, the particle beam invisible to our naked eyes in the vacuum but simulated nicely by the white flash in the computer simulation. Where the beam struck, centimeters-thick armor violently sublimated away and more air poured out, crystallizing into ice this time rather than catching fire.

"Transitioning," Villanueva warned, but not soon enough.

Existential fear and shock clutched the core of my being, and then we were somewhere else and it took me a second for my vision and my thoughts to clear enough to figure out where. We'd jumped inward another few thousand klicks along the path of travel of the Nova fleet, out of their firing arcs unless one of them took the time and fuel to adjust their attitude toward us. It would buy us a minute or two, and that was what Villanueva was looking for—time for the capacitors to recharge.

The cutter had two of the superconductive coils, and it needed one to charge for each Transition... which took nearly thirty seconds. The *Orion* had been upgraded but the cutters had not, and right now I was wishing they had been, imagining what we could have done if the Intercepts had Resscharr energy cannons and reactors.

"Brandano came in behind us," Villanueva told me, pointing to the ship we'd attacked. She was listing, knocked off her course by the expulsion of gas from the atmosphere, drive still burning, taking her out of the formation. "I think we got her."

I purposefully kept myself from feeling elation at the win. There were over three hundred and fifty of the things still left, spread across the main screen like a sea of red, and just three of us. The *Orion* was nowhere to be seen on the Tactical display, and I worried that we'd missed something while we were jumping, that she'd taken a hit and was already gone. Before the thought had fully formed, the *Orion* flashed back into existence at the other end of the gigantic formation, lashing out again.

The blue balefire turned two enemy ships into expanding balls of gas in the space of ten seconds, and Nance *should* have had time to take out one more of them, but the captain of the nearest cruiser was faster on the draw than the others had been. The Nova ship had hit maneuvering thrusters immediately on the *Orion*'s Transition, cutting his forward thrust to make the turn quicker, and a wash of star-white plasma coalesced in a half-sphere across Nance's shields.

Goddammit, I'd *told* the man not to get decisively engaged, told him that ship was more important to us than all the fucking Homeworlders on Homeworld, and I should have fucking *known* better, because there was no way a Fleet captain like Nance was going to back down from a fight.

"Get in there now!" I yelled at Villanueva, but her instincts as a pilot were faster than mine as a Marine, and we micro-Transitioned before I got the last word out.

Biting down against the gorge rising in my stomach, I couldn't even give an order when we popped back into existence just off the belly of the Nova ship that had fired on the *Orion*. I didn't need to. Villanueva's teeth bared in a snarl as she fired the proton cannon into the maw of the Nova plasma gun. It was what I would have told her to do, but the result wasn't what I expected. I thought the thing would just... you know, *break*. Like a proton cannon or a railgun might have done if someone had shot it in the middle of a battle. That wasn't what happened.

The ship swelled up like a balloon, except what was filling it wasn't air, it was fire. Pure white energy, slipping through cracks in the hull, until that metal balloon burst. Explosions in open space don't generally do anything. I knew that much just from osmosis, hanging around spacers for the last couple years. There was no atmosphere to conduct heat or concussion, which only left radiation as the media for damage, and most ships had enough shielding to keep that from being fatal.

This one was different, bigger, the reaction spreading out beyond the limits of the ship's lines and traveling across the two or three thousand kilometers to the next ship in the cluster and curling the armor away from the side facing the explosion like paint peeling in the sun. Then it all disappeared into darkness and dislocation and we were out again.

"What the *fuck* was that?" Villanueva exclaimed.

I didn't try to answer, didn't even *think* about the question, still reeling from the unanticipated jump and using what little concentration I could muster to search for the *Orion*. There. She'd jumped out as well, farther this time, as if Nance knew he'd need more time to recover from the hit. Close enough to radio though.

"*Orion*, this is Intercept One, what's your status?" My voice was hoarse, fire in the back of my throat, and I needed a drink. Water, if nothing else. I found a squeeze bulb tucked into the webbing at the side of my acceleration couch and sucked it down greedily.

"We're good," Nance replied, calm, steady, not at all like someone who'd just had his nose bloodied. "We were far enough away that the power conduit didn't fail. Thank God, because we only *have* so many spares on board."

"Antimatter."

I blinked at the non-sequitur, confused enough that it took me a moment to realize it was Dwight who'd uttered it.

"What?" Nance barked. "What are you talking about?"

"The Nova's main gun," the AI clarified, and I wondered if it was the version on the cutter or the more complex one over on the *Orion*... and if it mattered. "It's an antimatter weapon of some kind. That's the only thing that could explain the reaction when Intercept One fired on the mechanism. They undoubtedly have fail-safes that automatically separate and eject the antimatter if the ship is damaged too badly to contain it, but the strike on the actual weapon at close range was enough to allow an uncontrolled chain reaction."

"That's just dandy," Nance interrupted Dwight. "But unless it changes how we deal with these fuckers, it's irrelevant."

"It gives us a target," I suggested. "You catching this, Brandano?"

"Copy, Alvarez," the other Intercept pilot acknowledged. "Go for the big gun."

"And hurry," I added, checking the distance on the screen. "We only have a few hours before these guys engage the Grey forces in lunar orbit. And once they get there, it's too late for us. We do *not* get tangled up with these guys past minimum safe Transition distance. Are we all clear on that?"

"Yes, sir," Brandano said immediately. He didn't have to call me *sir*... he outranked me. But the man had been one of the first to back me taking command, and it was nice to know I wouldn't have to fight him at every turn, because he could be a real prick when he wanted to be.

Nance said nothing and I sighed.

"Captain, are we on the same page here?"

"Yeah, Alvarez, I got it. We don't risk the ship. But you tell me something... if you see those octopus-looking bastards laying waste to that planet, are you *really* going to be able to walk away from it?"

"Not if it were just me," I admitted. "But I promised the entire crew I'd get them home, and I didn't promise the people of Homeworld shit. Now, let's make good use of what time we have and start peeling ships off the front of their formation. The longer we can hold them out of lunar orbit, the better chance the Grey mines can take out even more of them. That's the only shot we have of saving these people, making the price of taking their world too high. Nance, you're the Fleet captain, but I'm going to tell you anyway. Transition in, no more than two shots, then Transition out. These guys aren't stupid. Two shots and you're out."

"Right." Nance growled the word, and I knew I was annoying him, but tough shit. It was my responsibility, and he'd agreed to that. "Two shots."

And I could believe that as much as I liked.

"Villanueva," I said, clenching my stomach for the micro-Transition, "take us back in."

"I don't want to jinx us," Awori said softly, his voice barely audible above the roar of the plasma drive, "but I think we might actually pull this off."

I'm ashamed to admit, I couldn't tell whether he was right or not, couldn't say in that moment where we were or how far we were from lunar orbit. We'd done at least twenty micro-Transitions in the last hour, and each one had hit me like a haymaker to the jaw. I didn't have a concussion—or at least, I was *fairly* sure I didn't—but my head lolled as if I'd gone twelve rounds with a professional fighter. I couldn't see straight, couldn't keep my thoughts together enough to give a coherent order.

Villanueva and Awori, on the other hand, didn't seem to be affected at all, or else knew much better how to hide it. I hated them both.

Slamming my fist into the armrest of my seat, I forced my eyes to focus and my brain to concentrate on what I was seeing. The cloud of Nova ships had shrunken visibly, down by nearly a hundred and fifty in the few hours it had taken us to get this close to lunar orbit. Instead of a red-tinted star map, it was a blood-spatter crime scene, the site of some historic massacre with markers for each of the victims. I should have felt bad for them, for the thousands we'd killed methodically, hunters slaughtering the plains bison from trains in the 19th century American west. I didn't, and not just because they were so different from us, from humans, and not just because the violence had been in the sterile vacuum, impersonal and faceless.

The truth was, I didn't feel anything, because nothing at all felt real about this place since we'd arrived. Whatever could be said about Yfingam and the other worlds we'd visited, there were humans and Tahni there. The Resscharr were alien to us, but we'd expected them, and the fact they'd evolved on our world had made them seem somehow familiar. The Homeworlders were *almost* human, which was probably why I'd allowed myself to let my guard down around them more than I should have. The Nova weren't even close, and everything beyond them was the stuff of fairy stories. I was having a hard time believing it even existed.

"You might be right, Chad," Villanueva admitted, lips pursed as she examined the screen. "There's not a damn thing they can do about the Transition Drive as long as we don't get bound up."

I squeezed my eyes shut. I was missing something. I remembered the command team in the back and twisted around in my seat.

"Sgt. Ruddy," I called, "you guys all right back there?"

I couldn't seem them, of course. They were all the way back in the utility bay with the suits, but the intercom speakers carried even if my voice wouldn't.

"We're okay, sir." The man's voice was gravelly, hoarser than usual. "You wanna tell that pilot up there that some of us need to go to the head? Unless she wants to hose this utility bay down after we land."

I tilted an eyebrow at Villanueva, and she sighed as if the whole thing was a huge bother.

"Fine. Go now. I'll call the *Orion* and Intercept Two and let them know we're going to be out of action for a few minutes."

It wasn't a bad idea, but I didn't need a potty break as much as I did something to eat. There were rat bars in a compartment just below the communications console, and I loosened my harness enough to dig through the thing and pull out three of them.

"Anyone?" I offered, holding out two of them. Pilots being all cool and aloof, I half expected them not to accept the food, but they both took them and chowed down eagerly. We'd been boosting and jumping for hours without anything except water.

The rat bar was cardboard as usual, but I downed it with all the enthusiasm of a starving man, knowing you could never predict when you'd get food or sleep in this business. The *Orion* and Intercept Two had disengaged as well, jumping out fifty thousand klicks, far enough away that the main guns of the Nova ships couldn't touch them. The Nova hadn't bothered to try launching missiles at us since the first few minutes of the fight. They were smart enough to understand we'd just Transition away, leaving their missiles to run out of reaction mass long before they could correct course.

Not smart enough to change their tactics on the run though. The Tahni had been better at this, but then they'd had more practice. If it had been me, as much of a groundpounder as I was, I would have launched those missiles every time the *Orion* jumped in and had them surround my ships like a mine field. Yeah, they'd have run out eventually, but they just needed to delay us until they got within striking distance of the planet.

Hell, if they had them, it would have worked better to launch planet-busters at Homeworld, forced us to deal with those, and delayed us engaging them.

And if I, a Marine company commander, could figure that out, then *they* should have been able to. The last swallow of ration bar stuck in my throat.

"Something's wrong," I said, though I wasn't sure who I was talking to. I slapped the communications control, urgency gathering like a predator ready to leap through my chest. "Captain Nance, do you read? Something's wrong here. They're keeping us busy for a reason."

"Alvarez," he replied, a grim note to the words, "we're detecting something at the gate."

"Oh, shit," I murmured. "More of their ships?" I had a vision of three or four hundred more Nova warships streaming through the gate, of doing this shit for another few *days*, of them wearing us away just by virtue of killing them. That, as it turned out, was the best-case scenario. What we got was the worst.

"No, just one."

"Cam." It was Lilandreth speaking this time, though why she'd be interrupting Nance, I didn't know. "I recognize the gravitic signature of the ship. It's one of ours... a Resscharr starship."

The image on the Tactical display of a vague, red dot coming through the distant jumpgate shifted, zooming in not with newfound optical abilities but with the estimate of the computer using the information fed to it by Lilandreth and probably Dwight. I'd seen it before on Yfingam, though this was bigger. An elongated cylinder, flattened at either end, glowing green.

"It's coming this way," Nance warned me. "At somewhere around seventy percent of the speed of light. It'll be here in minutes."

"It has a gravity drive," Lilandreth reminded, "gravitic defense shields, and gravitic weapons that will tear through the *Orion*'s shield with a range of thousands of kilometers."

"You're the commander, Alvarez," Nance said. "What the hell are we gonna do?"

[27]

"Are you sure this is going to work?" Nance asked me for what seemed like the tenth time. He was close, so there was next to no lightspeed delay. Both Intercepts were tucked in tight with the *Orion*, not quite docked but close enough that we could have within a minute.

Homeworld was behind us, a tiny blue marble, while its moon was larger. Too damn large. Spread out ahead of us was what remained of the Nova fleet, unyielding, unwavering. Knowing what was coming behind them and that we had to deal with it.

"Fuck no, I'm not sure!" I exploded, giving into the doubt and tension. "I'm a Marine, not a Fleet captain! And I sure as hell have never fought a Resscharr starship, but this is the only damn thing I can come up with, so either buy in or give me a better idea!"

Villanueva and Awori stared at me, the copilot's eyes wide but the pilot grinning in obvious amusement.

"For what it's worth," Dwight interjected, "the Tahni assault shuttles along with your Intercepts were able to destroy the smaller Resscharr ships on Yfingam using concentrated proton cannon fire. The key here is not allowing it to destroy *us* first."

"All right, all right," Nance sighed. "I'm not a hundred percent convinced but I don't have anything else to offer, so we'll do it your way. Though I'm not sure what good it's going to do keeping it from shooting that gravity gun at us if the Nova blow us into vapors with those antimatter cannons." He paused. "By the way, what happened to just taking the hell off if we thought there was any danger of them destroying our ship?"

"That thing's too fast. It'd take us hours to get the Marines off the planet, and it'd be on us long before then. The only way we all get out of here is if we take this damned thing out." A deep breath helped me to rein in my frustration with the man. "Just remember," I said, "Brandano, Villanueva... stay as close as you can to the *Orion*. We can't be popping out of T-space thousands of klicks away from each other."

"Yes, Mother," Villanueva muttered.

"Whatever we're gonna do," Awori said, "we'd better do it soon. That thing is only forty-five seconds away."

I knew the things could go that fast, but knowing it and seeing it were two different things. The green halo moved across the screen like we were playing a ViR video game, not showing any sign of turnover for deceleration because it didn't have to.

I scrolled through the menu on the comm control, finding the net for the ground forces.

"Vicky, it's me. You copy?"

It took a few seconds, and my gaze kept traveling back to the screen, to the approaching doom.

"I copy. What the hell's going on up there, Cam?"

"The Nova have a Resscharr starship," I said quickly, knowing we didn't have much time. "We're gonna try to take it out, but it's going to take all three of us, which means there'll be no one to oppose the Nova fleet except for the locals. Make sure the Grey commander knows that. It also probably means you're going to see ground troops land. Maybe a *lot* of them. You're going to have to handle them without orbital support from us, and I wouldn't expect much help from the Homeworlders on that. Not with the tech the Nova have been showing us. They'll rip right through any orbital weapons the Feds or the Grey have." The next part hurt to say, and I hoped no one was listening in on us. "This is their planet. Let them take the brunt of the ground combat, *use* them to set up the enemy. Don't get any of our Marines killed to save their soldiers. I have to go. Love you."

I cut off the transmission. I wanted to hear her reply, at least her confirmation, but the clock was running down. The Predecessor ship was ten seconds away. I wanted to wait until the last minute, and this was it.

"All ships," I called, "Transition now!"

I couldn't tell you why and I'm not sure if a physicist or an engineer could have either, but micro-Transitioning with the three ships together didn't feel as bad. Or maybe I'd just had a longer break this time and gotten some food in me and a bathroom break. Either way, when we popped back into existence at the center of the Nova fleet, I was immediately alert and aware with none of the psychological hangover.

I'm not sure that was a good thing, because it also meant I was *very* cognizant of the metal mountains rising around us in every direction, washing past us like a landslide. It would only take seconds for one or more of the approaching Nova ships to adjust course and aim their main guns our way, but they didn't *have* those seconds. Because the Resscharr ship didn't give a shit about them, didn't care that they were in the way... it just cared about destroying us.

The cylinder-shaped vessel homed in on us like a missile, spearing right through one of the Nova ships, twisting the larger starship apart like the angry hand of God when it struck. The green halo around the ship glowed stronger after the impact, ragged and angry, and its bullet-like pace across the space between us slowed to something approaching conceivable for a moment.

It didn't open fire immediately, but I had the sense that it would, that the only reason it hadn't was the collision, the loss of coherence of its drive field.

"Now!"

They'd been waiting for the command, and no one questioned it. Another jump, the shortest one a Transition Drive ship could possibly make, the reason why we'd stuck so close together, and we were on the other side of the glowing cigar.

It wouldn't take them long to spot us, though I think it would have taken them longer if they'd actually been Resscharr. I'm not sure when I'd decided they weren't, that it was the Nova themselves piloting the thing, and a moment's hesitation passed through me at the thought that maybe I was wrong, that this was the Reconstructors themselves trying to kill us. In the end, though, it made no difference either way.

.I didn't have to give the order to fire because none of the people manning our guns were idiots and none waited for it. This was the other part about keeping the Intercepts so close to the *Orion*, the need to focus both proton beams and the energy cannon on the same spot. The Resscharr ship was only a couple thousand klicks away, and when the beams struck, its verdant drive field shimmered and flared... and then expanded.

"Fuck!" Awori blurted, and I was sure the expression on my face mirrored the horrified clenching of muscles on his as the cutter tried to shake itself to pieces around us.

The feedback from the gravitic field shedding energy was nearly as bad as the hit from the main gun of one of the Nova ships, the vibration tossing me against my safety harness hard enough that I thought I'd dislocated my shoulder.

"Don't let up!" I'd tried to shout the words, but they came out as a pained groan and I didn't know whether anyone had heard me, even Villanueva.

Blue balefire on the main viewscreen told me that Wojtera had, or at least that he didn't need the encouragement. The cutters took a few seconds between shots to recharge the capacitors for the proton cannons, but the *Orion* had no such limitations, able to fire just as fast as the weapon could cycle. The green drive field went from St. Elmo's Fire to the crackling light of an aurora and past that into shades I couldn't describe, a fusion blast brought to life as a polychromatic fireworks display.

My gut told me we had the thing, that it couldn't take the sustained barrage. My gut was an idiot. Well, sort of. I knew the beam that shot out from the crackling halo of the alien ship's drive field wasn't at full power. If it had been, it would have torn the *Orion* to shreds and everything would have ended right there. Instead, her shields lit up like a Christmas tree ornament, blinding and actinic, and the blast of gravitic energy tossed the entire Fleet Intelligence ship tumbling backward like it had received a physical blow.

And us. No one cursed this time, but I think that was mostly because no one could even put together a coherent profanity. I'd been in one starship or another for most of my adult life and I'd never had the sensation of something *hitting* the hull, but I felt it now. The entire superstructure rang like a bell and gravity returned, not straight down as if we were in T-space, not straight back like we were boosting on the fusion drive, but random waves going through the ship, through *me*. I'd been in a lot of fights, but none of the bullies who'd beaten me up in those group homes had hit as hard as that wash of gravity.

Blood trickled down my nose and then beaded away into

tiny satellites spiraling toward the air vent along with a haze of smoke that had come from burnt-out controls, and I wondered what wasn't working anymore. Thank God Villanueva was still working.

"Goddammit," she ground out, grabbing the control yoke like she was drowning and it was a rope thrown to save her.

Her face refused to cohere into anything well delineated and solid, and at first I thought the haze obscured my vision, but then I realized it was my eyes refusing to focus. I shook my head and it hurt like a son of a bitch, but at least I could see. Which might not have been a good thing.

The *Orion* drifted, her shields down, powerless, and if the Predecessor-tech ship hadn't finished her off yet, it was only because of the damage the thing had taken. The halo of gravitic energy still crackled and sparked, not yet fully repropagated but building to it. We only had seconds. It might have been smarter, safer to Transition out of there, but if we lost the *Orion*, what would the point be?

"Intercept Two," I croaked, as close as I could come to a bark, "on my command, link targeting with us and fire." A nod from Villanueva told me she was ready. "Three, two, one... fire."

The two proton cannons spoke as one, the beams collimating onto the exact same spot, near the center of the Resscharr starship. I'd just been trying to buy time for the *Orion* to recover, maybe knock the enemy back on their heels for a minute to build up our capacitors. I hadn't realized how close to the edge that gravitic defense shield was. When the proton beams struck home, the ragged, angry splotches of green turned red, expanding outward again... and then faded to nothing.

I stared at the thing for another few seconds, sure that this was a ruse to lure us in, that it would lash out again and shred both Intercepts to scrap metal, but the green halo had evaporated and with it a luster, a translucence. The Resscharr ship seemed dull, tarnished. Old. Unspeakably old, a relic of another time.

In the stunned shock of the moment, I'd forgotten about the Nova cruisers, and I jerked upright in my seat as if waking from a dream. They were nowhere to be found. That shouldn't have been a surprise. Our own momentum had been sucked away by the micro-Transition, dumped into the nothingness of T-space, and the Resscharr ship had no reaction drive of its own, its only propulsion the manipulation of gravity... and that had faded with its drive field. The Nova cruisers, though, were still burning in toward Homeworld at around two gravities, and they'd been accelerating for a while.

They'd passed us by in seconds and hadn't looked back, counting on the Resscharr ship to take care of us. I stabbed at the controls between Villanueva and Awori, bringing the view from the rear cameras up on the main screen. The remaining Nova ships had performed turnover, their fusion drive flares pointed at Homeworld, decelerating at high Gs, higher than a human could have taken without going unconscious. Burning away momentum quickly enough that they could perform orbital insertion without bouncing off into interstellar space.

"*Orion*, can you hear me?" I called. "What's your status?"

If we could get the ship back up and running, we had maybe two minutes left to winnow down their numbers before the enemy fleet was too close to the planet. The reply was a long time coming, and with each passing second hope slipped away. When Nance finally answered, his tone plunged the knife into any ideas I'd had about him coming to the rescue.

"We're driftwood for the moment. That shot we took separated both main power conduits *physically* from the reactor. Repairs are going to take hours. Whatever's gonna happen on the planet is gonna be over before we can get there."

Hours. *Shit*. All it would take was one of those cruisers

deciding to come back and finish us off and there'd be nothing we could do about it. We could *still* evacuate, go grab the Marines, and leave, but there was no guarantee we'd be able to Transition out of the system before the Nova caught up with us. I had to make the call.

"Nance, send a lander with an engineering crew and a couple Marines over to that Predecessor ship... send Lilandreth along too. Dwight, you and Lilandreth get our people aboard that ship and see if it's salvageable. Intercept Two, you stay out here and guard the *Orion* while she affects repairs."

"What are *you* gonna do, Alvarez?" Nance asked. "Like I don't already know."

"The space battle is in the hands of the Homeworlders now," I told him. "There's nothing more we can do for them out here. Our people are down there, and that's where I'm going." I smiled without humor. "I've spent hours now watching other people pull the trigger. My turn."

[28]

We couldn't beat the Nova back to the planet. I'd hoped we might be able to by micro-Transitioning in closer to the lunar orbit, but we were, perversely, too close for that, and I wasn't ready to risk the Lagrangian jump back in toward the planet after Villanueva explained why it was exponentially more dangerous to jump *in* to the point than it was to jump out.

All I could do was grit my teeth, endure the misery of a high-gravity burn, and watch the show. Homeworld had dozens of new suns, temporary though they might have been, as Nova ships hit the minefield. I hadn't honestly expected it to work, and I still didn't know how much damage the fusion warheads were doing, but they certainly *looked* spectacular.

"We're not going to hit those things, are we?" I asked Villanueva, straining the words out past the acceleration.

"*Theoretically*," she replied, "we have the transponder codes to keep them from arming when we pass. Depending on how honest with us the Grey were being." I must have made a face that matched the trepidation in my gut, because she laughed. "Don't worry. There's a lot of mines, but space is big and our sensors are pretty good. I'm more worried about those idiots on the ground firing missiles and cannons at us."

As if putting the lie to her words, a fusion explosion lit up the darkness so close to us that radiation warnings flashed at the side of the screen. Yellow, not red, which was better I suppose.

"It looks as if they're taking some damage," Awori said, peering at the screen. I didn't know how he could tell because the whole tactical display looked like a mass of white and red lens flares, but I guess there was a reason they spent all that money sending him to pilot's school. "There's four... six... no, *twelve* of them with their drives cutting off already. Gotta be injector damage from the radiation. I don't know how tough those octopus people are, but I wouldn't want to be the crew after that much exposure."

"How many does that leave?" I asked him.

"Just under two hundred. They're through the minefield now... engaging with the Grey gunships."

"I thought you were a copilot, Chad," Villanueva muttered, "not a play-by-play announcer."

"The commander wanted a report," Awori objected, sounding hurt. If the jab hurt his feelings, it didn't stop him from narrating what he was seeing on the screen. "Damn, those things are so small, I can barely pick them up on the sensors. I *think* they're firing at each other, but the Nova aren't using the main guns, so it's hard to tell. Shit's blowing up in there, but I can't tell who."

"I'm pretty sure it's those little suicide sleds the Grey are flying," Villanueva said. "Damn things look like they might blow up just igniting the engines, much less trying to take on something the size of a cruiser."

"Don't we need to start decelerating?" I asked, watching the planet get closer in the screen. There was some magnification, sure, but we'd been burning for a while now.

"We're gonna do a serious, high-G braking burn, take less time," she explained so calmly, as if the agony we'd be going through didn't faze her at all. "Those cruisers are still gonna be hanging out in high orbit, and I don't want to paint a target on our ass and hang it out in the wind for too long."

I couldn't have sworn how much time passed. It might have been an eternity, surely *felt* like one between the tension of the destruction and death of a battle I could barely see combined with the anticipation of the pain to come. The only way I could judge time was by the arc of the planet growing in the screen... and the continued march of the fleet. The Grey ships had performed about as well as General Patton had predicted, and I don't know why that disappointed me. He knew them better than I did.

Now it was his turn, but I wouldn't get to see it.

"Hold onto those rat bars," Villanueva warned me. "Turnover and eight gravity braking boost in three seconds."

I started to clench my teeth but made myself stop, knowing that would be a good way to break a couple off. Instead, I simply relaxed every muscle in my body. The drive cut off and free fall took over from the three-gravity boost, but only for the few seconds it took to spin the cutter end for end. Steering jets hammered against the hull and the view from the nose camera spun in streaks of blue and green and black that my brain couldn't untangle.

Not that it had the chance. The second the image stabilized into the blackness of space, the drive fired again and over six hundred kilos of mass crushed me into the gel padding of the acceleration couch. I'd seen plenty of cows in my experiences fighting on the colony worlds during the war, and this was just like having one of them sitting on my chest. I'd been in a lot of uncomfortable positions in my career, including getting burned right down to the bone more than once, but I think I would have taken any of those experiences over the braking boost. At least when I got burned, I had painkillers from my suit to take the edge off. Here, there was no relief.

Breath came in minute, agonizing gasps, a fight worse than any battle of the war, and my vision glazed over before narrowing into a black-fringed tunnel. I was seconds from passing out, and I wished to hell I'd get there because I really didn't need to be conscious for this. It wouldn't happen. God hated me, I decided, and wanted me to experience every microsecond of this shit.

Some people thought Hell was eternal flame, demons poking at damned souls with pitchforks, while others thought it was outer darkness, separation from God and utter loneliness forever. I knew better. Hell was an eight-gravity burn that lasted the rest of your life, and I was convinced that would be my fate. Then God showed mercy and darkness closed in...

... until there was light. Atmospheric blue rushed in through the main screens, the nose of the cutter glittering, bathed in sunlight, and blessed, heavenly air filled my lungs. I'd passed out.

"What's happening?" I asked, pushing myself straight in my acceleration couch. "Where are we?"

"Welcome back to the world, Sleeping Beauty," Villanueva said, the words teasing but the tone underlying them utterly grim. "You've been out for a few minutes, and they haven't been good ones. Show him, Chad."

Awori's fingers danced on his controls and a section of the screen showed a computer-enhanced view of high orbit. The twenty Confederation warships waited in five diamond formations, four vessels each, not attacking yet. The reason why streaked across the blackness, sleek and streamlined, dozens of them reaching up from below, out from orbital defense platforms. The missiles were huge, each probably carrying warheads in the multiple megatons.

Most didn't make it close to their targets. The Nova cruisers peppered the space around them with defensive missiles, their chainfire eruptions scattering something tiny and metallic, a starfield of sensor readings. Probably nothing more high-tech than ball bearings, but they were enough. Where the Homeworlder missiles struck the objects, warheads detonated in spheres of destruction, often taking out more of their own, or the weapons simply went off course, heading out into space, guidance systems destroyed.

The missiles that made it through the screen of metal chaff were annihilated by gouts of plasma from the main guns or torn apart by defensive turrets. I couldn't tell what they fired, but it wasn't showing up on thermal, which probably meant coilguns.

Most of the Homeworlder missiles were taken out, but not all. Soundless spheres of white consumed a handful of the cruisers because no defense was perfect, but the missiles expended themselves in minutes, leaving well over a hundred and fifty of the enemy vessels. Twenty fusion drives ignited as one, the Confederation ships surging forward still in a tight formation, well-trained and well-disciplined. The government might be run by a social media maven, but their military didn't show it.

More missiles, dozens of them, smaller this time, shorter-ranged and not as successful. Not a single one of them struck home, the defensive turrets doing their job once more. Something did though. Again, no thermal signature except the flares of burning gas where the hulls of the Nova cruisers were breached, and I had to think the weapons were railguns this time, powerful enough to penetrate that armor.

A few more of the enemy ships fell by the wayside, their

drives going dark, the huge shapes listing off to the side as the blasts of evacuated air from the gaps in their hull acted as maneuvering jets. A few, but not enough. Spherical shapes separated from curved niches in the armored skirts of the cruisers, falling toward the planet like seed pods. Too many and too far away to count, but it had to be a thousand.

Their load delivered, the Nova threw themselves into battle against those twenty Confederation ships, and the outcome was as predestined as the fate of the universe. More of the Nova died, but raging starfire swallowed up the Confederation ships one after another. The last two diamond formations tried to boost out of orbit, away from the assured destruction, but they might as well have been moving in slow motion.

The entire Homeworld space defense network had been obliterated in minutes.

I blinked at the sudden disappearance of the playback screen, the corner where it had been merging back into the larger forward view. Below us, the northern continent stretched in browns and greens. We were heading to Two Rivers. And so were those Nova landers. For some reason, maybe the lingering haze of the long, grueling deceleration, I'd expected the things to spread out like a meteor shower, but that made no military sense. A few hundred troops here, a few hundred there, scattered through different cities would accomplish nothing. They'd be defeated in detail, and if they killed thousands or even tens of thousands, the end result would be the Confederation and the Grey still in power.

The Confederation forces—and ours—were concentrated in Two Rivers, the Fed capitol. If the Nova destroyed them, took over the largest city on the planet, the seat of power, the war would be over. The Grey might throw bodies at them, but the Nova could send reinforcements through the gates at will. One decisive battle. For them, and for us.

"The Confederation will have air support," I told Villanueva, "but I don't know how much they'll be worth. I'm counting on you. Coordinate with the assault shuttles and tell the drop-ships I want them off the ground and out of the combat zone. I don't want to have to thumb a ride off this planet."

"Copy that, sir," she said, all business now. "Where do you want me to drop you?"

A yank on the quick release of my harness set me free from its bruising grasp, and I steadied myself on the back of the acceleration couch as I scrambled out of the cockpit.

"Where else?" I threw back over my shoulder. "In the shit."

"Drop!"

Easier said than done. It was one thing to fall out the belly hatches of a drop-ship designed for it, something totally different to lumber off the ramp of a hovering Intercept cutter. More of a jump than a drop, and while the Vigilantes were versatile, agile weapons platforms, they didn't jump, which meant I had to fall forward and hit the jets in time to keep from slamming belly-first into the boarding ramp.

The thermal updraft from the shimmering heat of the cutter's belly jets tossed my suit around, threatening to send me into a fatal tumble three hundred meters off the ground, and I bit down on a yelp. More power to the jump-jets stabilized my flight, and I took a moment to check on the others. There were only four of us in the command team. Top *should* have been one of them, but I didn't want to rob Vicky of his leadership, particularly since I planned on running point on this team.

Sgt. Ruddy was a good Marine, responsible and disciplined, but no great shakes as a leader in combat. Corporal Feeney and two PFCs, Rawlins and Xu, rounded out the little team, just enough to watch my back and fill in gaps in our lines. By some miracle, all of them made it out of the bird in one piece and into a V-formation with me at the head.

The peaks of skyscrapers rose above us as we descended, artificial mountains hiding us from view and hiding the enemy from ours, but I'd seen them on the way down. They were hard to miss—I just had to follow the wreckage in their wake. Confederation fighter jets had tried to take the things down, but burning swathes of charred debris on the streets below told the story of how well that had gone. One of them had crashed into the side of a fifty-story building and smoke poured out of the ragged gap in the huge structure. I wondered how many people had died in the impact. I wondered how many more would die before the day was out.

At the center of the destruction were the landers, silver spheres ringed at the bottom by a flat platform with the drive bell beneath it. They were ancient temples towering above the crass, commercial structures of Two Rivers, and they were so much larger than I'd imagined when I'd watched them showering down on the planet from the Nova cruisers. Each could have carried a full company of Drop Troopers, making them twice as big as our drop-ships. I'd have thought that would make them more vulnerable, that even the relatively primitive fighter jets of the locals could knock one of the things out of the sky, but the landers bristled with weapons, missile launch tubes and gun turrets, still firing even as smoke wafted from the landing jets. The scorched areas surrounding the spheres had once been parking lots, train stations, open-air markets, but they were ash now, and the ash was spreading.

Confederation military vehicles, APCs and main battle tanks, and others I had no specific word for rolled through the streets, nothing but bugs compared to the huge spacecraft. And the landers swatted them aside negligently, like the insects they resembled. Missiles and gunfire shattered pavement and left charred ruin and twisted, burning metal behind. The Feds had agreed to coordinate with us, to use their forces in conjunction with ours instead of throwing them into the fire, but orders got lost and soldiers panicked at the sight of the destruction of their city and responded quickly rather than intelligently.

We weren't going to go after those ships, not with just battle-suits. Our target was what was streaming out of those landers. They were humanoid in shape, though the scale was off. If one of the things had been my height, then the lander would have been no larger than an assault shuttle. I wasn't particularly good at math, but that should mean that each of the mecha was near to ten meters tall. There was a qualitative difference between these things and the Tahni mobile artillery pieces I'd encountered during the war though. Those were slow and shambling, meant for fire support, but these things had a smooth, agile gait to them, fast enough for direct combat.

These weren't the first off the boat, and I didn't have to look far afield to find the first clash between their forces and ours. Vicky was smart and she knew that engaging the things under the fire support arc from the landers would be a very bad idea, so she'd put a few skyscrapers between them and her chosen battlefield. Explosions and the flare of energy weapons on thermal showed the free-fire zone, and I angled toward it.

"Intercept One, you read me?" I called. The cutter was gone from sight, but I didn't know if Villanueva had gone over the horizon or simply dipped beneath the level of the skyline.

"Gotcha, sir."

At least the Confederation had satellites we could bounce signals off. For now.

"Get with Assaults One and Two and start taking out those damned landers. That's your priority."

"Copy that. Good luck, sir."

We were nearly at street level now, the silver and gray of the faceless buildings reflecting our image back at us, four hulking, muscular titans from myth descending from the land of the gods to fight among men. The vision should have made me feel more confident, but there were just us four among a sea of sterling metal, and instead I felt very alone.

We could have stayed in the air, but I didn't feel like flying headlong into enemy fire. I cut the jets a block over from the nearest of the fighting and waited for the others to form up behind me. The streets were empty, deserted, not a soul in sight, not so much as a pet or a scavenger bird. Did they have underground shelters here? Had they stuffed the civilians into the basements of the buildings, or were they just huddled in offices and apartments, praying to whatever gods they believed in that they'd get through this?

There'd been so many like them through the years, so many innocent people who didn't care about the politics, didn't care whatever interstellar conflict had caused all this. They just wanted to live, wanted everything to go back to normal, wanted their families and friends to be okay. Over and over, I'd seen the disbelief in their eyes, the deep, soul-crushing grief. And what I came away thinking every time was how grateful I was to be in my Vigilante, armored against reality, too cynical to believe in that fairy-tale happily ever after. We'd fought for those who couldn't, but more than that, I fought for the right to make my own destiny rather than let impersonal, faceless forces of history do it for me.

"Vicky," I called, pausing with my shoulder against the mirrored glass of a ground-level window. "You copy?"

Nothing. I hadn't expected it. Here in the artificial canyons of the city streets, there'd be no satellite view, no line-of-sight comms, and the Nova were sophisticated enough to be jamming all EM signals, including from drones. We were going in blind.

"All right, Marines," I said to the command team. "Follow me."

[29]

Chaos and old night.

That was what Dak Shepherd had called the confusion of battle, and I suppose he knew as well as anyone. He'd gone through two interstellar wars, lost everything important to him. It was an apt description of the carnage I walked into. *Ran* into, because it was better to move fast on death ground.

Data and sight and sound washed over me like the crash of the surf and I let it, grabbing only onto the important bits. The battlespace was less than a hundred meters across and over three klicks long, three city blocks as Two Rivers laid things out, and the enemy had walked into a trap, thanks to Vicky.

Well, as much of a trap as we could spring on nearly a hundred ten-meter-tall mecha. No other infantry. I'd expected support infantry, treating the mecha like armor. That's what I would have done, what the Commonwealth military would have done if they'd been stupid enough to invest their budget in a huge target like a mecha. Mecha made sense if they were used as mobile artillery like the Tahni, but as armor not so much, and as an infantry replacement not at all. They were about to find out why.

The Confederation Army had lots of armor, but it was all conventional, tracked main battle tanks with coilguns for their main armament, and Vicky had clustered them at the other end of the kill zone, layered and behind the cover of rows of what looked like cargo containers, oblong metal cylinders dumped in the street in chevron formation, end to end. Farther back were heavier weapons, artillery, and rocket launchers, and squeezed into the gaps were the infantry firing crew-served weapons.

That was the data, the points of information that stuck in the analytical part of my brain, trained and honed in eight years of war. The sound and the sight were the chorus of chaos. A single coilgun firing was a chest-deep thrum, an electric snap and the thundercrack of the round in a drumbeat rhythm. Two or three hundred of them firing at once was a symphony orchestra conducted by an untalented madman, the static discharge from the combined electromagnetic coils sizzling and crackling in the heavy, afternoon air. It should have been fatal, an unrelenting barrage that should have penetrated the thickest armor something the size of the Nova mecha could carry. It didn't.

The metallic slugs from the coilguns were invisible, moving at hypersonic speeds, but their effect was easier to see... where they deflected off to the sides, spearing fist-sized holes through the buildings flanking the battlefield. Something was deflecting them, a wall of crackling, wavering air like a heat mirage in the desert. Electromagnetic deflectors. The Nova were smarter than I thought. The deflectors made the mecha less inane as a primary ground weapon.

Their main guns made them even less inane. Raw plasma, just like their ships, though I doubted they were powered by antimatter, and where the ionized gas touched three or four of the Confederation tanks burst into flames, flipping backward as the pavement beneath them exploded with a violent release of steam. Missiles flashed out on firefly tails of red, streaking smoke, but the EM deflectors turned them just as easily as the coilgun rounds, sending them corkscrewing into the ground, into the buildings around them, sometimes into an arc far over their towering heads and backward to an unknown fate.

Realtime caught up with the delayed perception from the wash of information, smacking me in the face like I'd run straight into one of those pillar-like legs, each three meters around. I knew what was going to happen next because I knew Vicky, knew we thought the same way, knew it before the IFF transponders of a company full of Vigilantes showed up, dropping from the rooftops around us.

And I knew what I had to do to support her plan.

The mecha were massive but they weren't as heavily armored as the Tahni version, depending more on their deflector shields, designed to fight the threats they expected, not at all worried about the threat they were actually facing.

"Hit him low, Marines," I told the rest of the team, designating the rearmost of the mecha with my targeting laser. "I'll hit him high."

The mecha were in a staggered file, only the first few ranks having clear fields of fire, and if I'd been running the formation I'd have had them turned to the rear, guarding their six. Maybe they had sensors turned behind them and maybe they saw me coming... but their main guns were turned the wrong way.

I hit the jets between one stride and the next and the burst kicked me in the ass, carrying me up and forward... right onto the shoulders of the machine. Static electricity snapped and crackled between the skin of my suit and the metal of the mech, the EM field from its deflector dishes strong enough to raise the hair on my arms. The thing was humanoid but not human-shaped, so it didn't have a head, just a wedge-shaped mass of metal armor guarding what was inside... but it *did* have shoulder joints, because the arms couldn't move otherwise.

I jammed the muzzle of my weapon between the armor shrouds over the right shoulder joint and pulled the trigger. If it had been a projectile weapon, or even the plasma gun I'd had before the upgrade, the backblast might have blown the thing up and killed me in the process, but this energy cannon was a level up from that. Raw, actinic power came out of every seam in the armor and the sinuous, segmented arm blew off the side of the machine. It had to have weighed tons, and when it struck the pavement the concrete cracked beneath it... and the sudden lack of that much mass threw the thing off-balance, sending it stumbling forward.

It might have caught itself, kept on its feet, but Ruddy and the others were blasting away at the legs, and as I rocketed off the mecha's shoulder, one of them separated at the knee. The mecha toppled, crashing face down, and as it hit at least two dozen of the things turned back toward us.

That might have been it for me. I had mobility on the things, but twenty-some plasma guns firing at the same time would probably have nailed all of us, but I hadn't forgotten about those Vigilantes falling out of the sky on their jump-jets. It was Bravo Company, the new suits fabricated on Yfingam, and I worried for a fraction of a second that they would be useless, that the coilguns that were their main armament would be useless against the deflectors, but Vicky was smarter than that. They didn't even try to use them.

The Vigilantes were three meters tall, and when they dropped onto the mecha it was like toddlers attacking a grown man. But these toddlers were a little more dangerous. Armor-sheathed fists ripped into the metal skin of the mecha, shredding huge strips of it away and exposing the internals. Two of them per mecha, and when one stripped away the armor, the other fired into the gap with their coilgun. It was risky, firing it that close to the electromagnetic projectors, but it worked. One after another, mecha seized up, some of them collapsing but others freezing into statues.

The right thing for me to do as a commander would have been to step back and watch the scenario unfold, but in the moment I wasn't the commander—Vicky was. I was a Marine, a grunt with only four others people in my team, and I reveled in the freedom of it. Bravo Company was keeping a handful of the mecha busy, but more important to us, they were distracting the entire enemy force.

Giving us an opening.

"Left," I barked on the command team net and led by example, loping around the left edge of the Nova perimeter. "Fire at the legs!"

I didn't know what exactly those energy cannons fired, but I knew whatever it was, it wasn't going to be deflected by the Nova deflectors. Flashes of blue lightning punched through the heavy armor over the legs of the mecha as we lumbered past them, painfully slow in my eyes but far faster than the machines or the pilots inside them could follow. Ten-meter-tall golems crashed to the ground, their supports kicked out from beneath them, and fifty tons of heavy metal shook the pavement with their impacts.

Plasma beams sought us out, and if their own people blocked the shot, it didn't stop the Nova from trying anyway. The air heated up around us as lances of fire cascaded in every direction, and all it would take was one of those shots just coming close to us and we'd be cooked. But through the carnage, Vicky led Alpha Company, descending from the rooftops on the other side of the street.

That would have been the hardest part for me, waiting up there with them, watching Bravo take the hits until just the right moment to jump in, but Vicky was always more calculating than I was in battle. She timed it just right. Not one of the mecha looked up, and when energy blasts started raining down from above, the Nova armor was caught flat-footed. It was a slaughter after that. For all that I'd worried myself sick over the mecha, the Nova had a bigger problem than technology. They didn't know how to fight a war.

The last shots were still finishing off the remnants when Vicky landed beside me, Top and Springfield flanking her.

"Casualties?" I asked her, looking around and checking the IFF but finding no dead. Top answered for her, like any good senior NCO.

"No KIA. No serious WIA either. Got a couple burns but nothing they can't fight through."

"What's the sitrep up there?" Vicky asked, no trace of sentimentality here on the battlefield.

"*Orion* is disabled," I told her, "but they can repair her, and I hope to hell she can make it back here, because there's not much left of the Homeworlders past low orbit and even if we win down here, there's nothing to stop the Nova ships up there from bombarding this fucking city."

As if on cue, jet engines thundered overhead and explosions shook the ground from kilometers away, smoke billowing past the tops of the surrounding buildings. I gestured upward.

"We got air support, but I tasked them with taking out the Nova landers. The damned things are sitting there like weapons installations, blasting everything that comes near on the ground."

"Speaking of air support, where's *theirs*?" Vicky wanted to know. "I haven't seen any shuttles, any fighters, nothing except those landers." She paused and I heard her bark orders over the command net. "Springfield, take Alpha and get back on the rooftops. They're going to be sending more troops to recon the area and see what happened to these poor bastards, and I want to know their disposition. Top, you go with Bravo and set up a perimeter three blocks out. These damned big-ass goofy things better not sneak up on us, or *somebody* is going to get demoted!"

The Marines scattered to carry out her commands, Alpha jetting back out almost immediately.

"Think about it," I told her, answering her original point. "Who the hell did they have to fight except the Homeworlders? If we hadn't been here, what would have happened?"

I couldn't see her face, but I heard the note of realization in her voice and knew the expression that went with it.

"They would have wiped them out. It wouldn't have even been close. The mecha could burn down anything they threw against it, especially with those shields."

"They don't know what they're up against," I agreed. "And maybe it's unsporting of me, but I'd like to take advantage of that while we can. We need to go punch them in the nose and let them know this isn't gonna be as easy as they thought it would. It might be the only way to get them to withdraw before we start getting serious civilian casualties."

"They're your Marines, Cam. And so am I."

I grinned. I hadn't imagined the challenge in that statement. Vicky loved me, but that didn't mean she was crazy about giving up command in a battle.

"Don't worry, you're still the ground commander. I'm having too much fun running around like a sergeant again. I'm going up over the top with Alpha. You take Bravo and circle west around the Nova landing site. Make sure you don't get caught in the airstrike corridor."

"And do what?" she demanded, motioning at Bravo as they scurried into position at the intersections of the road. "The coil-guns won't do shit unless we're right on top of them. And like you said, the Fed weapons are worse than useless."

"You and I know that," I agreed. "But the Nova don't. I want to keep it that way." I glanced behind us, saw the commander of the Confederation ground forces driving up in an armored vehicle, soot covering his face where it was exposed beneath his helmet. "And I know just how to pull it off."

[30]

A wild thunderstorm across the plains of Hausos. That was what the scene unfolding below us reminded me of. Intercept One and the two assault shuttles punched holes in the sky, the sonic booms of their passage warring with the thunderstrikes from proton cannon shots. Except of course, during a Hausos thunderstorm, the ground had never fired back at the lightning.

A dozen of the Nova landers burned fiercely, their spheres collapsed like broken eggs in a carton, but eye-searing plasma flashed across the sky from the rest of them, filling every square centimeter with fire, as if they thought they could bring the attacking spacecraft down with sheer volume. And they might have, God knows. There were hundreds of the things, and if they didn't put up their own air support, it might have been because they didn't think they'd need it.

So far our ships had avoided the return fire, but the Confederation fighter jets weren't so fortunate, one of the dagger-shaped planes tumbling out of the sky every few seconds. Their impacts seemed miniscule against the hellish outpouring of energy from the landers, but I winced at every one of them.

"Jesus H. Christ, sir," Springfield hissed, staring out at the scene as if it were an interactive art piece in a museum. *The End of the World Imagined.* "We're going into *that?*"

"No," I corrected her, pointing just south of the devastation, where columns of mecha were tromping through the streets as if the fire and destruction meant nothing to them. "They're gonna come to us."

The bait was out there, three klicks away from the front of the enemy lines. The Fed colonel, who the translator had informed me was named *Goes Quietly to the Task*, hadn't been very happy about the assignment I'd given him, not after the casualties his people had taken during the ambush, but he'd done it anyway. Lacking any connection to Dwight since the *Orion* was out of comm range and Intercept One dashed in and out of line-of-sight, I'd given the colonel my own nickname and dubbed him *Tasker*.

Colonel Tasker was a brave man, leading from the front, even though his command car was lightly armored compared to the tanks. I supposed it didn't matter, though, given that the plasma guns on those mecha could burn through either of them in seconds. He'd spread his tanks out on either side of the street, and I wondered for a second why the capitol city in a nation where they had aircars had such broad avenues. Maybe the aircar thing was a recent development and the cities had been built to accommodate ground transportation. They had plenty of room for tank battalions though, and the vehicles dutifully followed their orders despite what had to be a horrifying knowledge of how useless their weapons would be.

"Sucks being bait," Springfield said, following my gesture.

But they did their job well. Dozens of coilguns spoke as one, joined by flights of missiles and even a few lasers. The energy weapons were large and cumbersome, their focus mirrors fragile, and they were kept at the rear of the formation, but they were also the only thing the Confederation had that could touch those mecha. This far away, I could actually make out the metal slugs veering away from the deflector shields, tiny dots against the gray haze of the smoke-filled sky, and the missiles might as well have been fireworks launched for a city-wide celebration for all the good they did.

But the lasers were impressive. Their beams were visible as arcs of crackling red through the smoke, setting the particulates in the air afire with their passing, and even more visible where they struck the leading Nova mechs. Metal smoked and melted and sublimated away from the chest armor on the giant machines, and here and there a handful faltered under the focused barrage, the beam finding either some vital system or killing the pilot.

Both the coilguns and the lasers had a longer range than the Nova plasma weapons, but I knew the return fire was coming, the long legs of the mecha eating up distance by the tens of meters.

"It does," I agreed with Springfield's assessment, "but we're gonna make sure they don't pay for it." A flick of my forefinger on the control switched nets to the general company frequency. "Alpha, we're coming down at the rear of the enemy formation. Do *not* get between the two elements. Maybe your armor would stop a coilgun round from those tanks and maybe it wouldn't, but I don't want blue-on-blue casualties. We're going get low and stay below ten meters just in case those landers take a shot at us. Follow me in."

Stepping off the edge of a seventy-story building was something I'd never get used to, but I couldn't show hesitation in front of my Marines. *Not* hitting the jump-jets immediately took even more willpower, and I flashed back to Brigantia, where all of this had really begun, to plunging out of the sky and into the utter darkness of that lake. No cushioning water below this time though, just hard, unyielding pavement. I let it get way too close, barely fifty meters before I ignited the thrusters, the sudden, upward boost clacking my teeth together, and I could have sworn the soles of the suit's feet pads scraped the pavement before I started climbing.

We were at the edge of the city center, the border of the skyscrapers of the business district and the factories and warehouses of the industrial zones, and I'd just jumped off the last of the cover between us and the landers... and the mecha. No cover meant my only shelter was movement, and the fastest method of movement was the jets. I couldn't have done it a few months ago, not without the things overheating in seconds, but now I skimmed the ground, almost parallel to it, momentum keeping me airborne.

The IFF readout told me that the rest of Alpha Company was following, right behind Ruddy and my command team. Mansfield was running point for the rest of the company, and if I knew the man, he resented me for being out front. Warning flashes in my HUD made me wish I'd let him go first, ricocheting coilgun slugs and out-of-control missiles passing by only meters away. There was nothing I could do, no sure way to evade the random weapons, so I just prayed and kept going, trusting to God and luck and whatever had gotten me through the last ten years alive.

The hand of fate must have still been hanging over me, because none of the shit tumbling through the air hit anything but the ground and a few parked aircars, but what worried me even more than the possibility of being hit by unaimed friendly ordnance was the very real chance of being targeted by enemy weapons. The mecha were in the same sort of offset file formation they'd used before, their weapons and attention all turned forward, marching ever closer. I was a hundred meters to the side of their formation and ten ranks deep when they opened fire on the tank column.

Plasma so bright it outshone the afternoon sun cast long shadows in every direction, like a sign from God that I'd waited long enough. Flying parallel to the ground with the jump-jets was hard enough—firing sideways and trying to hit anything simultaneously was a few degrees of difficulty higher on the spectrum. I did it anyway. There was no hiding after that, no possibility of laying low or sneaking up on them. Energy bursts fanned out like searchlights and mecha shook, stumbled, fell as their legs took multiple hits, not just from my gun but from the Marines following me.

I only had a vague impression of the mecha toppling from the view at the edge of my HUD. The helmet could record video in 360 degrees from the cameras that ringed it, but I could pay attention to just so much at once, and there were more pressing matters ahead of me than behind. The column of enemy armor was hundreds deep, well over four klicks long, and the ones in the rear saw us long before we reached them.

I couldn't say how exactly I knew when to shift course. Maybe it was my subconscious mind paying more attention to the edges of my perception than I realized, or maybe it was an internal clock built from years of practice. Whatever it was yelling in my ear, I listened to it, changing my trajectory with a wild swing of arms and legs, shifting my center of gravity and angling the jump-jets downward.

My suit arced over the top of the file, squared-off shoulders and wedge-shaped heads below me, marching legs stomping cracks in the pavement, heavy plasma cannons stretched out along the right arm of the machines, thick cables tying the weapons to the bulge on the backs where I assumed the reactors were. They were ridiculously oversized toy soldiers matching step, and it almost seemed shameful to disrupt their rhythm by blasting down from above.

As much as I could, I targeted their weapon-bearing arms,

determined to keep them from shooting back even if I couldn't completely disable them. Over the top, another ten ranks passing by in a dull gray blur, and again I didn't know if I'd hit or how much effect the hits had. I just knew the others were following me and it was more important I provide a good example than work on my marksmanship.

Over the top, down the other side, and if I'd been in one of those mecha, I would have ignored the suits flying directly above me and concentrated on shooting the next few in line, but these weren't Marines. Hell, not only were they not humans, they weren't even that *humanoid*, other than being bipedal with bilateral symmetry and stereoscopic hearing and vision. God alone knew what a sentient octopus thought or how they trained their military. Plasma drowned out all sunlight, washed out even the radiant pulses from the energy cannons, but none of it touched me. IFF transponders blinked yellow, and in a couple cases red, showing damage, injuries, probably burn-throughs, but none flickered black. No direct hits, no deaths.

I shot from the other side, with the company still stretched over the top and back around the opposite flank, and the ranks of mecha no longer resembled a marching file of soldiers so much as a panic-stricken gaggle. Their guns turned in all directions, firing blindly, in a few cases shooting their own mecha, stirring enough confusion that I indulged in another pass around the rear of their lines.

Just as I passed the halfway point of their ranks, Vicky and Bravo took to the air, making a short hop from the next street over, just enough to be visible. Our half company had cut their numbers by a third in seconds, and now a full-sized complement was coming their way from the other side and *they* didn't know that Bravo only had coilguns.

That was it. That was enough, and all sense of cohesiveness vanished. They ran, not an organized withdrawal but a rout. We kept shooting, cutting down more of them as they fled, not wanting to let them think about it, definitely not wanting to give them the option of changing their mind.

"Hold up here!" I yelled, not because the system wouldn't amplify my voice to be heard but because I wanted the sharpness of the words to penetrate the bloodlust that always rose up when the enemy ran. "Do *not* pursue!"

A flight of missiles arced over my head and I turned sharply, staring back at the Confederation forces.

"Cease fucking fire!" I told them, remembering to shift frequencies. "You shoot one of us, I'm gonna come back there and kick somebody's ass." I wasn't sure if they heard me or not since they didn't acknowledge, but the coilguns and missile launchers stopped shooting.

Bravo Company touched down across the road, in the lee of a burning warehouse, the flames rippling across its roofline, black smoke a smudge against the sky. Vicky and Top had a handle on them and the Vergai volunteers spread out behind cover, or such cover as a three-meter-tall battlesuit could find here. Springfield didn't me to tell her how to handle Alpha either, spreading them along this side of the avenue, tucked into gaps in buildings and on rooftops.

Me, I stood in the middle of the street like an idiot, walking through the center of the downed mecha and watching the enemy regroup. We'd taken down at least fifty of them, damaged more, but there were still hundreds gathered a few klicks away, partially obscured by the wreckage of the buildings the landers had smashed to bits or burned to cinders when they'd come down. They were counting on the cover of their ships' guns to keep us from coming after them, and they were right about that.

An assault shuttle ripped a chunk out of the sky and a proton beam flashed out into one of the landers, blowing a ragged, glowing hole in the side, but there were dozens more of those, as well.

"Casualty report," I told Springfield.

"We have seven damaged suits," she said immediately. I'd given her time to get the data together, and she'd done it without prompting. "Two of them with burn-throughs. Griner and Wolf." I knew the names, could picture the faces. Corporals, both of them. "Serious injuries but not fatal. They can hold out until we get them back to the *Orion*'s med bay, but if they're hit again, they're dead. The rest are minor, nothing that can't wait."

"Post the two burn-throughs on a rooftop overwatch and tell them to stay there unless ordered to move."

"Already did, sir,"

Smart. She deserved the company, and I hoped when we got back that someone would recognize her leadership abilities the way we had.

"We knocked them on their heels," Vicky said, picking her way through the ruin of dozens of Nova mecha to stand beside me. "But the numbers are against us here, Cam. Eventually, they're gonna realize that and just wade back in with their entire force and wipe out the Confederation army troops. All we'll be able to do is snipe at them from the edges. Or maybe they'll get *real* smart and cagey and just hold up under the cover of their landers and dare us to come do something about it."

I sighed, looking from the far end of the road and the shifting silhouettes of mecha down to the broken and burnt machines scattered around us. One of the cockpits had split wide open, the ragged edges charred and smoking, and inside was the first of the Nova I'd seen close up. In person he looked even more alien than the ones I'd seen on the main screen of the *Orion*, his arms and legs less rigid here in death, more like the boneless tentacles they'd evolved from. Just one per mecha then. Individual pilots. I'd thought perhaps they might be drones and wondered why they weren't, whether there was some religious proscription as with the Tahni, or an ethical one based in their history, as was the case with the Commonwealth.

"You're right," I told Vicky. "But I don't know what else to do. Our only real choice is to hold them off until the *Orion* gets repaired." Which could be *hours* more...

"Alvarez." The voice was Nance's, and I almost replied until it continued, not giving me the chance. "Don't bother answering, I'm a good ten light-minutes away and I'm not looking to have a conversation. Just do as I say. Get you people together and under cover and make sure Intercept One and the assault shuttles clear the area around the landing site." I couldn't see his face but I could hear the grin. "And you might want to tune into the Nova laser comms frequency. The show's about to start."

[31]

"What the hell was he *talking* about?" Vicky demanded.

She'd left her position in the street beside me, instead following Nance's directive to get her Marines under cover. Springfield had done the same and I checked her work on IFF, making sure she'd pulled the lookouts off the rooftops just in case. Getting ahold of our air assets had taken a few minutes, but they'd obeyed my order and broke off engagement, patrolling a wide circle around the city.

"You heard the same thing I did," I replied, trying to find the settings for the Nova comm frequencies. It wasn't easy since they, like the Confederation, mostly used direct laser communications. "Whatever it is, I hope they hurry up. Without air cover, we're sitting ducks."

"Captain Alvarez, this is Colonel Tasker. Our orbital sensors are picking up something entering the upper atmosphere."

"Is it one of our ships?" I asked him, brightening. Maybe Nance had cut loose Intercept Two and sent it to back us up.

"Can your ships slow from relativistic speeds to nearly a standstill in less than ten thousand kilometers?"

A chill traveled up my spine as the implications of what he'd said sank in. I didn't have time to reply because it appeared in the sky overhead almost immediately, just a green glow at first. I couldn't make out the shape, but I knew it was a flat-ended cylinder, a cigar shape.

"How the hell?" Vicky murmured. "Didn't you say it was destroyed?"

"Disabled," I corrected her absently, staring at the thing as it descended like a meteor. I was sure it would crash into the city, adding another level of devastation to the tragedy, but it stopped as if by magic, the green halo flaring brighter at the exertion.

It stopped at a dead hover, not even bobbing with spent momentum, only a hundred meters above the ground. Silent, waiting like a sign from God, a pillar of cloud in the daytime, a pillar of fire at night.

God spoke.

"My children of the Nova," the voice said, though it spoke in English, "this is not what we wished for you."

An image filled the air around the ship, projected somehow onto nothing, no holotank required, the face of a Resscharr. The face of *Lilandreth*. And when she spoke again, I didn't hear it through my headphones. It wasn't exactly a loudspeaker, didn't conduct through the air. It was as if she was standing right beside my shoulder, whispering to me, to me personally, privately, in my own language. I wondered if that was what the Nova were experiencing... and if they'd buy it.

"I am Lilandreth of the Resscharr, and I say to you that this is not your destiny. We wish peace for all our children, and all you will accomplish here is senseless slaughter."

There was no reply for almost thirty seconds. Nothing stirred, even the mecha stock still as if the machines were staring upward along with the sentient beings inside them. When the Nova answered, it was on their laser comm network, and something bounced it back to me. I had a sense that the Resscharr ship was responsible, that Lilandreth was looping me into the conversation.

"I command these forces," the Nova said, even the translation sounding inhuman. "We were attacked without provocation, our cruiser destroyed, our people killed. You say you're of the Predecessors. If you are, we have waited eons for your return, for the blessing of your wisdom. How would you have us respond to such aggression?"

"I would have you discover the truth before you resort to open warfare, my children. What has happened has been a deception, an effort by an individual who wished power for herself. If you would have justice rather than vengeance, you will demand the woman known as Frost be delivered to you for judgement... and then you will make peace. This is my wisdom. Will you heed it?"

The projection of Lilandreth's face was replaced by security footage from the *Orion*, showing the Confederation contingent breaking out of the Ops Center, showing their military officers overpowering the duty crew in the docking bay and boarding their shuttle. Showing that shuttle dip below the belly of the *Orion* and fire the missile at the Nova cruiser.

Then the recording changed to the face of Bob, earnest and ashamed.

"My name," he said, "is Driftwood Floating Lazily at the Shore, and I was working as an asteroid miner when the Commonwealth ship *Orion* arrived in our system. I helped them understand our government and our society in preparation for them approaching us with the proposal for the agreement to trade their Transition Drive plans for our knowledge of the Predecessors. They trusted me, but when Ms. Frost approached me, offering me a job so that I could take care of my parents, I betrayed them. I helped Ms. Frost's representatives out of their locked compartment, and then I could only watch as they attacked the Nova cruiser the Commonwealth was trying to negotiate with. I can only offer my humble apologies both to the Nova and to my friends on the *Orion*."

Once the recording ended, Lilandreth's image returned, passive, patient.

Again, the wait was long, long enough that I wondered if the Nova commander was consulting with someone in orbit or maybe even passing a message back through the jumpgate. But that would probably take an hour, and the answer came in two or three minutes.

"We will withdraw our troops from the city and remain in orbit. If the guilty one is delivered to us within twenty hours, we will make peace. If not, we will return and there will be nothing left of this city but ash."

I wasn't sure when it had happened, but a grin had spread across my face and it wouldn't go away.

"Dwight, you did this, didn't you?"

"Oh, yes, Cam," the AI replied, though in my helmet headphones rather than as a voice coming out of thin air. "This ship is quite amazing and very nearly self-repairing. We just had to get aboard and have a little talk with the crew."

I shook my head.

"This I gotta hear."

"You are... a Predecessor?" Tasker asked hesitantly, staring up at Lilandreth, eyes wide. "One of the race who built the jumpgates?"

I shot the Resscharr a look, hoping she'd understand the message behind it. *Keep it simple.*

"Yes. I am of a mission sent to another place, and I am returning to my people with the help of the humans."

She hadn't attempted to take a seat in the office because none of the furniture suited her, but she showed no indication that standing for the two hours we'd waited had been any hardship. Me, I was about to fall dead asleep. Between the stress of the high-G maneuvering on Intercept One and the battle, I barely fought back utter exhaustion, and I wasn't going to be standing anywhere for long with the smart bandages wrapped around my right leg from ankle to knee.

I hadn't even realized I'd had the burns until I got out of the suit. There were black, blistered chars on the leg of the Vigilante, sure, but that was par for the course. No Drop Trooper came out of a battle without their suit covered with scars. I suppose I hadn't realized how powerful the mecha plasma guns were or how far away one of their blasts could be and still do damage.

I *really* could have used an auto-doc, but those were all on the *Orion* and I didn't have the luxury of shuttling up there at the moment. Vicky was out taking charge of the Marines, guarding the Predecessor starship. Not that anything the Feds had could touch it, nor could they just step into the cockpit and fly it out of here, but it made everyone feel better to have a guard around the thing. The *Orion* and both Intercepts were in high orbit, keeping an eye on the Nova ships, and just the fact that the Nova hadn't attacked them on sight was an indicator of how different they were from humans. If our ships had been within shooting distance of an enemy who'd killed thousands of our people and destroyed dozens of our vessels, I doubt we could have trusted ourselves not to try a sucker punch.

That meant that everyone else was busy and this duty fell to me. And Lilandreth. She had to be here because the Nova commander was on his way, and I had my doubts that we could pull this off without her to convince him we were serious. I still didn't know his name. He hadn't volunteered it, and I wondered if they even *had* names. Sure, every non-human society we'd come across had individual names, but they were also all descendants of humanoid life that had evolved on Earth. I tried to imagine a society where no one had a name and how that would work and only succeeded in giving myself a headache.

Tasker kept eyeing Lilandreth sidelong, as if he didn't feel comfortable being in the same room as her, but most of his attention was on his tab. There were three other Fed soldiers in the conference room with us, lined up beside the door, ostensibly as guards, though for whom and *against* whom wasn't clear. They had their rifles slung over their shoulders and had spent most of their time screwing around with their tabs. Normally, I would have had the former NCO's instinct to chew them out for being inattentive, but I was gonna let it slide this time. Their expressions weren't bored or amused... they were troubled. That was what I'd been hoping for. I said nothing to them, instead digging further into what Dwight and Lilandreth had told me earlier.

"How long ago was it?" I asked, looking at the Resscharr but knowing that Dwight would jump in if he saw fit. "How long ago did the Nova have contact with the Predecessors?"

"Near the beginning," she told me. "Ten thousand years ago." Lilandreth cast a baleful eye at Tasker, as if he was a representative of all the Homeworlders. "It's a good thing for these people that the Nova are like us, a slow and cautious species, not breakneck and headlong, else they would have adapted more of the technology that was left to them. Instead, they used merely what they thought they needed as they needed it."

"I wonder," Dwight interjected, and if he had a chin, I'd have pictured him rubbing it, "whether that may be the reason the Predecessors trusted the Nova to guard this approach to their realm... the fact that they needn't consider them a threat to their supremacy."

"Guard this approach?" I repeated, a frown tugging at the corners of my eyes. "Guard it from whom?"

"From *us*, I would imagine," Lilandreth said quietly. I was going to ask her what she meant, but I didn't have the chance.

Someone knocked on the door and the guards looked up from their tabs, stiffening as if they'd been caught goofing off. They exchanged a look with each other and one of them pulled the door open. I have to be honest, I couldn't tell a Grey from a Fed, not by clothes or features or mannerisms, but this particular one I'd already met, though I didn't know his name. He was the same intelligence officer who'd been in charge of watching Spinner, and I hoped he didn't know that the scientist had defected to our side, because that would make things awkward.

"I am," the man said gravely, "Colonel Graves. I was called here as a representative for my government."

And maybe it was just a coincidence that the *only* representative the Grey had handy for this was a military intelligence officer, but I had to think it said something about the relationship between the two governments. Or maybe something about the nature of the Grey, and it served as a reminder that no matter how corrupt I'd found the Feds, that didn't mean the Grey were any better.

"I'm Captain Alvarez," I told him. "Sorry if I don't get up." I gestured to my leg. "Have a seat."

The table was oval and polished bone white. It might have *been* bone, for all I knew, though I imagined it was probably marble, but the supports beneath it were clearly some sort of tusk or horns from animals we hadn't yet encountered. The chairs were upholstered with what felt like real leather, and I pondered how many millions of dollars the furniture would be worth back on Earth. Graves made no comment about the accommodations or my lack of decorum, just sat down across from me, his expression in line with the nickname Dwight had given him through the translation.

"My government is not happy about this situation," he told us. "The actions taken by Ms. Frost have endangered this entire planet and led to the deaths of thousands of colonists on the Glen. I find it even more disturbing that I've come here only to find no one of greater rank in your government than a colonel."

"I've been assured," Tasker told him, squirming under the harsh glare from Graves, "that there are others on the way."

"Don't worry, Colonel Graves," I told him. "I think you're going to be glad you came."

There was no knock this time. There wouldn't be. Frost burst through the door, her expression as dark and stormy as the proverbial night, flanked by General Patton and a pair of junior officers, each of them carrying handguns in chest holsters.

"Alvarez, what the fuck do you think you're trying to pull?" I didn't know what the words sounded like in her language, but Dwight's translation sure captured the tone. She slapped a palm on the table, ignoring Graves, even ignoring Lilandreth. "Do you *really* think you can take me down with your cheap theatrics?" She waved a hand around us demonstratively. "This is *my* battlefield, Marine, not yours. And in *this* nation, the people of the Confederation make the choices, not you!"

"Yeah," I acknowledged, still not getting up. "The people. And I'm sure you've been putting that gift I gave you to good use, haven't you?" I motioned at the tab still in Tasker's hand. The fact he hadn't bothered to put it away when she'd entered *should* have been a warning, but she hadn't noticed. When she saw it, she grinned broadly.

"Why, yes, I have, and I should thank you again for the generous donation."

"Cam," Vicky said, her voice a private mutter in my earbud,

"they're here. I have Top bringing them in along with an escort, out of their armor."

Now I finally did stand, moving to the door and pulling it open as the Fed soldiers stared between Frost and me. Master Sergeant Czarnecki walked through, a pulse carbine slung over his chest, and he eyed the armed Fed soldiers suspiciously as he stepped to the side, between them and the door.

Two more Drop Troopers came through behind him, both of them Vergai recruits. I couldn't remember their names, but I could always tell the Vergai by the lack of 'face jacks in their temples. We didn't have the equipment to implant them out here, so they were forced to use neural halos in the suits.

And behind them came the Nova. Four of them, the commander and his escort, and if they'd been creepy on video, standing face to face with them made the hair on the back of my neck stand on end. It wasn't their appearance. I'd been prepared for that, though seeing their purplish, slimy skin made my gut clench. I *should* have been prepared for the lack of clothes, though it did freak me out a little that they didn't seem to have any genitalia or distinguishing sexual characteristics at all. It wasn't even the smell, though that part I *hadn't* been prepared for. They smelled fishy, not like living near the shore but more like shoving myself headfirst into a cooler full of fresh catch, and that was enough to turn my stomach.

What got to me most was the way they moved. They weren't invertebrates like actual octopuses—at some point in their evolution, they'd developed a skeleton. But they retained something of that squishy, boneless motion and the juxtaposition was psychologically jarring, the most alien thing of all the alien things about them. That and their Goddamned fingers, which did *not* have bones and were constantly in motion, wriggling like tube worms at some underwater volcanic vent.

"Which one of you is the commander?" I asked, counting on

the speaker pinned to my jacket to translate it into the local language, which the things understood.

The one who'd been at the rear of the five shuffled forward with that eerie, squishing motion. When he spoke, the sounds were squeaking, gurgling, like nothing I'd ever heard, but just behind them a voice in the language of the Confederation came from a blue box affixed to his harness.

"I am."

Great. We were having a conversation in a language neither of us spoke running through two separate translation programs and talking through two external speakers. What could go wrong?

"Do you have a name?" I wondered. "An individual designation? I'm Cameron Alvarez, the commander of the Commonwealth forces here. What are you called?"

"I'm called commander." His deadpan face matched the neutral tone of the translation. "No other designation would be meaningful to you. I've come here to take possession of the one responsible for this conflict." His flat, dark eyes were hard to follow, but he turned toward Frost. "That would be you, Homeworlder."

Frost's sneer was admirably cold and defiant in the face of the aliens.

"Then you've come for nothing. We have a tradition here of yielding only to the vote of our citizens, not the whims of alien oppressors. General, have your soldiers arrest these enemies of the Confederation."

Patton regarded her silently for long seconds before sighing.

"I'm afraid I can't do that, ma'am." He pulled a tab from his belt and held the screen up for her. "There's been a vote. The people have spoken." Patton nodded to his subordinates. "Take her into custody."

The junior officers pulled their handguns and trained them

on the woman, one of them producing a pair of restraints. For the first time since I'd met her, Frost didn't seem in control. The color drained from her face and she stared not at the armed soldier, but at me.

"The computer," she hissed in realization.

"Among my people," I told her as the soldier slipped the cuffs over her wrists, "we have a saying for situations like this."

I shoved her toward the Nova commander, wondering what punishment they had in store for her and deciding I didn't care.

"Beware of Greeks bearing gifts."

[32]

"This could have been a hell of a lot worse."

I nodded, though I didn't look away from the window. The observation bubble was the only place on the ship that anyone could actually look out into space with their own eyes rather than having the view filtered through the external cameras, enhanced by computers. I didn't come here that often because the transparent aluminum dome wasn't left unshielded except when our situation was totally secure. And how often did *that* happen?

There was something satisfying, though, about seeing the world as it was, not how some computer thought it should look. From the bubble, Homeworld's moon seemed farther away than it had appeared on the main viewscreen of the *Orion*, the departing Nova ships barely visible at all beyond the faint glow of miniature stars that were their fusion drives.

The Predecessor starship was damn close though, so close I felt like I could reach right through the dome and touch it. I'd been shocked when they let us keep it... though not as shocked after Dwight and Lilandreth had explained to me how they'd come to have it in the first place.

"The Predecessors actually gave them one of their ships?" I'd asked once the Nova had left with Frost in tow. "Isn't that like giving a loaded gun to a toddler?"

It had been, perhaps, a little rude to talk about the matter in front of the Confederation military officers and Colonel Graves, but I'd about had my fill of the whole planet by that point.

"The Reconstructors gave it to them," Lilandreth had explained with a touch of amusement in her tone, "because it's broken." My mouth must have been hanging open, because she elaborated. "It can't enter Transition Space. Obviously the gravitic drive and weapons still function, but the only way it can travel between systems is via the wormhole jumpgates. I believe the jumpgate network was yet to be created at the time, though the Nova weren't totally clear on that."

"I'm surprised you got the crew to talk."

"They had no concept of operational security," Dwight had told me. "Nor of deception in general. Once they saw Lilandreth, it was difficult to shut them up."

Lilandreth was alone on the Resscharr ship, and I wondered if she planned on staying in there the whole journey.

"We didn't lose anybody," I told Vicky, though I wasn't sure if I was agreeing or disagreeing with her. "Lots of injuries, on the *Orion* and down with the Marines..."

"Including *you*," she reminded me, arm slipping through mine.

"Including me," I agreed, "but no fatalities. Could have been a hell of a lot worse, all right. It was worse for the people in Two Rivers."

The final tally had been five thousand dead, most of them in the military. Whatever their other failings, the Confederation had a good system of civilian shelters and a healthy sense of self-preservation.

"Frost got what she deserved, I hope." Vicky's lip curled in a snarl. "Having Dwight hack the quantum core to sabotage her propaganda campaign was a stroke of genius, by the way. My compliments."

"I knew you'd approve." I grinned aside at her. "And I knew she wouldn't be able to resist it."

"Alvarez, you done rubbernecking?" It was Nance, of course. Even if no one else knew where we were, Nance would. "We're going to be micro-Transitioning to the jumpgate in a few minutes, and I'd rather not get puke all over my observation bubble."

I sighed, then slapped the control to close the shielding over the transparent aluminum.

"We'll be right up," I told him, not trying to keep the annoyance out of my voice.

"He does that shit on purpose, you know," Vicky told me as we squeezed through the narrow hatchway back into the access passage. "Nance, I mean. He knows you're in charge, but he wants to remind you whose boat this is."

"I know. But as long as it keeps him happy."

The passageway from the observation bubble back into the crew quarters was long and, for most people who didn't make their living inside a Vigilante, claustrophobic, since it had to be sealed whenever the ship was in combat. Most of the crew didn't even know it was there, and the two of us got a lot of stares from unsuspecting Marines and Fleet spacers when we popped out of the other end.

One of them was Springfield, who stopped in mid-stride, blinking in surprise at our presence.

"Sir, ma'am," she said, nodding as she regained her composure. "Just wanted to let you know that the repairs on the suits are proceeding on schedule. No damage that couldn't be repaired with what we have on hand. The last of the wounded are being processed through the auto-docs and should be out in a few hours, according to Dr. Hallonen."

"Excellent," I said, not giving any indication that we'd had any business here other than to receive her report. "You did a damned good job down there, Lieutenant."

"Thank you, sir." Was she blushing? It was possible. There was an uncomfortable amount of hero worship from the Marines for the two of us, and I felt like I should discourage it, but Vicky had warned me otherwise. You never knew when you'd need just one moment of blind obedience without having to explain everything, and hero worship went a long way to making sure you got it.

"We're going to be transiting the wormhole in less than an hour," Vicky told the woman. "Make sure we have a platoon on standby from Alpha." She shrugged. "The Nova *said* they'd be guaranteeing us safe passage through the wormholes, but I hate depending on the kindness of strangers. Particularly when those strangers are octopus people."

"Will do, ma'am." Springfield nodded. "I already have First in their suits and loaded in a drop-ship, just in case. If everything is clear, I'll rotate Second in once we're in the next system." She opened her mouth, closed it again.

"Out with it, Springfield," I told her. "It's us. Remember, there are no stupid questions..."

"Only stupid people who *ask* questions," she finished for me, smiling crookedly. "Yes, sir. I was just wondering... well, being honest, the enlisted have been asking Top, and Top has been asking me. This is *it*, right? When we reach the end of this jumpgate system, we'll be going home?"

I exchanged an uncomfortable look with Vicky. This was the first time we'd heard the question, but we knew it wouldn't be the last.

"We don't know," I admitted. "We *think* the Reconstructors will be at the end of the line, but there's no way of knowing how far the Northwest Passage will be from there. We're just gonna have to roll with the punches."

"Yes, sir." Springfield tried to sound enthusiastic, but her eyes told the real story.

"After we transit the wormhole, go take some downtime. Eat, get some rest. This is a marathon, not a sprint."

The lieutenant nodded and headed off down the passage toward the lift bank. We had to go that way too, but I let her move off ahead of us, not wanting any awkward silences all the way up to the bridge.

"Shit," Vicky said softly, leaning against me. "She's about the most gung-ho Marine on this ship. If we can't count on her..."

"She'll be fine," I said, trying to reassure her but maybe more trying to reassure myself. "We'll keep them busy. That's the best way to keep Marines from thinking too much."

"Wish that would work for us."

I wasn't thinking about us though. Vicky paused and looked back at me, clearly wondering why I'd stopped.

"I think," I told her, "maybe I should make one more stop before I head to the bridge."

I knocked on the hatch. I don't know why, not when there was a perfectly good call button on the security plate beside it, but spending this much time away from the Core worlds had made me old-fashioned. And there was the audience to consider.

The hatch swung open and Jay's angular, narrow face stared at me with slack surprise.

"Oh, hey, boss," he said. "Didn't expect you to stop by."

And *I* certainly hadn't expected him to be here. Either of them.

"Hey, Bob," Jay called back into the compartment. "Boss is here." He turned back to me, stepping away from the door and waving invitingly. "Come on in, man... umm, I mean, *sir*."

"You're not in the military," I reminded him, stepping inside and pushing the hatch shut behind me. "You don't have to call me *sir*. *Cam* is fine."

The compartment was tiny, smaller than the one Vicky and I had shared before we'd moved into Hachette's command suite, and since neither Jay nor Bob were military, they hadn't had a lot of practice stowing their shit neatly. Which meant the place was a pigsty, with clothes jammed into webbing all over the bulkheads and hanging out of partially closed lockers. When we went to free- all, it was going to be an asteroid belt of underwear.

Bob stood up from his bunk, hands shoved awkwardly into his pockets, looking like he wasn't sure whether he should run away or give me a hug.

"I, uh..." he stuttered. "I wanted to thank you again, Cam, for giving me another chance. You didn't have to do that."

"You did right by us when it counted," I reminded him, "when you didn't have any expectation you'd be rewarded, when you could just as easily have been taken out and shot or whatever punishment Frost could sell to your people." I laughed softly. "Hell, someday I'll tell you how I wound up in the Marine Corps."

"So, like, what's up, man?" Jay wondered. "Is everything okay?"

"Yeah." I leaned against the bulkhead. "Look, there's a couple things we need to talk about. I didn't have a chance before we left because things were a little hectic, and now we're about to head through the gates and I don't know if there's going to be another opportunity." I waved them both to their bunks. "Have a seat."

I waited for them to both sit down in front of me, taking advantage of the time to try to put my thoughts into words.

"Okay, here's the deal. You're not in the military, like I said, but this *is* a military vessel, and I can't even start to tell you how many times we've had to fight for our lives since all this started." I snorted. "Sometimes, I don't think I remember what it's like *not* to fight for my life. But what that means is, we're probably not going to be lucky enough to get through all this without having to do it again."

"Um..." Jay raised his hand like a kid in school asking to go to the bathroom. "We're, like, not trained to be soldiers. I've never even fired a gun."

"I have," Bob offered. "Once. My uncle was a security police officer and he took me to the range when I was a teenager." He shrugged. "Uncle Garner said I was a natural though."

"We'll see about some range sessions, but I hope it won't come to either of you having to shoot anybody. What I'm telling you is that it might come down to one or both of you putting your lives at risk. You might die. I'm going to do the best I can to see that doesn't happen, but I need to know you understand."

"We understand," Jay told me, and for once he sounded serious. "This is the decision we made, Cam. This is what we wanted to do."

Bob nodded emphatically.

"We won't let you down."

I believed them. That didn't make me feel any better.

Because as much as I wanted to be like the rest of the crew, to think that all of our problems would be over when we reached the end of this line, I couldn't escape a gut-deep conviction that the hardest part of this journey was still ahead of us.

Out there, in the dark.

―――

The story will continue in **COLLATERAL EFFECTS!**

ALSO BY RICK PARTLOW

If you enjoyed Drop Trooper, you will love Recon and Holy War!

Start a new adventure today!

Start a new adventure today!

ALSO IN THE SERIES

CONTACT FRONT
KINETIC STRIKE
DANGER CLOSE
DIRECT FIRE
HOME FRONT
FIRE BASE
SHOCK ACTION
RELEASE POINT
KILL BOX
DROP ZONE
TANGO DOWN
BLUE FORCE
WEAPONS FREE
COLLATERAL EFFECTS

FROM THE PUBLISHER

Thank you for reading *Weapons Free*, book thirteen in Drop Trooper.

We hope you enjoyed it as much as we enjoyed bringing it to you. We just wanted to take a moment to encourage you to review the book on Amazon and Goodreads. Every review helps further the author's reach and, ultimately, helps them continue writing fantastic books for us all to enjoy.

If you liked this book, check out the rest of our catalogue at www.aethonbooks.com. To sign up to receive a FREE collection from some of our best authors as well as updates regarding all new releases, visit www.aethonbooks.com/sign-up.

JOIN THE STREET TEAM! Get advanced copies of all our books, plus other free stuff and help us put out hit after hit.

SEARCH ON FACEBOOK:
AETHON STREET TEAM

ABOUT RICK PARTLOW

RICK PARTLOW is that rarest of species, a native Floridian. Born in Tampa, he attended Florida Southern College and graduated with a degree in History and a commission in the US Army as an Infantry officer.

His lifelong love of science fiction began with Have Space Suit---Will Travel and the other Heinlein juveniles and traveled through Clifford Simak, Asimov, Clarke and on to William Gibson, Walter Jon Williams and Peter F Hamilton. And somewhere, submerged in the worlds of others, Rick began to create his own worlds.

He has written a ton of books in many different series, and his short stories have been included in seven different anthologies.

He currently lives in central Florida with his wife, two children and a willful mutt of a dog. Besides writing and reading science fiction and fantasy, he enjoys outdoor photography, hiking and camping.

www.rickpartlow.com

Printed in Dunstable, United Kingdom